SHAMANIC ALCHEMY

~~~~~~~~~

PRAISE FOR THE WORKS
OF JAMES ENDREDY

"With competence and authority James Endredy has written a powerful book with clear and precise instructions on advanced shamanic techniques learned directly from indigenous shamans. [*Advanced Shamanism*] is a wonderful contribution to shamanic literature. By bridging quantum physics with ancient shamanic practices, he immeasurably expands our access to the strange and wonderful world of the age-old shamanic path. This is the real deal."

JOSÉ LUIS STEVENS, PH.D., AUTHOR OF
AWAKEN THE INNER SHAMAN AND *ENCOUNTERS WITH POWER*

"James Endredy continues to tap into the primordial ways of healing. *Advanced Autogenic Training and Primal Awareness* is a marriage of his power of storytelling and his vast personal history with the practice. It is not often in this lifetime that one meets a true spiritual master, but this generation has James, and this book is a must-have for those desirous of deepening their connection with the I AM."

SHAWN TASSONE, M.D., PH.D., COAUTHOR OF
*SPIRITUAL PREGNANCY: DEVELOP, NURTURE & EMBRACE THE
JOURNEY TO MOTHERHOOD*

SHAMANIC ALCHEMY

The Great Work *of*
Inner Transformation

JAMES ENDREDY

Bear & Company
Rochester, Vermont

Bear & Company
One Park Street
Rochester, Vermont 05767
www.BearandCompanyBooks.com

Bear & Company is a division of Inner Traditions International

Library of Congress Cataloging-in-Publication Data

Names: Endredy, James, author.
Title: Shamanic alchemy : the great work of inner transformation / James
    Endredy.
Description: Rochester, Vermont : Bear & Company, 2019. | Includes
    bibliographical references and index.
Identifiers: LCCN 2018037981 (print) | LCCN 2018049768 (ebook) |
    ISBN 9781591433170 (pbk.) | ISBN 9781591433187 (ebook)
Subjects: LCSH: Shamanism. | Alchemy—Religious aspects.
Classification: LCC BF1611 .E658 2019 (print) | LCC BF1611 (ebook) |
    DDC 201/.44—dc23
LC record available at https://lccn.loc.gov/2018037981

Printed and bound in the United States by McNaughton & Gunn, Inc.

10 9 8 7 6 5 4 3 2 1

Text design by Priscilla Baker and layout by Debbie Glogover
This book was typeset in Garamond Premier Pro with Cache and Futura Sans used as display fonts

To send correspondence to the author of this book, mail a first-class letter to the author c/o Inner Traditions • Bear & Company, One Park Street, Rochester, VT 05767, and we will forward the communication, or contact the author directly at **www.JamesEndredy.com.**

CONTENTS

PART ONE

HISTORY, TERMS, AND THEORY OF ALCHEMY

PART TWO

PRAXIS FUNDAMENTALS

PART THREE

THE SEVEN STAGES OF SHAMANIC ALCHEMY TRANSFORMATION
The Azoth of Basil Valentine

ACKNOWLEDGMENTS

Writing a book takes a fair amount of time and effort, and without the support of friends, family, and professionals in the publishing industry, even the best books have little chance of reaching their intended audience. For this, my eleventh book, I give heartfelt thanks (in no particular order) to Old King Farm, my mom Irma, Big Ed, Luby, Jacki, Rick, Jessica, and Bandito del Kittycatos. Much appreciation goes to Ehud, Jon, Jeanie, and Kelly at Inner Traditions/Bear & Co. for the continued support of my work. Thanks go to my editors Jennie Marx and Kate Mueller, to Aaron Davis for the amazing cover art, and to Erica Robinson for the great catalog copy.

There are really no words to describe my immense gratitude to both my indigenous shaman mentors and the ancient alchemists. Without them the profound shamanic alchemy shared in this text would not be possible.

ALCHEMY AND SHAMANISM— TOOLS OF TRANSFORMATION

Alchemy—aka hermetic philosophy, the great art, the great work, the secret art, the divine art—is one of the most complex areas of study one can enter because of the vast variety of pursuits and goals associated with the term. It's also one of the oldest philosophies and disciplines, dating back some three thousand years or more.

So what is alchemy? The very simplest answer, and the one we will work from in this book, is: *alchemy is the art of transformation*. Paracelsus, probably the most important and consistent philosopher in the history of the alchemic tradition, and who I will speak of during the course of this book, put it this way: "Alchemy is the art that separates what is useful from what is not by transforming it into its ultimate matter and essence."[1]

For the actual work in this book, and truly learning alchemy is a lot of work, we will be employing alchemy as a practical vibrational science that will be enhanced and expanded upon by shamanic techniques. When we change the vibrational frequency within the structure of a substance or system via shamanic alchemy, it changes into a new form. For our purposes, we could say that we are here engaged in the art of transformation through the discipline of *mind over matter*. Or, as physicist Fred Allen Wolf puts it, mind *into* matter. Wolf promotes a new view of alchemy, some topics of which we will explore further in this book. On the new alchemy he writes:

In much the same way that modern dictionaries make alchemy a mere shadow of the chemistry to come, modern science has attempted to make the study of the subject a mere reflection of the objective and reducible science of matter. Some of us, including many scientists, don't agree with the new objective materialism. We believe in our heart of hearts, as did the alchemists that came before us, that something far richer than materialism is responsible for the universe . . . armed with the ancient knowledge and the modern vision that comes from modern physics, we can rediscover what the ancients may have known. All we need are a few basic concepts—a new way of seeing the old way. I call (these ways of seeing) the new alchemy.[2]

When seeing or hearing the word *alchemy,* one might think of old men in funny hats working at furnaces in ancient chemistry labs seeking to turn minerals into gold, create the philosopher's stone, or find the elixir of life. However, these popular modern stereotypes of the ancient alchemists are but a tiny fragment of alchemy. Alchemic author Stanislas Klossowski puts it nicely:

Alchemy is a rainbow bridging the chasm between earthly and heavenly planes, between matter and spirit. . . . Alchemy, the royal sacerdotal art, also called the hermetic philosophy, conceals in esoteric texts and enigmatic emblems, the means of penetrating the very secrets of Nature, Life and Death, of Unity, Eternity, and Infinity. Viewed in the context of these secrets, that of gold making is, relatively speaking, of little consequence: something comparable to the super-powers (siddhis) sometimes obtained by Great Yogis, which are sought not after for their own sake, but are important by-products of high spiritual attainment.[3]

In modern times the comprehensiveness of the alchemic art offers us innumerous insights into a wide spectrum of topics and disciplines, including alternative healing, psychology and parapsychology, spirituality, art, sociology, and quantum physics, to name a few. But remember, whether the alchemic subject is herbs, minerals, elements, or sociology, medicine,

Fig. I.1. Alchemical laboratory (Wellcome Images).

psychology, or shamanism, or even our own physical body, mind, or etheric body, alchemy is always about creative transformation; changing something that is inferior, imperfect, or unacceptable into something that is better, more perfect, and closer to what we desire.

Although alchemy in its various manifestations can be clearly viewed as a quite serious subject, reading through both ancient and modern texts on alchemy can be entertaining as well, and the history of alchemy has a plethora of interesting characters, some mythical, some shrouded in mystery, and many historical people.

Among these hundreds of fascinating personages, we have Hermes Trismegistus, regarded as a historical founder of alchemy and Hellenistic magical astral mysticism. The "Thrice Great Hermes" is often identified with Thoth, the ancient Egyptian scribe of the gods. There is of course the famous Paracelsus (the Latin name adopted by Dr. Theophrastus Bombastus von Hohenhiem)—a powerful sixteenth-century reformer in the history of medicine who boasted that his form of alchemical-medical philosophy transcended the learned medicine of the Galenist physicians of his day. Our modern adjective *bombastic* might be derived in part from his name, based on his dynamic attacks upon the contemporary authorities. And let's not forget Jabir ibn Hayyan (Latin, Geber), known as the father of European as well as Islamic alchemy. Born in Persia in the eighth century, Jabir was strongly influenced by the Islamic mysticism of the Shi'ites, yet he was extremely oriented toward laboratory practice and experimentation. One amusing theory of the etymology of the word *gibberish* is that it derives from the incomprehensible technical jargon used by Jabir (Geber) and other alchemists.

In more modern times, Franz Tausend stands out as one of the most successful quack alchemists, which helped give alchemy a bad rap in the early 1900s. Tausend boasted that through his new theories on atomic and molecular structure, he could transform lead into gold whenever he wished. His skill at persuasion was so great that he convinced many prominent persons, including princes, generals, bank directors, and well-known industrialists, to finance him. Unfortunately, his lavish lifestyle, which included two castles, eventually caught up with him. One of his dupes, a Munich banker, informed the police of his fraudulent activities, and he and his wife were jailed. The judge at his trial pronounced Tausend to be "a brazen and unscrupulous imposter whose guilt was attenuated only by the credulity of his dupes and the mischievous influence of his wife" and sentenced him to three years and eight months imprisonment.[4]

The full alchemic cast of characters throughout history is immense and beyond the scope of this book; however, leaving the imposters aside, I will present a simple lexicon, including some of the main personalities and their contributions to the art, as a means of imparting some of the key elements of alchemy.

Along with the innumerable people involved in alchemy through the ages is the vast amount of materials, tools, and process employed. Throughout the practical sections of this book, we will also be working with a variety of materials, tools, and processes, but before we get into all that, by way of introduction, let's take a quick peek into these topics of the great art through the eyes of a sixteenth-century author, which is both informative and, I think, at times very humorous.

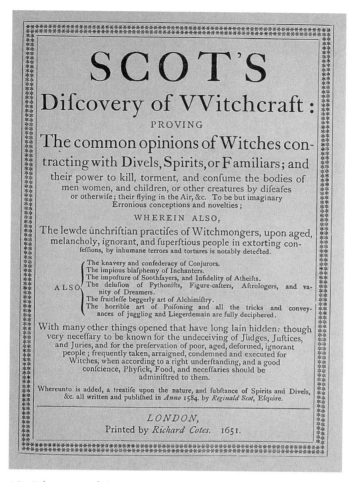

SCOT'S
Difcovery of VVitchcraft:
PROVING

The common opinions of Witches con-
tracting with Divels, Spirits, or Familiars; and
their power to kill, torment, and confume the bodies of
men women, and children, or other creatures by difeafes
or otherwife; their flying in the Air, &c. To be but imaginary
Erronious conceptions and novelties;

WHEREIN ALSO,

The lewde unchriftian practifes of Witchmongers, upon aged,
melancholy, ignorant, and fuperftious people in extorting con-
feffions, by inhumane terrors and tortures is notably detected.

ALSO
- The knavery and confederacy of Conjurors.
- The impious blafphemy of Inchanters.
- The impofture of Soothfayers, and Infidelity of Atheifts.
- The delufion of Pythonifts, Figure-cafters, Aftrologers, and va-
nity of Dreamers.
- The fruitleffe beggerly art of Alchimiftry.
- The horrible art of Poifoning and all the tricks and convey-
ances of juggling and Liegerdemain are fully deciphered.

With many other things opened that have long lain hidden: though
very neceffary to be known for the undeceiving of Judges, Juftices,
and Juries, and for the prefervation of poor, aged, deformed, ignorant
people; frequently taken, arraigned, condemned and executed for
Witches, when according to a right underftanding, and a good
confcience, Phyfick, Food, and neceffaries should be
adminiftred to them.

Whereunto is added, a treatife upon the nature, and fubftance of Spirits and Divels,
&c. all written and publifhed in *Anno* 1584. by *Reginald Scot*, Efquire.

LONDON,
Printed by *Richard Cotes*. 1651.

Fig. I.2. Title page of the 1651 edition of *The Discoverie of Witchcraft*.

During the time in England of Reginald Scot, the belief in witchcraft
flourished and the prosecution of witches was constant. However, this
member of Parliament believed that witches were either willful impostures
or illusions due to mental disturbance in the observers. Scot reasoned that
both witchcraft and conjuring could be explained by the art, or rather the
craft, of alcumystrie (alchemy), otherwise called multiplication.

He states:

In the bowels herof (Alcumystrie) dooth both witchcraft and con-
juration lie hidden. . . . And bicause the practisers heereof would be

thought wise, learned, cunning, and their crafts maisters, they have devised words of art, sentences and epithets obscure, and confectious so innu/merable (which are also compounded of strange and rare simples) as confound the capacities of them that are either set on worke heerein, or be brought to behold or expect their conclusions. For what plaine man would not beleeve, that they are learned and jollie fellowes, that have in such readinesse so many mysticall termes of art: as (for a tast) their subliming, amalgaming, engluting, imbibing, incorporating, cementing, ritrination, terminations, mollifications, and indurations of bodies, matters combust and coagulat, ingots, &c.[5]

Scots's list of materials (stuffe) used in alchemy is a treasure:

Or who is able to conceive (by reason of the abrupt confusion, contranetie, and multitude of drugs, simples, and confections) the operation and mysterie of their stuffe and workemanship. For these things and many more, are of necessitie to be prepared and used in the execution of this indevor ; namelie orpiment, sublimed Mercttrie, iron squames, Afercitfie crude, groundlie large, bole armoniake, verde-grece, borace, boles, gall, arsenicke, sal armoniake, brimstone,/ salt, paper, burnt bones, unsliked lime, claie, saltpeter, vitriall, saltartre, boles gall, alcalie, sal preparat, claie made with horsse doong, mans haire, oile of tartre, allum, glasse, woort, yest, argoll, resagor,f gleir of an eie, [t Resaigar] powders, ashes, doong, pisse, &c. Then have they waters corosive and lincall, waters of albification, and waters rubifieng, &c. Also oiles, ablutions, and metals fusible. Also their lamps, their urinalles, discensories, sublimatories, alembecks, viols, croslets, cucurbits, stillatories, and their fornace of calcination. . .[6]

So why would a modern person want to study and practice alchemy? For me, the answer is basically the same as why I study and practice shamanism, which has led me to combine them; however, as we will see, aspects of shamanism can easily be considered alchemy and vice versa. Shamanic alchemy, as presented in this book, will cover both the practical and spiritual sides of the topic; however, the practical applications (science) are innately spiritual in nature when regarded through the eyes of shamanism. Therefore, the answer to the above question is mostly found in a spiritual context, with practice in the art of alchemy a means to solidify the spiritual quest.

Many people, including myself, pursue a spiritual quest to *fill a void* that other activities cannot fulfill. Sex, drugs, alcohol, shopping, psychoanalytical therapy, wealth, power, sports, travel, or even a happy and fulfilling relationship, family life, or career does not satisfy our innate need for experiencing the numinous aspects of life. Alchemy and shamanism have nothing in common with those activities except for the fact that they can replace the negative aspects and uplift the positive ones. The same might be said for any for religious activity. However, with alchemy and shamanism, we can employ direct experience of numinous and invisible worlds not attainable through religious dogma. This direct form of experience is also known as gnosis—the Greek word for knowledge.

In the purest sense, both alchemy and shamanism are practical gnostic systems of enlightenment. Many of the early alchemists, such as the fathers of Hellenistic alchemy, Zosimos of Panoplis and Stephanus of Alexandria, considered themselves gnostics: the former belonged to the Poimandres gnostic sect and the latter was a gnostic Christian. The predominant reason for practicing gnostic systems such as alchemy and shamanism rather than blind faith in an organized religion is that direct experience is highly effective in relieving suffering, ignorance, and fear of death. The direct experience of practicing shamanic alchemy has the power to invoke peace of mind, a healthy and confident outlook on life, increased creativity, and physical and mental vitality.

As I stated in the second paragraph of this introduction: alchemy is the art of transformation. Shamanic alchemy provides tools for *inner transformation* in a dual process of personal-transpersonal and technical methods and procedures. The shamanic personal-transpersonal methods include but are not limited to vibrational energy work, connection to nature and the elements, regulation of the autonomic nervous system, and shamanic initiations. The alchemic technical procedures include the physical preparations and techniques in procuring energetically charged herbal tinctures, pertinent astronomy or astrology practices, spagyrics, and experiments with the various stages of alchemical separation and transformation. At the highest levels, this dual process evolves into one, each reinforcing the other in an expression of unity.

The answer to why a person would want to study and practice shamanic alchemy can be summed up in the following points.

Actually practicing (not just reading) shamanic alchemy opens the doors to occult knowledge of inner transformation through various methods and processes, both ancient and modern, providing numinous experiences that can fill our existential void and produce enhanced mental, physical, environmental, and spiritual health and vitality.

Although working with a partner or in a group can have advantages, for those who don't want to join or be part of an esoteric group, shamanic alchemy is ideal for the solo practitioner.

Experiences and the knowledge gained through shamanic alchemy have the power to stay with you so the energy can be used again later and during the course of everyday life. And alchemical products can be stored for later use without a reduction of potency.

As with most skills we learn in life, shamanic alchemy is learned through a *progression* of skills. This book is laid out to aide you in this progression. Therefore, it is imperative to read through the history, lexicon, and theories and then progress through the practices (praxis) in order, one by one, no matter how long it takes to accomplish each one. This is not a race! Some of the praxis may take months or even years to achieve.

It is most important to achieve the fundamental praxis first. Learning to enter an integrated state of consciousness, gaining tangible experience with phase-conjugate mirrors of the mind, taking the first steps toward direct shamanic viewing, and developing a concrete relationship with the Sacred Fire are the four cornerstones of shamanic alchemy. These fundamental praxis take time, patience, perseverance, and guts to achieve. Without these tools, the subsequent praxis cannot be fully realized, especially the seven stages of shamanic alchemy transformation.

I have personally experienced countless disappointments and failures and also many incredible and sometimes unbelievable successes during the over thirty years of learning the material contained in this book. It is my sincere hope that you will embrace both the ups and downs, the disappointments and the successes as you progress. With the completion of your *coagulation,* and the immense practical knowledge you have attained in order to achieve this transformation, you will have attained what few people have and be truly ready for what's next.

PART ONE

HISTORY, TERMS, AND THEORY OF ALCHEMY

1

THE DAWN OF ALCHEMY

Few academic writers on the subject acknowledge, or even realize, the complexity of true alchemical philosophy, and most never bother to even mention the most ancient alchemists of prehistory. Our modern studies of alchemy illuminate how alchemy flourished in many different cultures; however, what is often lost is the various magico-shamanic-religious systems that nourished the formation of alchemy since primitive man. To pigeon-hole alchemy as the isolated and eccentric pursuit of gold-makers beginning around the first century BCE is an extremely narrow and inaccurate view of the divine art. More accurately, alchemy can be viewed as a river that begins in prehistoric time and winds its way through history as it flows through an innumerable variety of landscapes (philosophies and operations) over the course of many thousands of years.

The most basic understanding of the origins of alchemy are rooted in what some scholars like to call the "conquest of matter," which began sometime in the Paleolithic Period when prehistoric people first succeeded in transforming stone into tools and control fire to change states of matter. But for our purposes, the subsequent Neolithic Period when pottery and agriculture were fully developed seems an appropriate time for identifying the dawn of alchemy.

MASTERS OF FIRE

One of the few scholars who enhanced our subject of the primitive roots of alchemy was Mircea Eliade with his fascinating study *The Forge and the*

Crucible. It would have been an amazing sight to see the face of the first alchemist of pottery around 25,000 BCE when that person realized he or she had hardened clay with fire. Eliade eloquently elucidates:

> The alchemist, like the smith, and the potter before him, is a "master of fire." It is with the fire that he controls the passage of matter from one state to the other. The first potter who, with the aid of live embers, was successful hardening those shapes which he had given to his clay, must have felt the intoxication of the demiurge: he had discovered a transmuting agent. That which natural heat—from the sun or bowels of the earth—took so long to ripen, was transformed by fire at a speed hitherto undreamed of. This demiurgic enthusiasm springs from that obscure presentiment that the great secret lay in discovering how to "perform" faster than nature, in other words (since it is always necessary to talk in terms of the spiritual experience of primitive man) how, without peril, to interfere in the process of the cosmic forces. Fire turned out to be the means by which man could "execute" faster, but it could also do something other than what already existed in nature. It was therefore a manifestation of a magico-religious power that could modify the world and which, consequently, did not belong to this world. This is why the most primitive cultures look upon the specialist in the sacred—the shaman, the medicine man, the magician—as "master of fire."[1]

In an integrated state of consciousness (see chapter 4), the shamanic master of fire can handle burning coals and with his inner heat easily stand frigid cold. The fire shaman is in direct contact with the numinous energy of the Sacred Fire. We will be discussing this at length in the practical sections of this book. Another master of fire that may or may not have had the skills of a shaman, but equally important in the ancient history of alchemy, were the first metallurgists and smiths. The alchemist's discovery around 8000 BCE of smelting an ore with fire to produce metal and later mixing ores to transform and create new metals impacted humanity to such an enormous degree that historians typically divide ancient human history into the Stone, Bronze, and Iron Ages.

When considering the conquest of matter by the ancient alchemists—the quest to influence, control, and shape the physical world of matter—we must remember that people are also matter. In this way the divine art also embraces the renewal and reshaping of the physical and inner person. The power generated by these processes becomes that which is spiritual. Alchemic metallurgy was surely a milestone in human history but so was the "spiritual gold" of the inner alchemist and also the alchemy of plants and herbs.

And so we also have masters of fire who involved themselves primarily with the making of tinctures, essences, and other products from medicinal plants. The use of fire was, and still is, vital in the art of making many of these curative products. This alchemic art, called spagyrics, we will practice in chapter 5.

The beginnings of this alchemic art is shrouded in mystery. Archaeologists have a much easier time dating metallurgic alchemy than plant alchemy in prehistory (before writing), but what we do have are later writings that explain prehistoric processes discovered and passed on by oral traditions. In this way it is clear that in ancient China, India, and Egypt, we find many important contributions to alchemical medicine. The first "published" material seems to come from China during the Han dynasty around 3000 BCE. Oriental scholar Masumi Chkashige explains:

> As to the bibliography of Chinese alchemy, Ko Hung's *Pao Pu Tsu* is the oldest complete book. We have a still older book entitled *Ts'an T'ung Chi,* which dates from the later Han dynasty. This book is without doubt one of the Taoist classics but is too abstract and esoteric for our study. One may also add *Pen Ts'ao Ching,* a treatise on Chinese materia medica, published towards the end of the Han dynasty. . . . A good many other alchemical books can be enumerated but they are of later date. An Chi' Sheng, an alchemist, is said to have lived considerably earlier than Ko Hung but he left no writings. In the final analysis, only the two works, *Pao Pu Tsu* and *Pen Ts'ao Ching* remain as authentic sources of information on the earlier Chinese alchemy.[2]

As noted in the introduction, there are many colorful figures in the history of alchemy. In his book Ko Hung states that through his teachers and the many secret books he was given, he was handed down the art of the immortals. It is said that after his death, Ko Hung's corpse was coffined but later upon opening it, nothing was to be found except his sloughed-off clothes. In the *Hsien Ching* it is said there are three levels that one may attain through life. A man of the highest ability ascends into heaven with all his earthly body and is called *t'ien hsien* (heavenly immortal). A man of moderate ability enters a sacred mountain and is called *t hsien* (earthly immortal). Here mountain probably means mine, where a man of moderate ability may, as a miner does, compound alchemical preparations. A man of the lowest ability first dies and then disappears, leaving only his clothes behind, and he is called *shih chien hsien* (immortal whose corpse disappears). Ko Hung's contemporaries wondered at the circumstances of his death and even laughed at him because, though he had been a devoted student of the art, he was unable to rise above even the lowest class.

THE SECRET ART

At the dawn of "historic" alchemy, it was regarded as a divine and sacred art, shrouded in mystery, and only to be approached with reverence. Its adepts, from its dawn and throughout more than four millennia of brilliance, kept its secrets to themselves and enshrouded their operations with symbolism and their materials with fantastic names to conceal their identity from the uninitiated. Common to alchemy are secret alphabets, ciphers, and emblematic drawings designed primarily for secrecy, but they also served as a sort of shorthand, just as chemists have today. In this way, adepts from different nations had a medium for understanding, while the uninitiated would have not a clue if they came upon these symbols and drawings. Novices were often bound by a sacred oath, and every precaution was taken to keep the processes of the sacred art secret.

Many now contend that alchemy originated in the attempt to demonstrate the applicability of the principles of mysticism to things of the physical realm. The chief principles are then concerned with the "soul" of human beings and are allegories dealing with spiritual truths. These ideas are supported in the fact that in the early periods, the divine art was practiced almost exclusively by the priesthood.

Roger Bacon, famous alchemist and writer of the 1500s, who based much of his work on the medieval *Secretum Secretorum* (The Secret of Secrets), has this to say about alchemic secrets and the nobility of the alchemist:

> All writers, because of the greatness of their secrets, conceal the science of alchemy in words and metaphors and figurative work, and God inspires them to this so that only the most wise and good men perceive it achieving the good of the republic. So the *Lapis* is to be taken first of all metaphorice, for that all upon which the *operacio alchimica* works. . . . But in all this are most difficult works and of great expense, to which works only the wisest and happiest can attain.[3]

ELEMENTS AND ALCHEMY

It's fair to say that alchemy in prehistory, medieval times, and even in more contemporary times has always been steeped in the grand theory of the four elements, which we will be working with throughout this book. For now, we can simply say that for the early alchemists water was seen as the solvent of all things. Air was regarded as the universal bond of nature that held in itself the substantial principles of all natural things—the universal world spirit. Fire was regarded as the cause of all motion and consequently of all change in nature. Seen in both the heavens and on Earth, it was the principle of all generation—the primal source of all forms in itself—the highest active element, one in essence but manifesting in four forms: celestial, subterranean, sacred (earthly, ceremonial), and mundane (culinary and other terrestrial uses). And earth, the fourth element, was the center in which all the others operated and the final receiver of all the influences of the heavenly bodies, our common mother from which all things sprang. Her abundance was produced by the operations of fire, air, and water.

In this theory of the four elements, the pairing of qualities arises—hot and cold, wet and dry. The alchemical transformation of an element is perfectly possible by a change of quality of the element. We shall see during this text that the alchemic word *element* is somewhat different from the modern scientific meaning. Renowned spagyric alchemist Manfred Junius says:

Scientific knowledge and formulation of transmutation led to a change in the concept of elements. "Element" in the modern meaning stands for a pure substance whose constituent atoms are all of the same kind. Elements are homogenous systems of a constant, nonvariable combination that cannot be divided by chemical means . . . the concept of elements in alchemy is totally different and rather resembles a state, since alchemy does not recognize stability in matter found in the realms of nature. In nature, nothing but change is stable, and nature itself represents a constantly occurring alchemy.[4]

In the Aristotelian theory of the third century BCE, which many if not most alchemists that came later held close to heart, especially Paracelsus and his followers, creation involved the separation of the elements, the division of heaven and Earth, and the emergence of land from sea. Beyond the sphere of the moon is found the fifth element—the *quintessence*. In alchemy the fifth element has a multitude of names and meanings. Early Greek theory identified *pneuma* (breath) with spirit and tended to regard it as the fifth element. In Sanskrit there is *prana,* which combines the idea of physical breath with that of spiritual energy.

Distillation is the alchemist's tool that frees the spirit-vapor from a body, and then this spirit can be reunited with another body and work as an active spiritual principle. A prime example of this was the discovery of the distillation of alcohol in the fourteenth century, which was given names such as *aqua ardens* (the soul in the spirit of wine) and *aqua vitae* (water of life). The extraction of the quintessence, the spiritual essence or fifth element, from various bodies is of major importance when practicing alchemy and one we will engage in during the shamanic alchemy practices in this book.

Another important process we will be practicing that relates to the elements and shamanic alchemy, among other matters, is *projection*. This method of transformation is manifested by projecting, throwing upon, or infusing a specific active vibratory principle into a body, including the human body. These are high-level techniques of mind into matter, with the aid of the elements, involving the acceleration and transmutation of energy and physical particles.

ASTROLOGY AND ALCHEMY

There is no doubt that astrology, which is probably the most ancient of occult activities, had a profound influence on alchemy. During the Middle Ages, the two so-called arts were constantly practiced together, and to this day modern spagyrics is steeped in astrology and the influence of celestial bodies on herbs and plants.

The sun and moon are believed to have the greatest effect on earthly life, including humans. The zodiac is generally attributed to the Sumerians, who were among the first to study the stars and create symbols. Celestial influences emanating from the thirty-six decans of the signs were thought to mysteriously affect life on Earth, including human life. As the science of astrology improved and expanded, parts of the human body were said to be affected by specific celestial bodies, and astrology gradually became an important part of the healing arts.

It is quite clear that practices of magic and divination that employ astrology came to be associated with alchemy. Magic, astrology, and alchemy all point to the stars and heavens as the source of the mysterious emanations (powers), whereby precious stones, metals, plants, and herbs derive their special properties.

SHAMANIC ALCHEMY

In the postmodern sense, shamanism and alchemy provide both practical and spiritual techniques of transformation. Physical-technical experiments and practices fuse with personal and transpersonal inner practices of enlightenment and spiritual growth. We will be exploring a wide variety of these practices and experiments in this book; however, it must be noted that the full range of these mystical studies is vast and beyond the scope of one book. Here we will begin wading down many streams of knowledge that eventually lead us to the river of alchemic teachings as it flows through time and space. These teachings can be found far and wide—in ancient manuscripts, the elements and celestial bodies, stones, trees, and plants and in the spiritual traditions of the mystical schools. As Eliade so aptly puts it:

Everywhere we find alchemy, it is always intimately related to a "mystical" tradition: in China with Taoism, in India with Yoga and Tantrism, in Hellenistic Egypt with gnosis, in Islamic countries with hermetic and esoteric mystical schools, in the Western Middle Ages and Renaissance with Hermeticism, Christian and sectarian mysticism, and Cabala. Consequently, to understand the meaning and function of alchemy, we must *not* judge the alchemical texts by the possible chemical insights which they may contain. Such an evaluation would be tantamount to judging—and classifying—great poetical creations by their scientific data or their historical accuracy.

That the alchemists *did* contribute also to the progress of the natural sciences is certainly true. But they did this indirectly and only as a consequence of their concern with mineral substance and living matter. For they were "experimenters," not abstract thinkers or erudite scholastics. Their inclination to "experiment," however, was not limited to the natural realm . . . the experiments with mineral or vegetal substances pursued a more ambitious goal: to change the alchemist's own mode of being.[5]

2

A DISTILLED LEXICON
OF ALCHEMY

To explain the word *alchemy* to those that simply relate to it in the pigeon-holed characterization of making gold from other materials, I'm providing a brief lexicon of personages, terms, places, and philosophies related to the fascinating history of this subject. To me this is far more interesting and informative than a history lesson. Even though this lexicon is packed with information, please know that it is not intended to encompass the full spectrum or history of the great art. For example, the classic book *A Lexicon of Alchemy* by Martinus Rulandus of 1612 (later translated by A. E. Waite) is close to five hundred pages with thousands of entries.

A

Air. See *Elements.*

Albertus Maᵹnus (1193–1280)
It is difficult to know which of the many texts attributed to Albertus Magnus were actually written by him because in the time of Albertus, due to the Catholic Church banning alchemical manuscripts, many authors would attribute their writing to authoritative figures such as Albertus whose reputation was legendary.

Albertus was born at Lauingen in Swabia of a noble family. During his life he earned the title of *doctor universalis,* was provincial of the

Dominicans in Saxony and bishop of Ratisbon (Regensburg), and is often regarded as the greatest German philosopher and theologian of the Middle Ages. His relics are in a sarcophagus displayed in the crypt of St. Andrew's Church, Cologne, Germany. Albertus was beatified in 1622 and canonized and proclaimed a doctor of the church on December 16, 1931, by Pope Pius XI, and the patron saint of natural scientists in 1941. St. Albert's feast day is November 15.

Albertus devoted much of his life to paraphrasing Aristotle, and two of his Aristotelian books—*De animalibus* (On animals) and *De mineralibus* (On minerals)—are well-regarded works. There are interesting stories and legends surrounding Albertus, including that he owned a magical talking head of brass (like Roger Bacon), which his famous pupil Thomas Aquinas (known for his natural theology and also later made a saint) smashed because it wouldn't shut up and was disturbing his work. It is also said that once Albertus made a garden bloom in winter for a duke in Holland.

If one has the desire (and time), there are many books a researcher can find about Albertus Magnus; some are questionable, but most are still in the same vein and most likely written by protégés or experienced followers, while others are surely authentic. I recently came across a truly fascinating hand-bound volume in the esoteric library of the retreat center where I currently live. It supposedly is "Faithfully Translated" from German from the works of Albertus Magnus. On the title page it reads:

Albertus Magnus

The Book of Nature and Hidden Secrets and Mysteries of Life Unveiled; Being the Forbidden Knowledge of Ancient Philosophers— By that Celebrated, Occult Student, Philospopher, Chemist, Naturalist, Psychomist, Astrologer, Alchemist, Metallurgist, Sorcerer, Explanator of the Mysteries of Wizards and Witchcraft: Together with Recondite Views of Numerous Secret Arts and Sciences—Obscure, Plain, Practical, Etc., Etc.

Of the numerous "secrets" contained in the text, here a few gems:

To make One's Self Invisible—You must obtain the ear of a black cat, boil it in the milk of a black cow, then make a thumb cover of it and wear it on the thumb, and no one will be able to see you.[1]

To Prevent Firearms from being Bewitched—Take nine blades of straw from under a sow while she is nursing her pigs, therefrom put nine knots into the shaft and insert them between the two barrel loops, and such a gun cannot be bewitched.[2]

To Compel a Thief to return Stolen Property—Obtain a new earthen pot with a cover, draw water from the undercurrent of a stream while calling out the three holiest names. Fill the vessel one-third, take the same to your home, set it upon the fire, take a piece of bread from the lower crust of the loaf, stick three pins into the bread, boil all in the vessel, and add a few nettles. Then say: "Thief, male or female, bring my stolen articles back, whether thou art boy or girl; thief, if thou art woman or man, I compel thee, in the name (most holiest name)."[3]

To Restore Manhood—Buy a pike as they are sold in the fish-market, carry it noiselessly to a running water, there let whale oil run into the snout of the fish, throw the fish into the running water, and then walk stream upward, and you will recover your strength and former powers.[4]

For Sore Breasts—Take distilled glori, five cents worth; juniperberry salt, five cents; white beeswax, three cents; mercury precipitate, two cents; and let the mass be mixed in an earthen pot, on the fire until it becomes stiff like salve. Stir it well, put some of it on linen, and apply once per day, upon the breast.[5]

Aludel
A pear-shaped vessel for chemical sublimation.

Antimony
A metal derived from stibnite that had tremendous significance to alchemists, especially those purifying gold. However, it is also said to purge the human body and for making a curing elixir.

Apparatus
There are numerous apparatus found in the alchemist's laboratory, and many famous engravings and paintings depict the alchemist working in

his lab with all kinds of strange devices and gadgets. Among these are the alembic, tribikos (a kind of alembic), kerotakis, bain-marie, crucible, and various types of furnaces. *See* Bain-Marie; Maria Prophetissa.

Aristotle (384–322 BCE)

With regard to alchemy, the teachings of Aristotle, especially his theories on the elements, laid the groundwork for alchemy, science, medicine, and magic. For centuries Aristotelian concepts greatly influenced the alchemists. He wrote on many subjects, including physics, biology, zoology, metaphysics, logic, ethics, aesthetics, poetry, theater, music, rhetoric, linguistics, politics, and government. Aristotle, student of Plato and tutor of Alexander the Great, left behind probably the most influential body of work of any philosopher in his time.

Arnald de Villanova (1235–1311)

Arnald de Villanova, reputable physician, has certain manuscripts ascribed to him that he might not have written. However, there are texts about both theoretical and practical alchemy that many believe were written by him, and in any case what is for sure is that his reputation in alchemic circles was unparalleled and he is often compared to Paracelsus in that both men were crucial in forming the connection between alchemy and medicine.

Astral Body

Esoteric alchemy includes the highly regarded notion that, as stated in the Emerald Tablet (a part of the *Hermetica,* Egyptian-Greek wisdom texts from the second century CE), what is below is like that which is above, and what is above is like that which is below. In the works of Paracelsus and many other alchemists, this is taken quite literally—man was created from heaven *and* earth and so he has inner stars due to his microcosmic nature (*see* Microcosm-Macrocosm). Therefore, the sun, moon, and all the other celestial bodies are also in man—the astral body.

Astrology

Many alchemists considered astrology supremely important to alchemic work, and planetary signs were often used in alchemical texts for the symbols of metals. Paraclesus mentions often in his works his belief that every physician should be both an alchemist and astrologer.

B

Bacon, Roger (1214–1294)

Roger Bacon was a Franciscan friar and esteemed philosopher who synthesized natural philosophy with mathematics and optics, along with theology, which included angels and magic. In Bacon's time science and theology scorned alchemy, but Bacon backed the "natural magic" of alchemy, greatly supported alchemist John Dee, and was vocal in his opinion that physicians should learn the ways of alchemy. It's said that Bacon's sympathies for those living in poverty, his interest in certain astrological doctrines, and his books on alchemy got him in trouble with the monks, and he was either jailed or under house arrest for a period of time. Bacon was a colorful, eccentric, and combative personality in the history of alchemy.

Fig. 2.1. Roger Bacon conducting an alchemical experiment in a vaulted cloister (etching by J. Nasmyth, 1845) (Wellcome Images).

Bain-Marie

The name of this heated bath is attributed to alchemist Maria Prophetissa who wrote about and invented various alchemic equipment, including the tribikos and kerotakis. Today, the simple bain-marie, or double boiler, is used in various culinary applications as well as in making soap, herbal essences, and butters. *See* Maria Prophetissa.

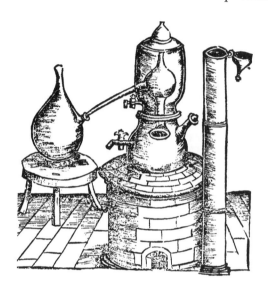

Fig. 2.2. An alchemical bain-marie or *balneum Mariae* (from *Coelum philosophorum* by Philipp Ulstad, 1528).

Beasts and Creatures

In alchemy there are many beasts that symbolize the various aspects of the art. Mythic beasts include red and green lions, the basilisk, dragons, winged serpents, and the phoenix. Animals such as eagles, lions, rams, snakes, and salamanders are also found in alchemic symbolism. These, and other creatures, are often viewed as protectors of sacred knowledge and pose obstacles on the path of enlightenment.

Birds

Bird symbolism in alchemy was mostly employed as an esoteric encoding device utilizing the colors of birds feathers to stand in for the colors of sequential stages of alchemic procedures. The movements of birds also conveyed these stages. *See* Stages for the complete list.

The crow or raven indicates the black phase operation of putrefaction, which involves the breaking down of structures by fire or decay. The white goose, white swan, or albatross symbolizes the white phase of dissolution. The peacock often signifies the turning point from black and white into the astral plane with shifting patterns of many colors. The pelican stands for the distillation operation, as well as the beginning of the red phase of alchemy. A famous image in alchemy is of a pelican stabbing her own breast with her beak and nourishing her young with her blood. The phoenix is often symbolized in the coagulation stage: through various processes before coagulation, the phoenix dies in flames and then rises from the ashes of its former self and flies into numinous unity.

The movements of birds in drawings also act as part of the secret language of the alchemist. To the uninitiated, a flock of birds ascending would be seen as just that—birds flying upward. However, in alchemic symbolism, ascending birds indicate the evaporation or volatilization of compounds. Descending birds indicate condensation or fixation. Birds shown both ascending and descending indicate the operation of distillation.

Boehme, Jacob (1575–1624)
Jacob Boehme was a shoemaker by trade, and his contribution to alchemic history is through his writings of his mystical visionary states. A student of the works of the alchemist Paracelsus, he is said to have seen into the book of nature, a Paracelsian term, and his popular writings of the Paracelsian cosmology of the world of nature and of astral influences helped facilitate the revival of Christian mysticism.

C

Caduceus
This short staff entwined by two serpents, usually surmounted by wings, is carried by Hermes Trismegistus. In alchemy the two entwined serpents symbolize the conjunction stage of alchemy (see Stages). The staff also represents the dynamic equilibrium of opposites. In modern times this symbol is often confused with the Rod of Asclepius, which is the symbol of the American Medical Association and many other medical organizations. The caduceus is often used as the symbol for commercial health care organizations.

Chinese Alchemy

The Chinese philosophers and alchemists, along with Taoists adepts, sought the secret of prolonging human life beyond its usual lifespan by reversing aging, with immortality as the ultimate goal. Thus, their work was mainly focused on the making of elixirs. Commonly used in the formation of elixirs were animal, mineral, and vegetable substances such as tortoise, fowl, crane and eggs of the crane, cinnabar, gold, silver, jade, peach, pine, and *chih* or *Ganoderma lucidum*. Chih is an herb, also called divine herb, but some say this substance is actually *G. lucidum,* which is a mushroom.

Symbols and allegories permeate Chinese alchemy where we find yin (cold and humidity), symbolized as the white tiger, and yang (heat and dryness), signified by the green dragon. Yin and yang, along with chi (vital energy force), explain how energy flows in the body, especially the vital organs.

Clyssus

In a clyssus, constituents of a single plant are extracted and then recombined, whereas an elixir is a mixture of extracts from various species of plants.

D

Dee, John (1527–1608)

John Dee was a renowned mathematician and cosmographer and a practitioner of alchemy, astrology, and angel magic. He had one of the largest libraries in England and devoted one wing of his house to an alchemic laboratory. Later in his life, with his friend alchemist Edward Kelley, he became deeply involved with séances and angel magic and was convinced that knowledge conveyed by the angels would greatly benefit mankind. But the publication of the conversations with the angels ruined his reputation, and in the end he died in poverty. The British Museum holds several artifacts presumed to be owned by Dee, including a crystal ball of the highest quality, wax seals that were placed under the feet of the table he used for scrying, an engraved gold amulet, and a black obsidian mirror that is said to be of Aztec origin.

Distillation

Quite possibly the most significant of the alchemical processes, distillation led to the design of apparatus, including the alembic, kerotakis, and tribikos.

Distillation of the *aqua vitae* (water of life), *aqua vini* (water of wine), and *aqua ardens* (burning water) and the mysterious mystical qualities of these distillations were important breakthroughs in the history of alchemy.

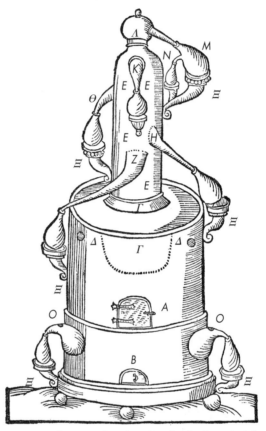

(A) Hypocaustum (combustion chamber for the fuel). (B) Ashpit. (Γ) Flask (still) with the matter to be distilled. (Δ) Airholes for regulating the fire. (E) Head with four beaks at various heights. (Λ) Mounted alembic with beak for the most spiritual (i.e., the subtlest) waters. (Z), (H), (Θ), (K) Beaks at various heights. The uppermost furnishes the subtler water, the lowest the least subtle. (M) Collecting retort for the condensation of the volatile spirits, i.e., the hard-to-coagulate vapors. (N) Receptacle for the collecting of the coagulated liquid. M and N together form an excipus geminus. (Ξ) Mounting supports for the receivers. (O) Rectificatoria (rectification vessels).

Fig. 2.3. Pentathlum, a multipurpose distilling appliance (from *Spagyrics: The Alchemical Preparation of Medicinal Essences, Tinctures, and Elixirs* by Manfred M. Junius).

Dragon

Probably the most famous alchemical symbol, the fire-breathing dragon is at once the guardian of the treasure of the opus and an archetype that undergoes numerous transformations. The *rebis,* an alchemical being with a male and a female head on a single body embodying qualities of both genders and representing the reconciliation of spirit and matter, is often depicted standing on top of a fire-breathing dragon.

E

Earth. See Elements.

Egg

The symbolism of an egg in alchemy and in general is open to a wide variety of interpretations. A chick hatching from an egg is an obvious symbol for growth. As an archetypal alchemic symbol, the hard shell could be seen as the earth, the albumen is the water, between the outer and inner membrane inside the shell is air, and the yolk is fire. In many alchemic texts the egg is seen as a hermetically sealed vessel, a model for alchemic vessels. Carl G. Jung compares the egg to the soul:

> In alchemy the egg stands for the chaos apprehended by the artifex, the *prima materia* containing the captive world-soul. Out of the egg—symbolized by the round cooking vessel—will rise the eagle or phoenix, the liberated soul.[6]

Elements

The four basic elements or energies in alchemy are fire, water, air, and earth. Operations and processes for manipulating these elements are a great part of alchemy. *See* "Elements and Alchemy" in chapter 1.

Elixir

In general, the Chinese alchemists were a lot more concerned with elixirs than in the West. They advanced the art of concocting elixirs to new levels with the hope of prolonging life or even becoming immortal. In the West there was in medieval times the search for the elixir of life, and famous alchemists such as Arnald de Villanova and Roger Bacon wrote popular texts on the subject. The term *elixir* has been used for essential oil blends, tinctures, and herbal teas; however, in spagyric alchemy, the term is for a specific process. In spagyrics, elixirs must be prepared in a philosophical manner from several plants, with the calcined plant salts added.

Emerald Tablet

Although relatively succinct in words, to many, the Emerald Tablet is considered the bible of alchemy. The actual origin of the tablet is shrouded in mystery. In a treatise by Albertus Magnus in the early fourteenth century, the tomb of Hermes was discovered by Alexander the Great in a cave near Hebron, and in the hands of Hermes was found a tablet of emerald that was taken by Sarah, the wife of Abraham. However, this version could easily have been produced to elevate certain religious dogmas. Another account by Roger Bacon states that a physician named Galienus Alfachim found the tablet in a cave, clasped in the hands of the corpse of the legendary Hermes Trismegistus.

There are numerous translations of the Phoenician inscription of the tablet, and throughout the centuries hundreds of philosophers, scholars, and alchemists have attempted to interpret its cryptic words. It is one of the most significant pillars of alchemy but also one of the biggest mysteries because everything concerning it is a great puzzle—its fabled and remarkable discovery, its author (was it written by Hermes or an anonymous writer who ascribed it to him to enhance its authority?). In any case, the Emerald Tablet is a cornerstone of the alchemic tradition that must be regarded carefully.

I have read numerous translations of the tablet, and it's readily apparent that the translations are often biased toward the translator's culture and cosmology. The translations are usually numbered by content to more easily compare them. This first one is more or less generic and uncolorful but supposedly translated directly from the Phoenician:

1. True it is without falsehood, certain most true.
2. That which is above is like to that which is below, and that which is below is like to that which is above, to accomplish the miracles of one thing.
3. And as in all things whereby contemplation of one, so in all

things arose from this one thing by a single act of adoption.

4. The father thereof is the Sun, the mother the moon.

5. The wind carried it in its womb, the earth is the source thereof.

6. It is the father of all works of wonder throughout the world.

6a. The power thereof is perfect.

7. If it be cast on to earth, it will separate the element of earth from that of fire, the subtle from the gross.

8. With great sagacity it doth ascend gently from earth to heaven. Again it doth descend to earth and uniteth in itself the force from things superior and things inferior.

9. Thus thou will possess the brightness of the world, and all obscurity will fly away from thee.

10. This thing is the strong fortitude of all strength, for it overcometh every subtle thing and doth penetrate every solid substance.

11. Thus was the world created.

12. Hence will there be marvelous adaptations achieved of which the manner is this.

13. For this reason I am called Hermes Trismegistus because I hold three parts of the wisdom of the whole world.[7]

This one, as you can see, has a noticeably Christian bent:

1. I speak not fictitious things, but that which is certain and most true.

2. What is below is like that which is above, and what is above is like that which is below to accomplish the miracles of One Thing.

3. And as all things were produced by the One Word of One Being, so all things were produced from the One Thing by adaptation.

4. Its father is the Sun, its mother the Moon.

5. The wind carries it in its belly, its nurse is the earth.

6. It is the father of all perfection throughout the world.

7. The power is vigorous if it be changed into earth.

7A. Separate the earth from the fire, the subtle from the gross, acting prudently and with judgement.

8. Ascend with the sagacity from the earth to heaven, and then

again descend to the earth and unite together the power of things superior and things inferior.

9. Thus you will obtain the glory of the whole world and obscurity will fly far from you.

10. This has more fortitude than fortitude itself, because it conquers every subtle thing and can penetrate every solid.

11. Thus was the world formed.

12. Hence proceed wonders which are here established.

13. Therefore I am called Hermes Trismegistus, having three parts of the philosophy of the whole world.[8]

There are many diverse interpretations of the Emerald Tablet; we have the tablet interpreted in light of the technical aspects of laboratory alchemy— to the creation of the world and everything in between. The mysteries it contains may never be full resolved. But one thing remains clear: it is a prime example, in so many ways, of the alchemic tradition. Therefore, my suggestion is that as you progress in the divine art, at times come back to it and see how (or if) your own interpretation changes and/or deepens as you progress.

F

Fermentation

In alchemy, fermentation has three distinct processes. It is the metabolic process that converts sugar to acids, gases, or alcohol. In spagyrics fermentation typically occurs through yeasts that convert sugar into alcohol and carbon dioxide. Unrefined salt can be used for the operation as well. Metaphorically, fermentation is the process of incubation and maturation of metals within the womb of Earth. On a spiritual or personal-growth level, fermentation is the beginning of our process of rebirth, symbolized by the birth of wine from the death of the grape.

Fire. See Elements.

Flamel, Nicholas (1330–1417)

An interesting alchemist of medieval times, Nicholas Flamel and his wife garnered enormous wealth during the fourteenth-century fervor for transmutation alchemy. Flamel is well known for his generous will, which included the founding of fourteen hospitals, construction of various chapels, and endowment for several churches.

Furnaces

Since prehistory, furnaces have played an integral part in the arts of alchemy, and their construction and use have taken on a spiritual connotation in many places and time periods throughout history. Alchemic furnaces come in many different configurations to accomplish various temperatures for specific tasks. Although used primarily in metallurgic processes, which is not the focus of this book, it's still pertinent to acknowledge these practices of alchemy for they are central to the concepts of transformation and transmutation. These processes are also employed in calcifying and distilling herbs for spagyrics. Sir Isaac Newton, whose "respectable" work in mathematics and chemistry are irrefutable and changed the course of history, was also a student of alchemy. Here we have a fascinating list of furnaces that he used:

1. Ye Wind furnace (for calcination, fusion, cementation, &c), weh blows itself by attracting ye air through a narrow passage 2. Ye distilling furnace by naked fire for things that ye require a strong fire for distillation. It differs not much from ye Wind furnace, only ye glasse rests on a cross barre of iron under weh bar is a hole to put in the fire, weh in ye Wind furnace it put in at ye top, 3. The Reverberatory furnace where ye flame only circulating under an arched roof acts upon ye body. 4. Ye Sand furnace when ye vessel is set in sand or sifted ashes heated by a fire made underneath. 5. Balneum or Balneum Mariae when ye body is set to distill or digest in hot water. 6. Balneum Roris or Vaporosum ye glasse hanging in the steame in boyling water instead of this may be used ye heat of hors dung (cald venter Equinis) i:e: brewsters whey wheat bran, Saw dust, chopt hay or straw, a little moistened closed pressed & covered. Or it may in an eggshell bee set under a hen. 7. Anathor, Piger Henricus, Furnace Acediae for long digestions ye vessel set in sand heated wth a Turret full of Charcoale weh is contrived to burn only at the bottom the upper onju continually sinking

downe for a supply. Or the sand may be heated by a Lamp and it is called the Lamp Furnace. These are made of fire, stones or brick.[9]

G

Gold

The main task of the metallurgic alchemists was the transmutation of base metals into gold for wealth. The Chinese alchemists generally used this science for the making of elixirs to prolong life and increase vitality, as did the esoteric Western alchemists in their search for the philosopher's stone and the elixir of life.

However, there is another side to the story about the alchemcial quest for gold. Jung and others believed the true search was for philosophic gold. Here is a quote by Eliphas Levi translated from the French original of 1854 on philosophical gold, the great work, and the operation of the sun (which Hermes also mentions in the Emerald Tablet):

> Like all magical Mysteries, the secrets of the Great Work possess a threefold significance: they are religious, philosophical and natural. Philosophical Gold is in religion the Absolute and Supreme reason; in philosophy it is Truth; in visible Nature it is the Sun; in the subterranean and visible world it is most pure and perfect gold. For this cause the search after the Great Work is called the Search for the Absolute, while the Work itself passes as an Operation of the Sun.[10]

H

Hellenic Alchemy

The culture of the Greeks, or the Hellenes, as the Romans named them, prospered around the Mediterranean and Black Seas. Greek language was the predominant language of both commerce and philosophy and brought with it more erudite linguistics for explaining sophisticated ideas, such as alchemical processes and philosophy, central themes being Pythagoras's holistic science; Demokritis's advanced ideas of the world being made up of material atoms; and the philosophies of Socrates, Plato, and Aristotle. While in China and India alchemists were mostly concerned with elixirs, Hellenic alchemy was more concerned with mystical-religious subjects and the tinging and dyeing of metals. *See* Maria Prophetissa; Zosimos of Panoplis.

Herbs

We will be exploring herbs deeply during the practical instructions in shamanic alchemy. Spagyrics is a common term for the alchemical transformation of herbs via the processes of dissolution, separation, and calcination. Shamanic intention is added to these steps of herbal transformation. Some herbs employed in shamanic alchemy have relaxing properties, while others contain a "magical" potency or have specific medicinal uses. *See* Spagyrics.

Hermaphrodite

In modern times the term *hermaphrodite* has been replaced with *intersex,* which describes various combinations of what are considered male and female biology in humans. This topic is too large and unnecessary for the scope of this book.

The etymology of the name comes from the supposed birth of Hermaphrodite to Hermes and Aphrodite (the goddess of love, beauty, pleasure, and procreation) in Greek mythology. In alchemy, the mystical marriage of mercury and sulfur is described as *conjunction,* which means to unite or bond together. Yin and yang and Shiva and Shakti are both cosmic symbols in Chinese and Indian alchemy, respectively. Early Hermetic texts include the notion that creation was brought about by a hermaphroditic mind, and that Adam was hermaphroditic in that Eve was created from his body. Gnostic texts include the idea that discovering a state of "sexual union" is a path to liberation and enlightenment. It is well to note that the uroboros symbolizes the unity in all things and is a central symbol of alchemy. *See* Uroboros.

Hermes Trismegistus

The writings of Hermes are immensely important to alchemy but also obscure in origin. Experts in the field commonly agree that Hermes was not a specific individual. As Duncan Greenlees, British writer, theosophist, and educationist, notes:

Hermes . . . was not a man as the Buddha, the Prophet Muhammed, Jesus, or Confucius were men. There was no special man who bore his name and who taught "the Religion of the Mind."

Hermes was the Greek God of the Mind, and so of Wisdom. Thus any writings held to be inspired by true Divine Wisdom could be, and were, attributed to the God of Wisdom, and were said to be written by Hermes himself. This pseudonymity, usual in ancient days, had no motive of deceit in it—the book was written by "Hermes" (*i.e.* Wisdom) through the hand of a pupil of Wisdom, who saw no significance in his own share of the work that his unimportant personal name should be recorded. Disciples thus habitually wrote in the names of their teachers, humbly acknowledging a debt where it rightly belonged.[11]

Hermes, the god of wisdom, reigned not only in Greece but also in Egypt and elsewhere. In the Nile Valley he was known under the ancient name of Thout at least five thousand years ago. He played a vital role in many myths and was known as the recorder of the gods; it is said that he invented writing.

The early Christian fathers mostly held that Hermes lived before Moses and was a pious man whom God used to reveal truths, which were later to be fully explained by Christianity.

Hermetic Tradition

The Hermetic tradition represents a non-Christian lineage of Hellenistic gnosticism. The central texts of the tradition, the Corpus Hermeticum, were lost to the West in classical times. Their rediscovery and translation during the late fifteenth century by the Renaissance court of Cosimo de Medici provided a seminal force in the development of Renaissance thought and culture. The fifteen tracts of the *Corpus Hermeticum,* along with *The Perfect Sermon or the Asclepius,* are the foundation documents of the Hermetic tradition.

The following is from the third book of the *Corpus Hermetica,* "The Sacred Sermon":

1. The glory of all things, God and that which is Divine, and the Divine Nature, the beginning of things that are.

2. God, and the Mind, and Nature, and Matter, and Operation, or Working and Necessity, and the End and Renovation.

3. For there were in the Chaos, an infinite darkness in the Abyss or bottomless Depth, and Water, and a subtle Spirit intelligible in Power; and there went out the Holy Light, and the Elements were coagulated from the Sand out of the moist Substance.

4. And all the Gods distinguished the Nature full of Seeds.

5. And when all things were interminated and unmade up, the light things were divided on high. And the heavy things were founded upon the moist sand, all things being Terminated or Divided by Fire; and being sustained or hung up by the Spirit they were so carried, and the Heaven was seen in Seven Circles.

6. And the Gods were seen in their Ideas of the Stars, with all their Signs, and the Stars were numbered, with the Gods in them. And the Sphere was all lined with Air, carried about in a circular, motion by the Spirit of God.

7. And every God by his internal power, did that which was commanded him; and there were made four footed things, and creeping things, and such as live in the Water, and such as fly, and every fruitful Seed, and Grass, and the Flowers of all Greens, and which had sowed in themselves the Seeds of Regeneration.

8. As also the Generations of men to the knowledge of the Divine Works, and a lively or working Testimony of Nature, and a multitude of men, and the Dominion of all things under Heaven and the knowledge of good things, and to be increased in increasing, and multiplied in multitude.

9. And every Soul in flesh, by the wonderful working of the Gods in the Circles, to the beholding of Heaven, the Gods, Divine Works, and the Operations of Nature; and for Signs of good things, and the knowledge of the Divine Power, and to find out every cunning workmanship of good things.

10. So it begineth to live in them, and to be wise according to the Operation of the course of the circular Gods; and to be resolved into that which shall be great Monuments; and Remembrances of

the cunning Works done upon Earth, leaving them to be read by the darkness of times.

11. And every generation of living flesh, of Fruit, Seed, and all Handicrafts, though they be lost, must of necessity be renewed by the renovation of the Gods, and of the Nature of a Circle, moving in number; for it is a Divine thing, that every world temperature should be renewed by nature, for in that which is Divine, is Nature also established.[12]

I

Indian Alchemy

The spirit of Indian alchemy lies both in the creation of elixirs and in the yoga-alchemy connection that Mircea Eliade speaks much of. In this regard, hatha yoga and tantra function in unity with the perception of the alchemic astral body. In alchemy, the microcosm (in this case spiritual man) is comparable to the yogic concept of the astral or diamond man. Through the unbroken yogic traditions, Indian alchemy is as alive now as the search for longevity was in ancient times.

Islamic Alchemy

The Arabs' conquest of Egypt, Syria, and Persia gave rise to a new scientific center of learning and the rise of Islam. The Islamic Arabs were eager seekers of knowledge and had a passion for alchemy. Historians tell us that an Arab prince, Khalid, assembled Greek philosophers in Egypt around the eighth century CE and commanded them to translate alchemic texts from Greek and Egyptian to Arabic. These are said to be the first translations made in Islam from one language to another. The most famous alchemist of this period was Jabir ibn Hayyan (*see* Jabir ibn Hayyan).

J

Jabir ibn Hayyan

According to tradition, Jabir ibn Hayyan is considered the father of Islamic alchemy and was possibly an apothecary or physician who lived mostly during the eighth century. There are close to three thousand articles and treatises attributed to Jabir, but historian Paul Kraus demonstrated in the 1940s that many of these were not written by him and more than likely were written by his subsequent followers in the ninth and tenth centuries.

One the most interesting aspects of Jabir's work is a type of numerology referred to as the method of the balance. In this method the quantity of the four natures (hot, cold, wet, and dry) is determined in a substance through the substance's name. Each letter of the Arabic alphabet was given a numerical value, and depending on the order of the letters, they were applied to the different natures.

Jung, Carl G. (1875–1961)

Visionary and dream experiences led Carl Jung to discover that the ancient art of alchemy was describing, in symbolic language, the journey that all of us must take toward embodying our own intrinsic wholeness, what he called the process of individuation. Although Jung was not an alchemist in the traditional sense, he found the study of historic alchemy helpful in explaining the archetypal roots of the modern mind. Jung wrote that he

> had very soon seen that analytical psychology [the psychology Jung developed] coincided in a most curious way with alchemy. The experiences of the alchemists, were, in a sense, my experiences, and their world was my world. This was, of course, a momentous discovery. I had stumbled upon the historical counterpart of my psychology of the unconscious.[13]

He goes on to say that "the process through which I had passed at that time corresponded to the process of alchemical transformation."[14] Jung proceeded to write *Psychology and Alchemy* where he lists many alchemic illustrations resembling mandalas as diagrams for meditation, reflection, and self-exploration. He also provides material concerning the visions of Zosimos and the works of Paracelsus. Although Jung lacked what practical alchemists call *praxis,* he is well noted as a kind of alchemist of the subconscious, and his place in alchemical history is significant in the resurgence of alchemic popularity since his writings.

Kelley, Edward (1555–1595)

Historically, Edward Kelley is viewed as a famous but dubious character in alchemic circles, said to have been involved with forging deeds, and was accused of necromancy. Most famous for his séances and angelic communication, he traveled with John Dee for a period in those pursuits but was ultimately jailed and tortured for his scheming. He was killed trying to flee custody.

M

Magic

From the earliest times, magic has been closely associated with alchemy. In ancient times magic was a common part of the everyday lives of people; although just as today, there were sure to be skeptics. Along with that, it must be said that magic is elusive and unpredictable. It can't be consistently replicated with each person achieving the same results—that's the work of science. Also, magic has always been the domain of special people and groups, and it is only revealed to people by an act of the divine, with this sacred knowledge then passed along through secret lineages. We can say that people knowledgeable in magic were and are special because even if a nonchosen person is given a magical secret or spell he or she can't necessarily make it work. In essence, the principles of magic are hidden to the ordinary mind because the ordinary mind simply can't perceive them. Alchemical magic is not simply a set of theories; it is a practical, energetic, vibratory praxis with sympathetic and antipathic powers that influence events.

Maier, Michael (1568–1622)

Michael Maier was a physician and alchemist whose most noteworthy contribution to the divine art was his remarkable books of emblems. His most famous emblem book is *Atalanta Fugiens,* which has a series of fifty emblems each containing a motto, a copper-plate engraving by Matthäus Merian, an epigram, a fugue for three voices, and an explanation of the emblem's alchemical meaning. *Atalanta Fugiens* presents a brilliant view into alchemic tradition enhanced by Paracelsian and Rosicrucian philosophy. Engravings from this text are included throughout this book.

Manuscripts and Texts

One of the principal ways alchemy was spread and advanced through the ages was via manuscripts and texts that were translated and handed down generation to generation. Especially during the Middle Ages, there were a great many manuscripts and texts on various subjects, including experiments, tincturing, inspiration, and philosophy. Included in these were texts by Plato, Aristotle, and Albertus Magnus. During the early part of this period a work entitled *Compositiones ad tingenda musiva* or *Compositiones variae* contains a number of recipes that were apparently used in the alchemic crafts of the time. Alchemic scholar C. J. S. Thompson explains:

> In this manuscript we find formulae for dyeing skins, for gilding iron, for writing in letters of gold, and for soldering metals. It also contains recipes for colouring artificial stones used in making mosaics, directions for staining glass and the staining of wood, bone, and horn, together with a list of ores, metals, earths and metallic oxides employed by craftsman in making jewelry, in enamelling, and painting. Instructions are given for gilding glass, wood, metals and fabrics. Mention is also made of gums, resins and other vegetable substances used in the arts, of products derived from the sea, such as salt coral, and molluscs yielding a purple dye.[15]

Among the most interesting of the ancient alchemic manuscripts are those illuminated in gold that illustrate various processes. Examples of these are still preserved in the National Library of France and the Library of the Arsenal in Paris, the British Museum in London, and principal libraries in Italy such as the Vatican Library, among others.

I have found the reading and study of alchemic manuscripts and texts extremely illuminating and quite enjoyable. In this modern age of computers and digitizing, we are given the ability to examine vast amounts of literature like no other time before. Publishers such as Kessinger, among others, have digitized ancient and rare books for preservation, and many rare books on alchemy are now available that we (the general public) may not have otherwise even known about.

Maria Prophetissa (ca. first to third centuries)

Maria Prophetissa, or Mary the Jewess, is known as one of the first alchemic writers and is attributed to inventing important alchemic equipment such as the tribikos. In the writings of Zosimos she is regarded as a revered figure in alchemy. Probably the most famous alchemic precept is the Axiom of Maria, attributed to Maria: one becomes two, two becomes three, and out of the third comes the one as the fourth.

Fig. 2.4. Maria Prophetissa (engraving by Matthäus Merian, from *Atalanta Fugiens* by Michael Maier, 1617).

Mercury. See Philosophical Principles.

Metals

Although we won't be dealing much with metals in this book, it is good to recognize the significance of this subject in alchemy. Mircea Eliade postulates that mining and metallurgy were prominent in ancient alchemy and that gold and copper were used as far back as the fourth millennium BCE. Even before that, meteoric rock was used for tools and weapons. Some alchemists of the Middle Ages were consumed with the relationship of mercury and sulfur in the creation of gold.

Mind-Soul-Spirit-Matter

I am including this topic due to the enormous current interest in mind-spirit-body modalities and because it is core to many alchemic philosophies. The alchemic point of view is fascinating and if nothing else good food for thought. This quote comes from the introduction to an alchemic textbook on the art of self-regeneration written by A. S. Raleigh, the late official scribe of the Hermetic Brotherhood, which includes lessons inspired by a sermon of Hermes entitled "About the Common Mind":

> The sermon . . . deals with the Common or General Mind as the principle or Energy radiating from God Beyond All Name, and its relation to the individual mind in man, as well as all other forms of life, in so far as they are dominated by Mind. The position taken by Hermes is that the thinking of the Supreme Divinity is radiated forth as Mind, possessing the same essentiality as does the very Esse of God. This Mind it is that dominates all the creative life of the Cosmos. All else is the product of this Mind. This is termed the Common Mind, because it is the Mind common to all. In man it becomes individualized as the mind, which becomes the energizing principle of the soul."[16]

In "Lesson VII" (chapter 7) of Raleigh's book, which relates to the fourteenth part of Hermes's sermon, we get to the crux of matter-spirit-soul-mind or mind-soul-spirit-matter. The relationships among the four are looked at from both directions, a perspective also suggested by the famous alchemic adage from the Emerald Tablet: "What is below is like that which is above, and what is above is like that which is below." In this passage it is made clear that these principles are perfectly united, joined together, one acting as the vehicle for the other.

> This is why we are told that the subtlest part of Matter is Air. Air as used in this connection means Spirit, or Pneuma, while Matter in this sense is of course the Physical Matter of which bodies are composed. We are told that there is in reality no sharp line of demarcation between the Spirit and Matter, but rather the Spirit has entered into Matter, and so united to it, as to become the subtlest part physical matter, so

that it is difficult to determine where Spirit ceases and Matter begins. In the same way, Psyche or Soul enters into Spirit or Pneuma, blending with it, and becoming the subtlest part of Spirit. Mind, likewise, enters into Psyche or Soul, uniting with it in such a way as to become the subtlest energy of Psyche or Soul. And God enters into Mind and is the subtlest part of Mind. God energizes Mind, Mind energized Soul, Soul energizes Spirit, and Spirit energizes Matter. . . . In this way are all the Principles merged the one into the other.[17]

Microcosm-Macrocosm

The notion that each human is a microcosm of the universal macrocosm is prevalent in alchemic texts. Humanity was created of the four elements, and the stars are within us (the astral body). Paracelsus illustrates:

Fig. 2.5. Microcosm-macrocosm, earth-heaven (engraving by Matthäus Merian, from *Atalanta Fugiens* by Michael Maier, 1618).

Since man is a child of the cosmos, and is himself the microcosm, he must be begotton, each time anew, by his mother. And just as he was created by the four elements of the world even in the beginning, even so he will be created in the future again and again. . . . Thus life in the world is life in the matrix (i.e., the womb). The child in the maternal body lives in the firmament and outside the mother's body it lives in the outer firmament. . . . The inner stars of man are in their properties, kind and mature, by their course and position, like his outer stars and different only in form and in material. For as regards their nature, it is the same in the ether and in the microcosm of man. . . . Man consists of the four elements, not only—as some hold—because he has four tempers, but also because he partakes of the nature, essence, and properties of these elements. In him there lies the "young heaven," that is to say, all the planets are part of man's structure and they are children of the great heaven which is their father. For man was created from heaven and earth, and is therefore like them!"[18]

N

Newton, Sir Isaac (1643–1727)

We know from recent research that the great mathematician was also passionately into the mysteries and riddles of alchemy. Modern scholars suggest that Isaac Newton was not entirely satisfied with physical and mathematical answers, and as a deeply religious man he was in constant search for the One God and the divine unity in nature. It is said that during his alchemical pursuits, he would sleep only a few hours a night, and that his alchemic furnaces would burn constantly for weeks at a time. It has also been noted that he was extremely well read on the subject. Researcher Betty Jo Dobbs writes:

He had read Greek alchemists, Arabic alchemists, the alchemists of the medieval Latin West, of the Renaissance, and his own period. He had read Aristotelian alchemists. Medical alchemists, Neoplatonic alchemists, and mechanical alchemists. He had read the most mystical and the most pragmatic.[19]

O

Ouroboros

The word *ouroboros* comes from the Greek *oura* meaning "tail" and *boros* meaning "eating"—thus "he who eats the tail." This symbolizes the cyclic nature of the universe: creation out of destruction, life out of death. The ouroboros eats its own tail to sustain its life, in an eternal cycle of renewal.

Fig. 2.6. Ouroboros (engraving by Matthäus Merian, from *Atalanta Fugiens* by Michael Maier, 1617).

P

Paracelsus (1493–1541)

Paracelsus is the Latin name adopted by Philippus Theophrastus Aureolus Bombastus von Hohenheim. It was the well-known quotes of Paracelsus relating to nature and philosophy that originally motivated my study of

Fig. 2.7. Paracelsus (image from the book *Zweihundert deutsche Männer in Bildnissen und Lebensbeschreibungen* [Two hundred German men in portraits and biographies], Leipzig 1854, edited by Ludwig Bechstein).

alchemy, and as "bombastic" as some of his writings are, I'm a big fan. I will let a scholar of Paracelsus begin his story. This text comes from the translation from German of *Four Treatises of Theophrastus Bombastus von Hohenheim Called Paracelsus*. I am fortunate to have an original copy of this book produced in 1941 by Publications of the Institute of the History of Medicine by Johns Hopkins University.

> Four hundred years ago, on September 24, 1541, Paracelsus died in Salzburg. He died misunderstood by the world, embittered, and poor. With him went one of the most forceful personalities of the Renaissance. . .
>
> Paracelsus wanted to be a physician like his father. He studied the arts, possibly in Vienna, then medicine in Italy at the University of Ferrara. But he was thoroughly disappointed with the instruction he was given at the time. From his father he had learned to see nature with his own eyes, not through the medium of books, and he had learned much biology with him. In Villach, laboring in mines and smelting

works, he had acquired a thorough knowledge of chemistry. And now, in Italy, he found that there was too wide a gap between science and the Graeco-Arabic theories that were still the foundation of medicine. He was a rebellious spirit, at that time already hard-headed and stubborn. Since he could not find at the university the enlightenment he was seeking he looked for other teachers and started on a voyage of discovery which, with short interruptions, was to last until his death.[20]

For many years Paracelsus traveled all through Europe including Sweden, Poland, Lithuania, Turkey, Greece, the Ionian Islands, Alexandria, and the British Isles. During his wanderings he practiced medicine but more importantly developed his own system of medicine and also a unique philosophy and theology. He conceived of disease much differently than the physicians of his time and applied science and mysticism "through the eyes of nature" to try and determine the place of humanity in the world and the causes and meanings of disease. He tried to reform the medical establishment, but no one would listen. In frustration, he would yell at his medical colleagues, incurring their opprobrium. He wrote many books, but there was a deliberate conspiracy against him and only a few were published during his lifetime. After a brief stint teaching at the university in Basel, Switzerland, he resumed his wanderings, after being antagonized by his colleagues and misunderstood by his students. Always hoping to have his books published, but rarely ever realizing this, he went to Salzburg a bitter and worn-out man, to die at only forty-eight years old.

Although he was undoubtedly a reputable physician, his often-violent tirades against physicians backfired because his most important works were never published during his lifetime. Fortunately, he did have a few disciples who eventually published his manuscripts, and during the sixteenth and throughout the seventeenth century, they attracted wide attention. Many of his remedies became widely accepted. Whenever medicine went through a speculative and/or mystical phase, such as in Germany in the 1800s and also today, the figure of Paracelsus comes forth. We now have access to many works of Paracelsus; however, they are quite obscure and not easy to read, and many of the problems he ventured to solve remain unsolved today.

Throughout this book you will find quotes on various topics by

Paracelsus, but here are two important ones that reveal the man himself. The first is by the bombastic Theophrastus Bombastus:

Since you, O Sophist,* everywhere abuse me with such fatuous and mendacious words, on the ground that being sprung from rude Helvetia I can understand and know nothing: and also because being a duly qualified physician I still wander from one district to another; therefore I have proposed by means of this treatise to disclose to the ignorant and inexperienced: what good arts existed in the first age; what my art avails against you and yours against me; what should be thought of each, and how my posterity in this age of grace will imitate me. Look at Hermes, Archelaus, and others in the first age: see what Spagyrists and what Philosophers then existed. By this they testify that their enemies, who are your patrons, O Sophist, at the present time are but mere empty forms and idols. Although this would not be attested by those who are falsely considered your authentic fathers and saints, yet the ancient Emerald Table shews more art and experience in Philosophy, Alchemy, Magic, and the like, than could ever be taught by you and your crowd of followers. . . . Now at this time, I, Theophrastus Paracelsus Bombast, Monarch of the Arcana, am endowed by God with special gifts for this end, that every searcher after this supreme philosophic work may be forced to imitate and to follow me, be he Italian, Pole, Gaul, German, or whatsoever or whosoever he be. Come hither after me, all you philosophers, astronomers, and spagyrists, of however lofty a name ye may be, I will show and open to you, Alchemists and Doctors, who are exalted by me with the most consummate labours, this corporeal regeneration.[21]

The next passage, titled "The Fourth Defence: Concerning My Journeyings," has Paracelsus as the author. This second passage hits home to me and also affords me some comfort that I am not alone on the wayfarers' path of knowledge.

---

*A sophist was a specific kind of respected teacher in both ancient Greece and in the Roman Empire, but the sophists' practice of charging money for education and providing wisdom only to those who could pay resulted in the condemnations made by Socrates through Plato.

It is necessary that I answer for my journeyings and for the fact that I am resident nowhere. Now how can I be against that or force that, which to force it is not possible for me? Or, what can I give to or take from predestination? Yet I have to exonerate myself in some measure to you, since I am so much harangued to you, to vex me and ridicule me too, because I am a wayfarer and as though I were therefore the less worthy. No one should take it amiss, if I should complain about this. The journeys which I have thus far made have profited me much, for the reason that no man's master is in his home and none has his teacher in the chimney-corner. Thus the arts are not all confirmed with one's fatherland, but they are distributed over the whole world. Not that they are in one man alone, or in one place: on the contrary they must be gathered together, sought out and captured, where they are. . . Is it not just and very fitting that I should investigate and seek out these goals, and see what is wrote in each one? . . . Is it not true, art pursues no man, but must be pursued? . . . Thus it follows: if a man desire to see a person, to see a country, to see a city, to know these same places and customs, the nature of heaven and the elements, he must go after them. For, for them to go after him is not possible.[22]

Paracelsus and Elemental Spirits

The famous alchemist Paracelsus was a rebel, not only in medical matters (*see* Paracelsus), but his intense individualism made it impossible for him to accept the integral dogmas of the dominant Catholic Church of his time. For one, he believed in elemental spirits.

Christianity had a difficult time overcoming the ancient gods, and soon the Christian heaven was populated with angels and saints, many of whom took the place of the ancient gods. However, the church had no place for the pagan elemental spirits that were so deeply rooted in popular belief and a part of everyday life. Unable to either successfully deny their existence or make them a part of Christian theology, the church theologians simply deemed these spirits to be devils.

Paracelsus had totally different views; he believed firmly in their existence and that they were not devils but creatures of God and, like all other creatures, were testimonies of God's miraculous works. Paracelsus considered these creatures important enough to write a whole treatise about them. For him, each element of the four is inhabited by a kind of being peculiar to it and to whom the element is called *chaos*. We live between heaven and earth where there is air. Man, therefore, lives in air, and air is his chaos. Thus water is chaos to the nymphs: they are at home in their chaos so do not drown in water. Likewise, gnomes are not choked in earth, and salamanders do not burn in fire.

Here is a small excerpt from Paracelsus's treaty titled *A Book on Nymphs, Sylphs, Pygmies, Etc.* This comes from the section "About their Abode":

> Their abode is of four kinds, namely, according to the four elements. . . . Those in the water are nymphs, those in the air are sylphs, those in the earth are pygmies, those in the fire salamanders. . . . The names have been given them by people who did not understand them. . . . The name of the water people is also undina, and of the air people sylvestres, and of the mountain people gnomi, and of the fire people vulcani rather than salamandri. . . . that the undinae have their abode in water, and the water is given to them as to us the air, and just as we are astonished that they should live in water, they are astonished about us being in air. The same applies to the gnomi in the mountains: the earth is their air and is their chaos. (For everything lives in chaos, that is: everything has its abode in chaos, walks and stands therein.) Now, the earth is not more than mere chaos to the mountain manikins. For they walk through solid walls, through rocks and stones, like a spirit; this is why these things are all chaos to them, that is, nothing. That amounts to: as little as we are hampered by the air, as little they are hampered by the mountain, by earth and rocks . . . the coarser the chaos, the more subtile is the creature; and the more subtile the chaos the coarser the creature. The mountain people have a coarse chaos: therefore they must be more subtile; and man has a subtile chaos; therefore, he is all the coarser. And thus there are different kinds of chaos, and the inhabitants are adapted in nature and quality to live in them.[23]

Philosophical Principles

In alchemic terminology there are three principles or elements—mercury, sulfur, and salt—but these principles are different from their meaning in modern chemistry. In alchemy, the principles are considered as follows:

Mercury represents the passive or feminine principle of life, the vital force or power.

Sulfur represents the masculine or active principle, consciousness or soul, individual soul and world soul.

Salt represents matter, body, the solid.

Phoenix

The mythical phoenix is the classic alchemic symbol of sacrifice. In medieval legend, it is said that the phoenix came from Arabia and flew to Egypt to undertake its death and rebirth. To Christian alchemists this is plainly seen in the death and resurrection of Christ, to others the colors of the bird—red, gold, black, and white—symbolize processes in the alchemic stages of transmutation.

Prima Materia

Definitions of this term, also called prime matter or first matter, vary throughout different alchemic disciplines. In his analysis of the subject Jung writes:

The basis of the opus, the *prima materia*, is one of the most famous secrets of alchemy. This is hardly surprising since it represents the unknown substance that carries the projection of the autonomous psychic content.[24]

According to Paracelsus, all created things proceed from one matter, not each one separately from its own peculiar nature. This common matter of all things is the great mystery (*mysterium magnum*). This great mystery is the mother of all elements.

Other concepts in alchemy of the prima materia include numerology where numbers compounded together exist from one atom, a natural monad that comprehends and rules over the infinite as emanating from itself. In terms easier to comprehend, alchemic philosophy is often asserted to have five principles, with one being prima materia and five being quintessence:

1. The divine principle, the unity of prima materia and prima energia that form the foundation of creation.
2. Duality or polarity; in alchemy the opposition between fixed and volatile, sun and moon, yin and yang, and so on.
3. Triad or trinity; in alchemy this is often expressed by the duality of sulfur and mercury to which salt is added.
4. Quaternity; referring to the four elements: fire, water, air, and earth.
5. Quintuplicity: the four manifestations of elemental nature with the quintessence.

Quintessence

This is another one of those alchemic terms that has various meanings. One way to look at it is that within the four elements a fifth is present, the quintessence, but it is actually none of the four elements. It is the element that permeates all of creation and the force that binds everything. Without quintessence the elements would be dead. Paracelsus, in his usual obscure style, explains that in relation to the elements, quintessence is their incorruptible eternal substratum.

Distillation is often cited in alchemical practices for the extraction of quintessence, which in this case is synonymous with spirit or elixir, especially in the case of spagyrics.

R

Rosicrucians

For many historians the mystery of the Rosicrucians, the strange and secret fraternity of the Rosy Cross, which supposedly flourished between the fifteenth and seventeenth centuries, has never been satisfactorily solved. The German alchemist Michael Maier was very interested in the subject as were the famous alchemists Robert Fludd and Thomas Vaughan. What can be ascertained is that forms of Rosicrucianism and other philosophical colleges have existed from earliest times for the study of medicine and natural secrets.

The discoveries made were perpetuated from generation to generation by the initiation of new members. Some believe this is still going on today.

S

Salt. See *Philosophical Principles.*

Secretum Secrectorum

This text, meaning "secret of secrets," was popular during medieval times and one that Roger Bacon and other alchemists believed in wholeheartedly. The topics in the text include astrology, magical and medical properties of plants and gems, natural philosophy, physiognomy, ethics, and other alchemic ideas. The source of the text is controversial; Bacon apparently believed it was the work of Aristotle, but many scholars believe it derived from Islamic and Persian legends. The work has been translated into many languages.

Sol and Luna

The image of the sun and moon together, along with ouroboros, is the most enigmatic and ubiquitous hermetic symbol. In alchemy the sun is conceived of as masculine and the moon as feminine. According to these ancient ideas, the moon is a vessel of the sun: she is a universal receptacle of the sun in particular, and she was called *infundibulum terrae* (the funnel of the earth) because she "receives and pours out" the powers of heaven. In alchemic symbolism, sun and moon are almost always shown together, or when one is represented the other is too.

Spaᵹyrics

Spagyrics, also called spagyria, is an ancient practice that has garnered new interest in modern times and one that I explore in this book. Spagyrics is the application of alchemical methods to prepare tinctures, essences, and other products from the vibrational and medicinal properties of plants. Spagyria differs from the usual processes of making these products and also from analytical chemistry and pharmacology, even though these sciences in their own way can explain the effects of spagyric remedies. As Paracelsus said, the spagyrist has to "stand in the light of nature" to truly

Fig. 2.8. Hermes points out the mystical connection between the sun and the moon (from *Viridarium Chymicum: The Chemical Pleasure-Garden* by Daniel Stoltzius Von Stoltzenbert, 1624).

understand the natural laws and bases. Spagyrics takes into account the three alchemic philosophical principles or essentials. At the practical level, spagyric preparations always contain the salts obtained through incineration and calcination of the plant residue, unlike simpler preparations of tinctures and essences, which remove the plant residues after extraction.

Stages

Practical alchemy has a variety of laboratory stages or processes that can differ from alchemist to alchemist and in the order they are done, depending on the desired result. In most modern books on alchemy, especially as relates to "spiritual" or personal growth alchemy, there are usually seven stages. We will discuss this more in chapter 6. For now, what follows are two sample lists of common processes or stages.

1. Calcination: drying up

2. Dissolution: likened to death and burial

3. Conjunction: the combining of separate substances

4. Putrefaction: necessary for germination of the seed

5. Congelation: gathering together or cohesion of the substances

6. Sublimation: the body flies upward

7. Fermentation: the substance becomes soft and fluid

8. Exaltation: the perfection or essence

1. Division: the separation of the parts of the compound

2. Coitus: the natural act of two, a joining of both body and spirit

3. Calcination: pulverization of dry matter by fire

4. Sublimation: the elevation of dry matter by fire, when the extract is driven to the highest part of the vessel

5. Solution: the reduction of dry matter in a liquid

6. Generation: the generation of nature contained in matter and form

7. Putrefaction: the corruption of the proper and natural heat in every moist thing

8. Fermentation: the incorporation of the inanimate or that which giveth life, the restoration of taste, the inspiration of smell

9. Conjunction: the joining of two or more bodies

10. Separation: the division or separation of bodies

11. Imbibition: a soaking or maceration of a body in a liquid

12. Fixation: the body receives the tangent spirit, which takes away its volatility

Tinctures

Simply, tinctures are liquid extracts made from herbs that you take orally. They are usually extracted in alcohol, but they can also be extracted in vegetable glycerin or apple cider vinegar (nonalcoholic). *See* Spagyrics.

Transmutation and Transformation

The word *transmutation* gets used a lot in esoteric traditions, often as a synonym for *transformation*. But though these words are similar, they don't mean the same thing. Transmutation implies completely changing something—*trans* meaning "across, beyond, through" and *mutare* "to change." Except for a radioactive element, or through a nuclear reaction, strictly speaking, transmutation rarely happens in nature. It has become popular in recent times to use the word in relation to states of consciousness. On this subject we can find examples of temporary transmutation, such as spirit possession and high (or deep) levels of shamanic trance. More often than not, the word *transformation* more aptly describes the alchemists' work both in the laboratory and at the levels of personal and spiritual growth.

Trees

One the most ancient symbols found cross-culturally, trees were and still are used with reference to spirituality and knowledge. Two main examples of this include the world tree or cosmic tree of shamanism and the tree of life of the kabbalah. There are many alchemic illustrations of trees, with symbols of plants and metals sometimes inserted in the branches. Jung explores tree symbolism at great length as an archetypal representation of spiritual growth in the human psyche.

Sulfur. See Philosophical Principles.

V

Valentine, Basil (1394–1450)

Valentine is a legendary alchemist who is included here simply due to the influence that his writing had on other famous alchemists. Legend has it that he was a fifteenth-century monk and alchemist, but there is no physical evidence that he ever existed. Whoever wrote the books attributed to Basil Valentine was a very astute chemist, to the point that those who disliked Paracelsus claimed that he stole his ideas from Valentine.

W

Water. See Elements.

Wei Po Yang

Considered one of, if not the, father of Chinese alchemy. A popular tale about him goes like this:

The Story of Wei Po-Yang, the Pupil, and the Dog

Wei Po-Yang worked on the creation of the Elixir of Immortality. In order to do so, he believed that he needed to study in isolation. With this in mind, he moved his laboratory to the mountains, taking with him only a dog and three of his most trusted pupils. Many nights and days later, he had completed his first elixir, though whether it was the true Elixir of Immortality, that still remained to be seen.

In order to test its potency, Wei Po-Yang administers the elixir to his dog. The unfortunate dog, however, dies in the process, which leads to Wei Po-Yang's mistrust of his potion. With his pupils reluctant in ingesting such an elixir, and no one else to test it on, he drinks the potion himself. One of his pupils, loyal to a fault, also tests the elixir, and both he and his master die in the process. The remaining two pupils, seeing the fate of their master and colleague, opt out of taking the elixir, and instead remove themselves from the mountain.

However, the end of Wei Po-Yang isn't as tragic as it seems, for after the two pupils leave, Wei Po-Yang revives from his deathly state. He rouses his pupil and his dog, and all three transcend to become hsien (immortals).

Z

Zosimos of Panoplis

Scholars tell us that Zosimos is the first alchemist of whom we have authentic records. He flourished sometime around the fourth century and is commonly recognized as the father of Hellenistic alchemy. His skill in the art may be gathered from venerated references to him in the eighth and ninth centuries by Photius and other historians. Zosimos was acutely interested in alchemic equipment and writes that Maria Prophetissa was an expert in their making.

Zosimos believed that apart from the doctrines and texts contained in hermetic and alchemic books, there was a "secret knowledge" enjoyed only by the priests that was forbidden to reveal. He wrote a kind of encyclopedia of alchemy (some say with his sister) known as the *Cheirokmeta*. Full of secretive language, allegories, and dream sequences, his texts established a permanent connection between practical laboratory work and spiritual perfection. Despite the fragmentary nature of what survives of his work, and the difficulty in interpreting it, these writings provide the best window we have into Greek alchemy. These early texts establish many concepts and styles that would remain fundamental for much of later alchemy.

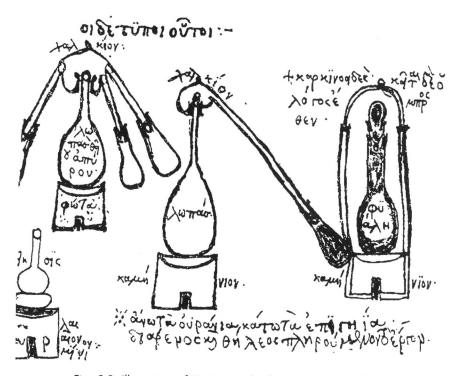

Fig. 2.9. Illustration of Zosimos's distillation equipment by an unknown author from the fifteenth-century Byzantine Greek manuscript *Parisinus graces* (as reproduced in *Collection des anciens alchimistes grecs* [3 vol., Paris, 1887–1888, p. 161] by Marcelin Berthelot).

3

SHAMANIC AND ALCHEMICAL COSMOLOGIES

Throughout the ages, humanity has had a burning thirst to comprehend the way in which the universe came into being and runs, what the universe is composed of, what causes natural phenomena to occur, and the primal force that created the whole cosmic order. Although the basic questions have always been the same, the answers have varied greatly throughout time and in different places because the *approaches* for answering the questions are as varied as the questions themselves. Approaches include the philosophical, spiritual-religious, artistic, and scientific. For our work here, we can say that a person's *cosmology* is how he or she looks at the answers to the questions.

COSMOLOGICAL THEORIES

In preparation for practical applications of shamanic alchemy, it's important to realize the different cosmologies of the people that formed the shamanic and alchemic processes and how they have changed, spread, and evolved throughout history up to the present day. The nature-based transcendental cosmology of the ancients is much different from the rational-scientific cosmology prevalent today. Both viewpoints or worldviews and all points in-between are simply part of our human history; there is no point arguing whose cosmology is right or wrong. The intent here is simply to acknowledge the differences in cosmologies and learn more about them. In doing so we widen our knowledge and prepare ourselves for further explorations.

I present here a brief outline of each belief system in an attempt to wrangle all the various theories into some kind of order. I have divided cosmology into three main theories and periods only for the sake of distinguishing the major differences, knowing that in many cases a person, during his or her lifetime, could believe in varying degrees in any one of the three. Please recognize I am simply providing information toward preparing for the practical work of shamanic alchemy. It is certainly not my intent to discuss creationism *versus* the big bang theory.

Transcendental Theory
1. A person believes that a higher, unseen, numinous reality coexists with the visible, physical reality.
2. A person believes that a select few have had experiential access to that higher, unseen reality and have passed down those experiences through spoken word and in writing.
3. A person believes that the very basis for his or her whole view in life (belief about God, heaven and hell, afterlife, etc.) is ultimately based on these experiences of a higher, unseen reality, which have been recorded.

Intuitional Theory
1. A person believes that the physical, visible world has a higher, harmonious order to it, other than that which he or she can perceive.
2. A person believes in the various ideas that philosophers, poets, and astronomers have developed about that cosmic, unperceived harmony.
3. A person believes that order to the cosmos exists and just fits or is, even if the various ideas proposed by different philosophers, poets, and astronomers don't always harmonize.
4. A person (if aware of history) believes that the specific theories of the cosmic harmony have altered over the centuries because we have gained insights into, or acquired knowledge of, the cosmic order.

Rational Theory

1. A person believes in purely empirical, scientific facts.
2. A person believes in an existing, harmonious cosmic order, but one that can be revealed only through empirical, scientific exploring, not by theorizing or philosophizing.

Within these three, broad theoretical and philosophical forms or cosmic structures are the different means or methods that humans throughout time have used to attempt to analyze, or simply make sense of, the cosmos. The chart below depicts six means that humanity has developed.

Means	Form
1. Mystical Shamanism	Transcendental
2. Mystical-Shamanistic Philosophy	Transcendental and Intuitional
3. Intuitional Philosophy	Intuitional
4. Intuitional Astronomy	Intuitional and Rational
5. Rational Philosophy	Rational
6. Rational Astronomy	Rational

This simple chart depicts humanity's gradual movement from transcendental forms to rational forms of cosmology.

1. Mystical shamanism is a transcendental means of cosmology obtained through direct experiences with the numinous. In this case the numinous includes super-sensual phenomena that not only include the sun, moon, and stars but also mountains, rivers, trees, animals, wind, rain, rock, flowers, and the spirits that animate them.
2. Mystical-shamanistic philosophy is transcendental but also intuitional, the difference being that these thinkers, although they describe a transcendental form, obtain their knowledge from mental or imaginative ideas (intuitional form) and not from direct experience with the numinous.

3. Intuitional philosophy is a cosmological means that philosophically and poetically describes intuitional theory. The ancient poets and philosophers did an amazing job communicating their ideas about the workings of the cosmos. These philosophies, along with intuitional astrology, formed the prevalent cosmological scheme of Western civilization for over two thousand years, up to the seventeenth century.

4. Intuitional astronomy combines intuitional description with rational empirical knowledge gathered from mathematical data of celestial motions.

5. Rational philosophy contains those philosophers who helped create the new rational-scientific cosmology without using empirical evidence but simply their own mental reasoning.

6. Rational astronomy is the gaining of knowledge by gathering and investigating data. Through this method, modern astronomers have formulated a mathematical scheme of the cosmos. For the last three centuries, the basis for humanity's understanding of the cosmos has relied almost exclusively on rational astronomy.

The Philosophical Principles of Alchemy and the Elements

One of the main concepts of alchemy, especially since the time of Paracelsus, is that all matter is maintained through the cooperation of three philosophical principles, also sometimes referred to as the three essentials: mercury, sulfur, and salt. The different proportions of these three principles accounts for the countless manifestations of matter. In this way, the names of these principles are not to be mistaken for their normal meanings, nor their meanings in chemistry.

Within the philosophical principles of alchemy, forget about your chemistry lessons. Alchemical mercury is not quicksilver (Hg), sulfur is not the element sulfur (S), and salt is not sodium chloride (NaCl). So important are these principles in alchemy that when written they are almost always capitalized. Briefly, here are the meanings of the alchemic philosophical principles:

Mercury is the feminine principle associated with life, vital force, the etheric. It is subtle but can also be corrosive. It is akin to the vital force of inhalation, breathing techniques such as pranayama, etheric space such as akasha, and vital force such as chi. It is also associated with blood, often referred to as moon, and in Indian alchemy with the semen of Siva.

Sulfur is the masculine principle associated with soul, both in the individual and in the world, and is assciated with consciousness, activity, and the sun. Sulfur is known in alchemy as the invisible fire.

Salt is basically matter, a solid. It's a body or vehicle and works together with mercury and sulfur, whereas mercury and sulfur alone form the law of polarity. The two snakes of the caduceus represent mercury and sulfur, which dissolve and bind.

These three building blocks construct the universe we observe: matter (salt principle), life-spirit (mercury principle), consciousness and intelligence (sulfur principle). Through our senses we are aware of the three philosophical principles via the manner in which matter manifests. They manifest in four forms that correlate to the elements and their properties:

1. Solid: earth, cold
2. Liquid: water, moist
3. Gaseous: air, dry
4. Radiant, etheric: fire, hot

Elements have the ability to separate and combine, and each element contains something of the other three. In this way, the elements of alchemy, like the three philosophies, are not basic substances as in chemistry; they are manifestations of states of matter. In alchemy they are often represented by triangles, which you can see at the bottom of figure 3.1, from left to right: earth, water, air, fire.

Combined, they form the symbol for ether or unity, also known as the symbol of Solomon and the Star of David, and in alchemy the quintessence. As we can see, earth and water are depicted as descending triangles and are manifested or fixed. Fire and air are ascending and are inflowing or volatile. The quintessence is the force that binds everything and as such is the spiritual core of all things. One of the goals of spagyrics, which we

Fig. 3.1. The four elements (from *Viridarium Chymicum:
The Chemical Pleasure-Garden* by Daniel Stoltzius Von Stoltzenbert, 1624).

Fig. 3.2. Symbol for ether
or quintessence.

will discuss later, is to liberate the quintessence of plant matter. In this
way, quintessence in alchemy often also refers to one of the philosophical
principles.

Shamanic Cosmology

For most shamanic cultures, including the complex cosmologies of the Siberian, Mayan, and Huichol shamans, three worlds exist from which all existence is contained called the upper, middle, and lower worlds, also known as heaven, earth, and the underworld. The world tree, or axis mundi, connects all three levels. Some cultures use a specific mountain or even a sacred pillar in a temple or home as metaphor for the axis mundi.

It truly is a metaphor because there is no way to experience the axis mundi without being in an altered state of consciousness. But if we want to talk about experiences of shamanic reality, we must use these types of metaphors. We can describe the movement of consciousness as down into the underworld or up into heaven. Either way, these are just metaphors for the movement or expansion of our consciousness.

Even though indigenous cultures throughout the world consider groves and individual trees to be sacred, the World Tree is a metaphor for the center of creation in the middle of the quantum foam. In this way, every tree, every place, and every person is at the center of creation. When we climb up or down or simply swing on the branches of the World Tree, our lives are changed forever as we break the spell of the consensus and expand our consciousness into the cosmic foam. We experience the unity of consciousness, matter, time, and space and the interconnectedness of all life. This is the perennial journey of the shaman.

Although many cultural differences exist among ancient and modern shamanic communities worldwide, a few basic commonalities exist in the underlying worldview of nearly all the people in the broader shamanic community. These include:

- An individual is both unique and indistinguishable from his or her environment. The entire world shares one body, one flesh.
- Identity is formed through intimate relationship with the natural world, especially the home territory and sacred places.
- Service to the human community as well as to the community of nature is inseparable from the goals of the individual.
- Daily activities emphasize giving as much as possible while asking for no more than what is necessary.

- All life has intrinsic value that is not dependent on human economic valuation.
- The community is completely dependent on the local environment for material sustenance and therefore is treated with utmost respect and reciprocity.[1]

As Nicholas Wood notes in his book *Voices from the Earth:*

There is a Native American phrase, "For All My Relations." The Lakota words for this are "Mitakuya Oyasin." This doesn't mean just your mother and father, your brothers and sisters, your aunt and uncle. It means your cat. The bird your cat catches. The mites in the bird's feathers. The tree the bird lived in. The clouds it flew beneath. And the stars above the clouds.[2]

This is the basis of the shaman's world. Shamanic states of consciousness are used by shamans to enter other realities than the ones that we are normally accustomed to. This may sound "far out" to some, but modern science is now joining the ancient shamans and mystics in agreeing on this. For the shaman, probably the most important dimension, other than our physical reality, can be best described as the spirit world. This does not necessarily mean the world of human spirits or souls of the dead. Most shamanic cultures list many layers of the spirit world, existing at once together and separate, as does our physical reality and the other dimensions.

The very basis of shamanism is that some ineffable essence (consciousness, spirit, soul, etc.) can leave the physical body and travel to other dimensions or worlds. Normally, our culture only recognizes death as the one time our spirit crosses over to another dimension, but if we examine dreaming, which we do every night, we can see that our consciousness can move around without our controlling it. How many of us have had a dream that has later come true? Or in a dream have spoken to a deceased relative or friend as if he or she were still alive? I know I have. An argument could be made that the altered state of consciousness employed by shamans is simply a controlled form of dreaming learned through shamanic teachings.

Modern physics has many new theories about the nature of reality and consciousness that may shed light on how shamans work. In his book *Mysticism and the New Physics,* Michael Talbot states that "every point in space-time is connected via the 'quantum foam' to every other point in space-time, (which) makes our universe into an immense dream space." He also suggests that "consciousness is a biogravitational field similar to the gravitational field governing matter. This is akin to saying that mind and matter are different vibrations or ripples in the same pond."[3]

Both of these perspectives, which arise from modern physics, are exactly what forms the basis for the techniques and practices of shamans to reach altered states of consciousness. To go one step further, we could say that, out of all possible realities, we are the ones who choose the reality we subscribe to during the course of our everyday lives. Usually, we follow the consensus of what those around us consider to be reality.

Shamans do not limit themselves to the consensus. This is one of the most important things to learn about shamans and one of the hardest for the Western mind to realize: that we have limited ourselves to our strictly personal human consciousness and the worldview of the society we live in. But the universe is not quite that simple . . .

Here are some key points about who shamans are and what they do:

- All of the duties and practices of the shaman work within and around the specific culture of the tribe the he or she is part of.
- Although the vocation is sometimes passed from one generation to the next in the same family, more often an individual is chosen by the spirits and called to the practice, and therefore the initiate has no choice. If the potential shaman refuses the call, it is common for this person or someone in his or her family to become seriously ill or die.
- Once the spirits select a person to become a shaman, the individual almost always passes through an intense and life-threatening initiation or near-death experience that radically and permanently shifts the perception of the potential shaman.
- If the individual survives the initiation period, being a shaman becomes a full-time, lifetime vocation.

- Although a novice shaman is usually guided by either an elder shaman and/or the community he or she serves, the actual lessons, skills, and power of the shaman are acquired through direct encounters with the spirit world after the novice has passed through the near-death experience or initiation period.
- A relationship with the spirits is maintained through continuous personal offerings and, at certain times, blood sacrifices to the spirits.
- Offerings vary in intensity depending on the situation and desired outcome. It is not uncommon for an important offering to represent a full year's wages or equivalent amount of work. This high level of commitment is what gives power to the offering and the shaman.
- The shaman radically and often alters his or her perception through a variety of means, some of which may include ingestion of hallucinogenic plants, multiple day and night ceremonies, fasting, many hours of continuous dancing, prolonged exposure to the elements, sleep deprivation, ritualized animal sacrifice, and body mortification, among others.
- The shaman commonly makes agreements and bargains with the local nature spirits and wild animals. If the agreements are not carried out, the shaman often becomes seriously ill or the recipient of some sort of physical tragedy or "accident," such as slipping off a cliff or falling off a horse.
- Because tribes are usually completely or partially dependent on crops and domesticated animals for survival, the shaman is in constant contact with the spirits to ensure the life, growth, and health of these plants and animals.
- Ceremonies, rituals, and offerings are made at appropriate times during the year according to the cyclical realities of nature and the cosmos to ensure adequate sustenance for the tribe.

PART TWO

PRAXIS
FUNDAMENTALS

4

INITIATION AND THEURGY

Most postmodern shamanic-alchemic initiations will of necessity be self-initiations. Self-initiations are very fruitful in that without intermediaries the initiate directly experiences the numinous through his or her own will and effort. As the novice progresses, symbolic and experiential initiations conducted by an experienced shaman can mark the completion or beginning of higher stages of development, but to start, self-initiations are powerful rites of passage that are employed to transform mundane conscious to higher states.

Shamanic initiation is a *progression* from one state of being to another. To understand something at a certain level, one must *be* at that level. Arriving at that level is accomplished through both knowledge and experience. Experience must be gained both psychically and physically. In most cases shamanic initiation isn't so much what a person would elect to do, like going to the movies, but rather is a situation born of necessity, such as a calling received by the initiate to undertake the work. Nothing is more powerful than this calling, and since you are reading this you have probably received it in one way or the other.

In the modern cultures of the West, we tend to view the unfolding of our lives as a relatively uniform and continuous process punctuated at times by secondary changes and events. But in the shamanic world, the tendency is to view personal development as a series of leaps or jumps from one dimension of existence to another, to the point that a person's name and identity may change many times during the course of a lifetime as the individual evolves from one mode of being to another. This seems a little strange to us because we don't engage in powerful rites of passage whereby a person is purged, purified, and initiated throughout the various life stages, as is common in the shamanic world.

In the life of a shamanic tribe the important stages in a person's life are marked by activities of inner purification that sweep clean the past, disrupt routine thought processes, and remove unwanted distractions so that the individual can proceed unimpeded into a new dimension of existence. Purification can take many forms, including physical processes, such as fasting, sweating, exposure to extreme heat or cold, vomiting, pain, or bleeding, and cleansing by natural energies, such as water, wind, earth, smoke, steam, and fire. The purification may alternatively or jointly be combined with psychic cleansing through prolonged isolation, repetitive actions, severe exhaustion, or psychic bombardment by presiding shamans. All these purification processes serve to diminish the controlling side of the initiate's ego, making the ego become small, which then enables the initiate to enter a new life stage.

This idea of "becoming small" is extremely important for modern people because we have been taught our whole lives to strive to be independent, successful, and "big," but by doing so we miss the undercurrent of magic in organic reality. All of the above-mentioned forms of purification, as well as many of the theurgic techniques I am sharing in this book, are designed to foster an entry into the flowing force or stream of power that spontaneously arises during prolonged entry into heightened states of awareness, peak emotional experiences, moments of ecstatic bliss, unbearable pain, and, especially, mystical union. When the controlling aspects of our ego are quieted and we engage the primal flow of consciousness that animates our world, we become acutely aware of our insignificance when compared to the incomprehensible vastness of the universe. Touching the stream of universal power goes hand in hand with the ritual purification of becoming small in the face of the great mystery.

The relevance of this experience for modern people can not be overstated because our culture teaches us to utterly reject the idea that we are no better or worse than all that surrounds us. When we become small and humble, even if it's only during periodic rituals or ceremonies, we allow our grandiose ego to shrink and move out of the way so that we can perceive life as a magnificent gift and fully appreciate the scope of our time here. Making the most of our time here is one of the key reasons to engage in rites of passage because they spur you out of complacency, give you a kick in the ass, and push you to claim your own authentic and unique abilities and creative power.

Before getting into physical alchemic practices, we will prepare shamanically through initiatory rites of passage, which will energize our alchemic work. This is one of the main differences between shamanic alchemy and the alchemy of the so-called puffers. These alchemists fanatically puffed fires with bellows in a misguided attempt to manufacture gold using alchemical transmutation, often wasting their entire lives and fortunes in the effort.

STATES OF CONSCIOUSNESS

Because states of consciousness are such an important subject when conversing about or learning and practicing shamanism, it is appropriate to briefly discuss this topic before entering into the practices.

Our ordinary or normal state of consciousness can be described simply as that with which we typically interact and view the world. If you are reading this, you are conscious; you are currently experiencing the world around you, including the words you're reading and what they mean, as well as your environment, thoughts, feelings, and body. During normal consciousness, we typically also view the world through the consensus reality supported by those around us.

Altered States of Consciousness
The term *altered states of consciousness* (ASC) was popularized in 1969 by transpersonal psychologist Charles Tart in his book *Altered States of Consciousness,* a collection of thirty-five scientific papers describing various altered states. An ASC can be described as a change in one's normal mental state (usually temporary) without being considered unconscious. Altered states of consciousness can be created intentionally, or they can happen by accident or due to illness.[1]

Accidental or pathological circumstances that can induce ASC include a traumatic experience on either a physical or mental level (especially near-death experiences), epileptic seizure, sleep deprivation, infection (such as meningitis), fasting, and spontaneous psychosis. Intentional activities that can induce ASC include meditation, dreaming (especially lucid dreaming), sex, hypnosis, contemplation of art (including music) and nature, sensory deprivation, sensory stimulation (especially deep connection to natural energies, such as fire, wind, water, earth, and animals), yoga, dance (especially ecstatic dance), psychic activities (telepathy, psychokinesis, remote viewing, especially shamanic viewing), and use of mind-altering drugs and plant entheogens.[2]

Shamanic States of Consciousness

As far as I know, the term *shamanic state of consciousness* (SSC) was coined by Michael Harner in 1982 with his famous book *The Way of the Shaman*. Unfortunately, although many of the topics covered in Harner's book are shamanic, since the publication of that book, many people have, and still are, using the term SSC for activities that are not shamanic. For example, I have been to classes on shamanic journeying where, after the leader sits everyone in a circle and does some drumming, the first thing he or she says is "close your eyes and imagine that you are in a beautiful meadow, or on top of a mountain, or in a cave," and so on. This is not shamanism. This is a very useful therapeutic technique more aptly described as guided visualization that is often employed by a trained practitioner in treating social anxiety, depression, bipolar disorder, and post-traumatic stress, among others.[3]

Although SSC would be a convenient way to describe the states of consciousness produced by the practices in this book, I will not use it for the above reasons.

Integrative States of Consciousness

The integrative state of consciousness (ISC) is the term I will use to best describe the states of consciousness that the practices in this book produce. An ISC involves enhanced access to normally unconscious information through integration of different brain systems (which induces emotional, behavioral, and cognitive integration), passive manipulation of our autonomic nervous system, and psychic-energetic integration with our environment via our holographic field and phase-conjugate mirrors.[4] These last two terms will be explained shortly.

To simplify this discussion on how human consciousness relates to the world, I divide human consciousness into six levels to illustrate the marked differences between the various levels:

1. The first level I refer to as ordinary consciousness for our modern culture, and for other cultures that have lost a sense of unity with nature and the cosmos. At this level the ego is almost completely self-centered and isolated from the occurrences of the more-than-human world.

2. In the second level there is a slight awareness of fusion between the self and the surrounding environment of nature and other beings. At this level, an individual manifests the capacity for empathy but not to the degree that the person would refrain from doing harm or damage to something or someone outside his or her narrow sphere of compassion if deemed necessary.

3. At the third level, the individual experiences temporarily melding with the environment or other beings.

4. The fourth level is significant for shamanism because the individual begins to identify his or her human organism with a much larger unified body—with plants and animals and other phenomena and forms of communication not accessible to the lower levels. At this level, the individual can experience consciousness free of human evaluations and judgments.

5. At the fifth level the feeling of unity between self and environment leads to experiences of silent knowledge, such as telepathy and the ability to transfer energy, to heal, and to compress or lengthen the perception of time, among other abilities and perceptions commonly thought to be supernatural or extrasensory. At this level many experiences cannot be explained by words.

6. The sixth level is the level free from all human attachments; the individual's personal organism and consciousness are completely indistinguishable from the unified consciousness of the cosmos.

Shamanic experience generally happens at levels three, four, and five. Through intentionally practicing and purposefully struggling through various actions, ceremonies, and rituals with the more-than-human world, a person realizes increasing states of unity, first with other people and his or her immediate environment, then with other beings and the wider world, and eventually with powers and forces inconceivable to the linear-rational mode of perception.

Praxis 1

Developing an Integrated State of Consciousness

Intentionally creating an ISC is vital to truly experiencing the various numinous realities of shamanic alchemy. (The following text and exercise is adapted from my book *Advanced Shamanism: The Practice of Conscious Transformation;* if you are already familiar with this material, please enter an ISC and proceed to page 85.) While in an ordinary state of consciousness, the practices in this book will still be valuable; however, when performed in an ISC, the magical nature of shamanism and the mysteries and nuances of alchemy are experienced at a heightened level as the scope of perception becomes unlimited. This is achieved by altering the way we perceive via what we place our attention on.

The shamanic practice for entering an ISC is called the five points of attention. This is an advanced practice taught to me by Huichol/Wirrarika shamans. The story of how I learned it is recounted in my book *Teachings of the Peyote Shamans: The Five Points of Attention.* The crux of this technique is to both focus and expand our attention. Expansion in this practice happens via splitting our attention by consciously placing our attention on first three and then, much later, five points. This splitting of attention is achieved without a reduction in any of the points. For example, we will first split our attention into three points, but we will not be using only a third of our capacity on each. Each point will receive 100 percent of our attention.

This situation is a shamanic paradox that is not easily achieved even with training and practice. Most modern people will never experience this ISC because they don't know it exists or that it's even possible. However, if you can experience the five points of attention, you open the door of shamanic consciousness to infinite possibilities in the realms of attention and perception. At this level all shamanic practices are more easily mastered. The added bonus of this practice is that in our everyday lives, we become infinitely more aware, which fosters a calm and humble confidence during any situation. Grasping and then practicing this technique can take time. If you are patient and dedicated to learning it, in time it will become second nature, and you will wonder how you ever got through life without it.

By focusing on two points of attention in this part of the practice, you will create a drawing that will serve as an instructional tool for learning about the five attentions.

1. Draw a circle with an even-sided cross inside it. The four ends of the cross should intersect and stop at the circle.
2. In the center of the cross, write the word *me*.
3. Where the right arm of the cross meets the circle, write *object*.
4. Left of the center of the right arm, draw an arrow pointing to the word *me*.
5. Right of center of the right arm, draw an arrow pointing to the word *object*.[5]

We can see the drawing has five points: four at the intersections of the cross and the circle and one in the middle. All the points are connected and illustrate the five points of attention. Right now, we have labeled

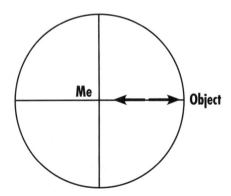

Fig. 4.1. Two points of attention

two points: *me* (me, myself, I) and *object* (object, entity, thing, situation). The arrow pointing to me illustrates your attention focusing on yourself. The arrow pointing to object illustrates the placement of attention on something other than you. As you can see, we now have two arrows, two points of attention. If you can place your attention on the object and still focus on yourself, then you have split your attention in two. This is not a normal state of consciousness for most people.

During most of the day attention is placed outward to what we are doing. In some moments we pay attention to our self, especially when we are being careful about what we say or when we are looking in the mirror or when we stub a toe. But we almost always are placing our awareness on one or the other. Rarely do we place our attention on both at the same time. When I explain this to my students, someone will often ask, "How is this different from multitasking?" Shaman Jesús provides an answer, excerpted from my book *Teachings of the Peyote Shamans: The Five Points of Attention*:[6]

Jesús looked at me quizzically. I wondered if I used the proper words in Spanish. So I added, "We call multitasking doing various things at the same time. Like many people drive their car, talk on their cell phone, read a map, and eat a bagel all at the same time. Isn't our attention split most of the time?"

Chuckling, Jesús replied, "The attention of the object can be used in a multitude of ways. But I am betting that the person driving that car is not paying attention to their essence, to their true being, while they are doing all those other things. That takes a special effort of concentration. And if they were to do that, I also bet that they would immediately stop talking and eating and pay closer attention on their driving. Or maybe they would give up driving altogether. In your other example, thinking about a situation, even one that has to do with yourself, is not the same as paying attention to your inner self. You are placing attention on the details of the situation."[7]

According to Jesús, we have three important aspects that make us who we are. We have our ego: I am this and I am that. We have our essence: our true being that we are born with. And we have our individual personality:

our acquired characteristics. Our essence is what lives inherently inside each one of us—it is our inner quality, our level of being, our innermost values. It asks us to seek questions: Who am I? Where did I come from? Where am I going? When people live their life centered in ego, they are imbalanced and in disharmony, like someone trapped on an island alone his whole life. There needs to be harmony among essence, personality, and ego. Harmony opens the door to true self-knowledge and the light of the divine.

Maintaining the first two points—simultaneously thinking of self and object—is the beginning of looking outward, beyond self. You place your attention internally in the direction toward your feelings and overall health, surveying yourself both physically and mentally, while also paying attention to the object, that which is outside yourself. However, once you have experienced enough times doing this, you will come to a point where the exercise becomes completely different because you will begin to touch your essence.[8]

FOCUSING ON THREE POINTS OF ATTENTION

Now we come to another paradoxical shamanic situation: it is incredibly difficult to divide human attention in two, but it is actually easier to divide it into three and later five. These unexplainable situations are a big part of why I practice shamanism—the thrill of diving into the unknown, knowing sheer intellect will not reach the goal. It is only through experience that we learn about things that are true, even if we cannot explain it.

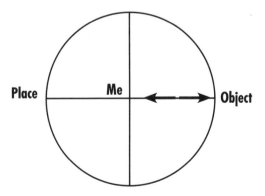

Fig. 4.2. Three points of attention

The third point of attention is place. This depicts where you are and why you are there. Now write *place* on your drawing at the point where the left arm meets the circle. In the same way as you did on the right arm, draw an arrow pointing to me and one pointing to place. From now on, focus on these three points of attention.

1. *Me.* Do not forget yourself. Always watch yourself. Pay attention at all times to your words, actions, gestures, and habits, even your thoughts and emotions.
2. *Object.* Be thoroughly attentive to objects, entities, situations, anything outside you that you can interpret with your senses.
3. *Place.* Observe at all times where you are and be cognizant of why you are there.[9]

It is most important to remember not to become infatuated with one point of attention. Whether it is yourself, an object, or a place, no matter how interesting, beautiful, horrible, entrancing, or atrocious something is, don't focus on one point of attention to such an extent that the others are left out. If you do that you will miss the whole point. When attending to the three points at once becomes natural during your daily life, the challenge is then to keep that attention during special circumstances. The goal is to maintain attention on all three points, even during stressful moments.

My teacher had me experience the three attentions while crawling on the ground in the high-altitude desert where his tribe lives. I do this with students in my training classes in the Green Mountains: the woods are kinder on the knees but the experience is still very potent and appropriate. Placing yourself in a situation that is completely foreign to you makes splitting your attention from one to three easier because you are not as tempted to fall back on the habitual ways you use your attention. Without talking and having lots of people and media distractions around upholding your ego and personality, breaking through and experiencing the three-way split of attention can unfold naturally and in accordance with your true essence.

The idea is simple. In a natural setting have a partner go approximately one to two hundred yards away from you. It's helpful for your partner to be ahead of you on a trail so you will know when you reach your destination (your partner). If you don't have a partner, you can use something to mark your destination. Wear whatever clothing you need to be safe but avoid gloves if possible.

To begin, simply get down on your knees and focus on each of the three points of attention. Place attention on yourself: feel your body and notice your feelings and emotions. Place attention on objects: notice all the different plants, rocks, colors, sounds, tastes, smells—everything that is outside your body and your head. Place attention on this place: keep cognizant of where you are in the bigger picture, beyond the ground you are crawling on. You are in the middle of a vast and magical place. These three states of attention are completely different from one another, although you will try to experience them all at the same time.

When you feel ready, begin to crawl toward your destination while keeping in mind that the physical destination is secondary to your real destination—simultaneous awareness of the three points of attention. The act of crawling in nature is a wonderful way to break down our feelings of superiority toward nature and allows us to place our attention outside the sphere of our merely human concerns.

In this setting the awareness of the three points of attention typically comes fairly easily. It is common when experiencing this to also feel a state of inner silence. Attending to the three points of attention while crawling in nature tends to quiet the incessant talking of our inner voice. When this happens, paying attention to yourself won't be through words in your mind anymore. It will be more like a sort of pure knowing and feeling.

You will perceive everything purely through your senses—no filters, biases, or analysis: the feeling of the ground under your hands and knees and your movement as you crawl along, the sight of the shapes and colors of rocks, earth, plants, twigs, and insects, the taste of dust and sweat, the sounds of birds and the wind in the leaves.

The attention of place can be bolstered a couple of ways—by raising your head and fully realizing where you are on a grand or planetary level and also feeling the energy of the place on an intimate level. How does the place feel? What season is it? What's going on right now in this place?

This initial experience of splitting but being aware of the three attentions all at once is a remarkable achievement.[10]

While in this integrative state of consciousness, your ego and personality are temporarily placed in the backseat and your true essence shines through. You may not have experienced your true essence since you were a very young child. For some of us, our true essence is only experienced during a dangerous or extremely special situation, such as a severe accident, the miracle of childbirth, or the death of a loved one. This practice opens the door to experiencing our essence on a daily basis without extreme circumstances being the catalyst. When I asked the Huichol shaman about the practical use of the three attentions, he replied, "The experience you just had will only be truly practical when you employ it to other life situations. For example, when talking to people, working, writing, and so on. If you can focus on your three points of attention during your ordinary life, you will see extraordinary results with regard to your quality of life."

It is almost impossible to be living in your true essence and still have unhealthy feelings of anger, depression, arrogance, jealousy, or selfishness. Your essence wants you to discover and live with your true talents and in states of happiness, kindness, cooperation, unity, and wonder. Also, once you have become proficient in living with the attention of the three points, you will then be able to raise your level to five points, which is a most magnificent and mature state of conscious living. People who live solely within their ego and personality cannot possibly comprehend this state of being. When I teach this initial exercise of perceiving the three attentions at once, most people experience it on their first try. If you don't, simply try again right away or on another day. Don't pressure yourself. If you do feel you have accomplished this first step, be aware that you may feel tired or energetically drained. This is common for us modern people.

Our first attempt at reaching the three attentions tends to use up our current available energy. It takes great effort for modern people to make the breakthrough. This can be referred to as the "little death" because the dominating ego and personality are switched off. Your attention was split and pulled so far away from where it normally resides that when released from that far-off place, it snaps back and goes past its usual place. Kind of like the band of a slingshot. The best thing is to do something nice for yourself right away (I'm talking about something healthy): take a walk, take a bath, go swimming, get a massage, eat a delicious meal. Also, I recommend not jumping straight back into everyday life. Give your energy some time to recharge. Through time and practice with this technique, you will find that not only will you not use up your energy, you will gain available energy through living closer to your true essence. Once you have initially experienced the three attentions, the practical use of this amazing ISC is the goal. At this stage of the training we attempt to cultivate the awareness of the three attentions during our everyday life.

The most difficult aspect of this practice is learning how to experience the three attentions at will and hold onto this ISC over long periods or all the time, which is a tremendous achievement. Because of the way we have been trained to think our whole lives, we easily slip back into one attention without even realizing it. When I first came back home after learning this technique, I would very naturally simply get sucked into whatever it was I was doing, which placed my attention squarely on the object. I would first have to intentionally realize what I was doing and then try to go back to the attention of three. It amazed me how well trained my awareness was to constantly remain on one attention. I could easily expand to three when I intended to, but in the beginning, without even realizing it, I would revert to one. Eventually, the more you practice, the easier it becomes to stay aware of where your attention is going.

I developed a little trick that I used during my first six months of trying to master this technique (my teachers laughed when I told them about this trick, but it really works). Get a timer; a sports watch works well. Set it for a hour or less (half an hour was best for me). During the beginning of your day, enter the awareness of the three attentions and try to stay there. If you are like me and most of my students when they started, you will quickly revert to one. When your timer goes off, check where your attention is. If not on three (which will probably be the case), reset your timer and refocus your attention to three and try to stay there as long as you can before your timer goes off. You will experience a wordless feeling of humble accomplishment when you finally hear your timer and you are still in the attention of three.[11]

It is crucial to master the three attentions before attempting the jump to five. My shaman teachers would not tell me about the other two attentions at all, nothing except that they exist, until I could prove mastery of the first three attentions. Once you know what the other two are, it's pretty much impossible not to try them, even if you haven't mastered three. But attempting to do the five attentions too soon can be devastating for your chances of learning the first three; if you don't learn the first three first, you won't make the ultimate goal of five. So please take this advice: don't ruin your chances of attaining the five attentions by reading my other book or asking someone about it. Someone who has mastered the five and knows you haven't mastered three will not tell you anyway. During the course of learning the techniques in this book, you will be frequently asked to practice the first three attentions, which over time will lead to mastery of them. When I say "enter an ISC," or something similar, at the start of an exercise, the main thing I'm asking you to do is enter into the three points of attention if you haven't already. When you have mastered the three attentions, then go ahead and read about, practice, and master the five attentions, no matter where you are in the other practices in this book, or later on in your life.

DIRECT SHAMANIC VIEWING

The following text and the next three exercises in this section are excerpted from my book *Advanced Shamanism*. If you are already familiar with this material, then enter an ISC and proceed to chapter 5. This material is so important for the practice of shamanic alchemy that it needs to be included here before we move on. As stated above, learning to enter an ISC via holding the three points of attention has many benefits, one of these not mentioned yet is the learned ability of direct shamanic viewing (DSV). At the highest levels, DSV is employed in shamanic healing after the five points of attention are mastered. However, for shamanic alchemy practices, we can employ DSV while in an ISC cultivated by the three points of attention. In attempting to explain DSV, a short discussion on quantum theory, holographic fields, and phase-conjugate mirrors is necessary.

Many who study physics today agree that there are many dimensions beyond the four dimensions of space-time, but there is disagreement on how many there might be. Whatever the number (and the number may be infinite), these multiple dimensions constitute the hyperspace of our larger reality. DSV is possible because imbedded in the hyperspace are fields of consciousness. This is important since our lifetime of experiences are not stored solely within the brain but in what can be called a holographic field that imbeds the brain and the body. This field has a staggering storage capacity and resolves the puzzle of adequate information storage within the brain. In an ISC it is possible during DSV to access this holographic field of information.[12]

For the operations of shamanic alchemy elucidated in this book, DSV is employed to view multidimensional hyperspace, which includes the holographic field, by viewing life-forms other than people. Learning to view people is beyond the scope of this book and not necessary for learning shamanic alchemy. Here it is most important to learn to view natural phenomena such as plants, trees, animals, and elements such as fire, water, air, and soil.

It is my belief that the old-time alchemists were intimately familiar, as are shamans, with DSV although they didn't name it as such. It is quite easy to see that the alchemists that drew, and were portrayed in, alchemic art and symbols could see much more than someone in a state of normal consciousness. The images I have supplied in this book, many of which are hundreds of years old, are perfect examples. Even if we simply look at the Azoth drawing of the seven alchemic stages, we see many examples (see page 123). I explain this drawing later in the book, but for now I just ask that you ponder this in relation to this one drawing: Would a person in a normal state of consciousness perceive a man's body connected to the four elements? See a salamander as living in the fire? A crow perched on a human skull as death of the profane? An androgynous youth emerging from an open grave as the attainment of the seven stages of coagulation?

During DSV it is quite common to see a subject morph, and it seems quite clear that the alchemists were experiencing this at least to some degree or maybe more profoundly than I am able to comprehend. There are thousands of such examples in the alchemic literature. I have many examples through my own experiences. Here is an example of one from when I first began DSV:

I was lying on my couch reading. It was fairly late on a warm summer night. My canine companion Sophie was with me. Earlier that year when I moved from Sedona, Arizona, to Northern California, I not only brought Sophie with me but also our little friend El Gato. El Gato Bandito de Kitty-Cat-O (his full funny name) came to us as a stray, not more than five inches long. We found him sleeping on our porch one night, and after extensive searching for the owners and putting up flyers with no luck, we adopted him. Sophie and he became very close, like brother and sister.

El Gato was more or less an outdoor cat that would come home every few days to eat cat food and sleep with us. On this night I had not realized he was out (the screen door was slightly open) as I had just seen him in the house.

While reading quietly I heard a gut-wrenching scream of agony from outside and knew right away it was El Gato. We lived in the woods surrounded by thousands of acres of forest. My main fear for El Gato at this place was the coyotes, and from the sounds I was hearing it appeared he got caught. Not worrying that I was in my underwear (we had no neighbors close enough to see me), I jumped up, grabbed a flashlight, and Sophie and I were out the door in two seconds.

Following the screams, we ran down the wooded slope behind the house at full speed with Sophie in the lead. After a hundred yards or so Sophie stopped, and in the light of my flashlight I picked up five sets of eyeballs looking at us. That was the moment I realized I was direct viewing. The severity of the moment automatically caused my resources to emerge.

I looked down at Sophie and an incredible thing happened: she took off straight for the coyotes and my perception went with her. I had intentionally experienced this before with other animals but never before with Sophie. I was seeing through her eyes as she ran. Her sight was amazingly different from mine, so I staggered for a few seconds until I got used to it.

Sophie was a big confident dog who had fought with coyotes, javelinas, and other dogs her whole life and had never lost. She was raised in the woods and had no fear. As she approached the coyotes at full speed I felt her adrenaline and fearlessness but some part of me was still aware of myself and in that moment I felt afraid for her. I didn't want her to get hurt.

Those feelings brought me back into my perception but in a way I didn't expect. I was viewing the scene in hyperspace. The darkness meant nothing. I could clearly see the coyotes in the dark without my flashlight. Except the coyotes weren't coyotes. The most aggressive one was a wasp, two were flies, one a rat, and one a fox. All were the same size as a coyote. Sophie was a brown bear about twice her normal size.

The coyotes took one look at her running toward them, and they wanted no part of a fight and ran off. Sophie didn't chase them, as she figured her job was done. My normal perception was restored, and I watched Sophie walk up the hill to me. But where was El Gato?

In my normal state I had the feeling that unfortunately El Gato had been taken by the coyotes. I sat down in the dark and was overwhelmed by the sadness of never seeing my little buddy again. But Sophie had other ideas. After giving me a wet kiss, she began walking back to the house; however, she was not walking normally—she was tracking. Sophie was an experienced tracker and could find me hidden in the woods over five miles away. Once I knew what she was doing, I followed her and joined my perception once again with hers. It took her less than two minutes to find El Gato who was curled up under a log and severely injured.

I'm thankful to say that after two surgeries for internal injuries and many months of healing, El Gato made a full recovery. After that incident he rarely left Sophie's side. It was actually quite humorous that when the three of us were outside he would actually walk right under Sophie's belly.

The zoomorphic type changes that my perception experienced with the coyotes and Sophie while viewing in the hyperspace may seem bizarre or imaginative to those who have not experienced something similar. However, this is not uncommon to the Huichol and other indigenous shaman. The Huichol often use a term that could be roughly translated to "spirit" in these situations. For example, it is common for them to see the spirit of certain flowering plants as different kinds of spiders. The powerful Datura and Solandra hold the wolf spirit; the sacred peyote transforms into Kahullumari, the blue spirit deer, who is the guide, messenger, and guardian of the sacred desert of Wirikuta. There are many other examples *that can be cited, including those from non-shamanic modalities such as the Holy Spirit as a white dove in Christianity and the many zoomorphic Egyptian gods, among others. In terms of intentional DSV, once we are in an ISC and are viewing in the hyperspace it is necessary to be open to all possibilities of what can be seen or felt beyond our normal senses.*[13]

The manner in which I will describe the practice of DSV is a combination of how my shaman mentors taught me and what I have discovered on my own and through teaching other people. DSV is a *learned* technique. Practice, including successes and failures, is the only thing that will make you proficient.

Listed below are the main components to DSV:

Integrated state of consciousness (ISC). Without entering an ISC, intentional DSV is not possible. As previously stated, an ISC cultivated by the five points of attention is the recommended technique for DSV.

Passive volition. We are not trying to force our viewing but rather set ourselves up for success and passively view what is there.

Viewing target. This is the plant, tree, animal, or element that you desire to view.

Viewing focal point. Similar to an adjustable lens on a camera, we can view at a wide angle, normal view, or zoom.

Viewing physical data. In the clear-minded ISC fostered by the five points of attention we are still cognizant of the physical world and information received by our physical senses.

Viewing hyperspace and holographic field data. This is information we receive that is not limited to our physical senses.

Decoding viewing data. We determine the meaning of what we are viewing.[14]

Praxis 2

Phase-Conjugate Mirrors of the Mind

Phase conjugation is a complicated subject that need not be explained in its entirety here. For this praxis we will briefly explore phase-conjugate (p-c) mirrors and how this pertains to DSV. Jean Millay, Ph.D., in her book *Multidimensional Mind: Remote Viewing and the Evolution of Intelligence,* brings to light a fascinating correlation between phase conjugated mirrors and remote viewing based on the work of researcher Ray Gottlieb, OD, Ph.D.

Gottlieb explains that perceptual unity has long perplexed neuroscientists. How does the brain gather scattered sensations such as shape, size, color, distance, motion, name, associated memories, and effective meaning instantaneously into whole, meaningful perceptions? Gottlieb postulates that phase-conjugate mirrors suggest a possible mechanism for this unity. He cites the experiments of the pioneers of holography who constructed four phase-conjugate mirrors from three lasers. Two lasers meet head on, when a third is aimed into this configuration it reflects much like raindrops reflect sunlight to make a rainbow. In *Multidimensional Mind,* Millay explains how the reflections from millions of p-c mirrors synthesize information in the brain.[15]

> Ordinary mirrors reflect light according to the angle the light strikes the mirror, but P-C mirrors "self-target"—the reflection retraces the path back to its source at any angle of incidence. . . .
>
> The reflection merges spatial and temporal information from all three input beams so data from several sources can be combined and fed back to a specific location. Mirrors of different light frequencies cannot interact so many can function at the same site. Mirrors form and vanish instantly as the lasers go on and off. No threshold power of the object [third] beam is required for conjugation to occur. . . .
>
> Here we see how this light apparatus might mirror actual brain function. Imagine millions of coherent packets of light traveling through white and gray matter, meeting in strategic places, creating millions of P-C mirrors that synthesize and reflect information automatically and accurately to meaningful sites.
>
> And where might we find an ideal medium for such light works? The ventricles come to mind. They're four in all, linked into a winged structure. The two lateral ventricles are centered in the cerebral hemispheres, the third between the two halves of the thalamus and hypothalamus, and the fourth between the cerebellum and the brain stem.[16]

Gottlieb's concept is interesting and thought provoking: the brain communicates with itself via phase-conjugate mirrors and coherent light energy is involved with the process of translating information from the hyperspace into sensory memory and then into awareness and the ability of expression. However, I bring it up here simply because when I read Millay's description of Gottlieb's theory, I had already "viewed" this phenomenon and was extremely surprised to learn of a scientific theory or explanation for it. I just sat there with my mouth open in disbelief.

I will explain. During my shamanic viewing training with Huichol shamans, I was very fortunate to be able to view my teachers as they were viewing in hyperspace. What I have viewed on several occasions is so close to what Gottlieb describes that it can't be overlooked. While in an ISC sitting in circle with shamans and the Sacred Fire, I viewed millions of tiny reflections of light in the area of the brain of multiple shamans while they were in an ISC or trance state during various ceremonies. It was like viewing a whole galaxy of stars in the night sky inside the mind of the shaman.

This viewing of millions (or billions) of tiny light reflections was also the precursor to my viewing the holographic field of the shamans and so viewing what they were viewing. And I know for sure that they were doing the same thing with me. There were even times when I viewed two shamans viewing me while I viewed them, and we created four phase-conjugate mirrors just like the three lasers in Gottlieb's hypothesis. These four phase-conjugate mirrors appeared like doorways in each of the cardinal directions with the Sacred Fire in the middle. The multidimensional doorways were similar in impression to the doorways and windows experienced in shamanic dreaming.

The major point here is that when you are in an ISC, you can passively intend to view the phase-conjugate mirrors of your own mind, which is a gateway to DSV. The easiest time to begin viewing your own phase-conjugate mirrors is during hypnagogic and hypnopompic states. These terms refer to the borderline state between wakefulness and falling asleep, either falling asleep (hypnagogic) or waking up (hypnopompic). During these states, but especially the hypnagogic, the phosphenes and colored specks of light you can see even with your eyes closed are akin to viewing p-c mirrors while in a fully awake ISC. However, once you practice viewing the p-c mirrors in a hypnagogic state with eyes either open or closed it is easier to passively intend them in a fully awake ISC.

Although it is common to view p-c mirrors spontaneously during an ISC, the natural progression in training to passively intend to see them has proven to be very helpful in developing this ability. First practice in a hypnagogic state, then in an awake ISC with closed eyes, followed by an awake ISC alternating eyes open and closed, and finally in an ISC with eyes open. Viewing p-c mirrors with eyes open is easier in the dark. When you can passively intend to view them at will in daylight, you have mastered the technique.[17]

<u>**Praxis 3**</u>

Direct Shamanic Viewing— Targets Other Than People

Once you have mastered viewing p-c mirrors at will, the next step is viewing natural objects. I suggest you train outdoors when possible and in a natural setting that is both inspiring and free from the distractions of people and noise and light pollution (if practicing when dark). If this is not possible, you can train indoors with natural items from this type of place.

In this step choose various viewing targets over the course of weeks or months but for the time being resist the temptation to view people. Until you learn the technique, the viewing of seemingly inanimate objects such as rocks or animal parts (feathers, bones, etc.) is more difficult, so I suggest starting with live plants and trees or even animals if you see them. Here is the basic practice:

1. View your target and collect physical and emotional data with all of your senses, intellect, and feelings.
2. Engage the three points of attention to enter an ISC.
3. While in the ISC, bring forth your p-c mirrors.
4. Passively view your target with the intention of viewing it in hyperspace. Many situations can happen in this step depending on which dimension you are viewing. You may see the target's field of energy; it may morph into something completely different; in some way it might connect or communicate with you through your normal senses or nonverbal communication. Remain open to any and all possibilities.

5. If and/or when you feel inclined for whatever reason, change your focal point of viewing.

6. Continue viewing and collecting information about your target from hyperspace. Your target may remain the same as when you first began viewing, or it could change once or many times. Be patient and receive whatever you view or feel.

7. While still in an ISC, attempt to decode the information you are receiving.[18]

The last step can be, by far, the most difficult. Sometimes the meaning of the information will be apparent, and you will understand immediately, as in my example with the sequoias. But often the meaning of what you view will be baffling. Why has a flowering plant turned into a spider or a deer into a blue jay? As in my example with the coyotes: Why did each morph into a different animal? In this step you may understand the meaning of what you are viewing in the context of the hyperspace, which may or may not have any meaning to you in normal reality.

In the coyote example I understood the meaning to be that I was viewing characteristics that each coyote shared with another species. I was more or less viewing the personality traits of each coyote. When I have seen a running deer morph into a blue jay, it didn't make much sense to my mind while viewing in hyperspace, but my rational mind knew that the blue jay is an ally to the deer. Throughout many years of hunting deer when I was younger, I know that the loudmouthed blue jay is a security guard for the forest and will alert all the animals of threats. A running or jumping deer with its white tail up is doing the same job as the blue jay in that moment by signaling to any other deer around that there is an intruder nearby.[19]

It's common, especially when first learning, to not immediately ascertain what is viewed in hyperspace. Don't worry; this is normal and many times the meaning will appear later. It is important to note that over time, as you practice collecting information, you will gradually learn to decode information with greater accuracy. It is also helpful to learn DSV with a partner or other people. Those with more experience can help beginners to decode information, which helps the novice viewers advance to a deeper understanding of what they are viewing. The suggestion here is that during the course of this book the experiences are greatly enhanced when you intentionally employ an ISC and at moments DSV.

Praxis 4
Bringing Forth the Sacred Fire

This exercise is adapted from *Advanced Shamanism*. There are several praxes in this book that require a Sacred Fire, so I will describe here my preferred ritual practice of bring forth the Fire in a sacred way so that when working with the Fire we have a time-tested shamanic method when engaging this powerful form of numinous energy. So important is this practice that I teach it to all my students and have written about it in previous books. Here is the core explanation for those who are not yet familiar with it.

The rituals surrounding the preparation, ignition, and maintenance of the Sacred Fire vary greatly from one shamanic tradition to the next. I'm going to describe one way to go about these processes, a way that has evolved from many hundreds of experiences with indigenous shamans, work groups, and my own personal initiations and ceremonies with Fire. Please keep in mind that my suggestion is to always stay true to your own inner guidance in developing and employing rituals and ceremonies, especially when dealing with metaphysical powers in a shamanic setting; however, the way of relating to the Fire that I am about to describe contains ancient and time-tested formulas that are successful at merging our human consciousness with the Fire, and I invite you try it this way whether or not you have previous experience with the fundamental energy of Fire.

The first step is to take a moment, clear your thoughts, and enter an ISC by focusing on the three points of attention. Now clear a small area where you will lay the Sacred Fire. There is no need to make a giant fire. If you clear a circular area approximately thirty-six inches in diameter and make a bed for the fire eighteen inches in diameter that should work nicely. Clearing the area implies removing all vegetative matter, and anything else that might be there, so that you have nothing but soil under and around the fire.

To make the bed for the fire, collect stones, preferably the size of your heart or fist, and place them in a circle on the area you have cleared. This formally delineates the space for the Sacred Fire to manifest and also solidifies the fact that you are ritually inviting and calling to the spirit of the Fire to join you.

Next, you place the pillow for the Sacred Fire, a medium diameter log (around six to ten inches in diameter), inside the stone circle and position it on the eastern side of the inside edge of the circle (the ends of the log will be facing north and south). Resting on this pillow will be the arrows of wood (usually thinner pieces of wood than the pillow) that will be the food of the Sacred Fire. The sticks used to the feed Fire are called arrows because they point to a specific direction both physically and symbolically, and they are the vehicle of flight that delivers yours messages to the spirit. If you placed your pillow in the east, all the arrows rest on the pillow and point in the same direction toward the east and to the rising sun. Each time you give wood to Fire, you place the food in the same direction on the pillow, and in this way you are continually focusing your attention to the sun, which is the Fire that gives life to our planet. East is the default position; however, if or when you have a reason to point your arrows in a different direction, for example, toward a trip you taking or to a special place or person, simply position your pillow so that your arrows will point in the desired direction. The Huichol/Wirrarika shamans point their arrows to a pilgrimage site until they get there, and when they leave, they reverse the pillow so that their arrows point to home for the trip back.

How you actually ignite your fire will depend entirely on your skill and relationship with Fire. Since this is a sacred practice of working with Fire and not a lesson in survival training, using matches or a lighter is fine. In all cases, whether experienced or not, remember that this Sacred Fire is fed exclusively with wood sticks placed only in one direction, placing them across one another would introduce opposing and distracting forces to the ritual. Making a quick and hot fire by crisscrossing sticks of wood can work well to maximize the efficiency of oxygen and fuel when making a fire for cooking or in a survival situation, but this is a Sacred Fire that is being induced into being for completely different reasons. The flame of the Sacred Fire is brought to life by a mixture of physical realities and metaphysical inputs. So please throw out all of your purely logical and scientific formulas and make the fire with your heart and not your head.

I suggest to start by placing very dry and thin diameter sticks as the first layer of arrows and then slowly adding larger diameter sticks until the fire is established. If there are pine trees in the area you are working, dead, thin, lower branches are perfect for this. I usually carry a small supply of lower pine tree branches and resinous wood, which ignite easily. If you have trouble and need to use some sort of natural fire-starting material, that's OK because, as stated earlier, this is a ritual with Fire, not a course in survival fire starting.

As soon as your Sacred Fire comes to life, start talking to the unique energetic phenomena that is front of you. I refer to Fire as Grandfather, as do my shaman mentors. Although the visions Fire delivers aren't necessarily male, as suggested by the name grandfather, I find it extremely useful to name Fire in this way as a form of both respect and personal human connection. In a world that is sometimes confusing, it is comforting and empowering to refer on a personal level to Mother Earth, Father Sun, Grandmother Growth, and Grandfather Fire, not just as a form of delineation but as a way to personally identify with the enormous powers that they imply.

To begin speaking with Grandfather Fire, it is proper to respectfully greet him and briefly state your intention. If you are alone, you will obviously do this by yourself; if you have a group, everyone can greet Grandfather at the same time or individually, with the person who lit the fire talking first. The greeting goes like this: "Welcome Grandfather Fire, thank you joining me (us) with your light, energy, and ancient wisdom. I am here before you tonight to [briefly describe what you intend to do with the fire, you will go into more specifics when you actually do your work]."

When you begin your work, it is proper to begin by directly addressing Grandfather Fire once by saying, "Grandfather Fire, in front of you, Grandmother Growth, and all my companions, I [clearly state the first item of your work with Grandfather Fire]." When you say "all my companions," you are not only referring to any human companions but all the living entities and elements around you—trees, grass, animals, wind, sky, stars, worms, insects, and so on. This is the formal setup for working shamanically with Grandfather Fire. From here you continue to feed

Grandfather (all sticks on the pillow in the same direction) when needed and/or place a stick arrow as an offering of intent while passing through the different phases of your work.

This is the general format for working with Grandfather Fire or the Sacred Fire for any reason and for practices outlined in this book.[20]

Fig. 4.3. Author energetically conversing with Grandfather Fire
(photo by Nancy Bartell).

5

SHAMANIC SPAGYRICS

If not coined by, certainly promoted by, Paracelsus, a spagyric is an herbal elixir or medicine prepared through alchemic procedures. Alchemists, through carefully observing and imitating nature's slow-moving processes, can speed up these processes and transformations by way of certain procedures. The word *spagyria,* from the ancient Greek, is a combination of *spao,* meaning "to draw out or divide," and *ageiro,* meaning "to gather or bind or join." A common alchemic phrase states: *Solve et coagula, et habebis magisterium!* (Dissolve and bind, and you will have the magistery!)

Spagyrics takes place in three stages: (1) separation, (2) purification, and (3) cohabitation or coagulation (known as the alchemical wedding). These alchemical procedures lead to an increase and release of vibratory energy contained in the plant. Spagyric preparations differ from nonspagyric herbal preparations, such as ordinary tinctures, infusions, or decoctions, in that they are much more complete by the recombining of the purified ash of the calcined plant used to make the initial preparation. In other words, when making an ordinary tincture or infusion, the original plant material is discarded once the essential oils of the plant are removed, but with spagyrics the alchemical salt (body) of the plant is purified (calcinated) and returned back (recombined) to the preparation to create a holistic preparation with increased power and energy. Paracelsus based many of his famous medicines and elixirs on spagyric procedures.

In chapter 6 we will engage the seven stages of shamanic alchemy transformation through specific personal practices and ceremonies of calcination, dissolution, separation, conjunction, fermentation, distillation, and coagulation. To begin the process of shamanic alchemy, first we will engage in "laboratory" techniques of these seven stages, which help to tangibly enter the great work.

It is important to note that what you are engaging in here is utterly real. We began our praxis with the shamanic processes of entering an ISC, learning DSV, and making a connection with the Sacred Fire. Now we move on to laboratory-type techniques before we move on to personal-growth techniques of transformation. I bring this up simply because many modern instructional books on alchemy include zero or little hands-on training.* Instead, the authors ask us to imagine we are doing something related to a specific alchemic process or to meditate on it. Although imagination and meditation certainly have their place in enriching our lives, the ancient and old-time alchemists would be rolling in their graves if they heard a teacher of alchemy tell a student or adept to imagine calcination or meditate about distillation. I am not saying this to put down either of these modalities, as I use them both myself. However, the fact remains the same; meditating on shoveling snow or visualizing cooking a beautiful and delicious meal may help your performance when you actually do it, but if you don't do it, the snow on your walkway will still be there and the ingredients for the meal will still be in the fridge.

I have fond memories of an intern we had one season who is a dedicated Buddhist adept that meditates and prays for hours every day. He walked into the barn, and I asked him if he had gotten around to shoveling the walkways. Sheepishly he answered no. But then with a big grin he added, "but I meditated on it!" We both laughed at his comical reply and also because he had volunteered to do the walkways and was a good worker who would surely get them shoveled.

Dear reader, please acknowledge that here you are engaging in actual practices of alchemy and shamanism, not visualization or meditation techniques. What I am attempting to teach you is work. Many times, especially during the personal transformation techniques of chapter 6, this work will

---

*Mark Stavish's book *The Path of Alchemy* (listed in the bibliography) is recommended. Stavish uniquely combines explanations of laboratory processes with meditation exercises.

push you past anything you ever experienced, and you *will* come out of it *changed.*

I realize that some of you reading this may have previous knowledge of alchemic laboratory processes. That's great! I encourage you to proceed through this section to be more readily prepared for chapter 6. For those of you coming from a more shamanic background or who are new to both alchemy and shamanism, this chapter lays the foundation for higher level alchemic-shamanic practices to come.

ALCHEMIC HERBS

Both historically and today, herbal alchemy is a skilled art form whose applications reach far and wide. Herbal alchemists usually designate the properties of an herb to various astrological and medicinal uses. For example, a commonly agreed-upon astrological correspondence for basil is Mars; its day is Tuesday, and the associated human organ is gall. However, I found that even the most experienced alchemic herbalists don't always agree on an herb's designations. For example, some herbalists believe comfrey is ruled by Saturn (Saturday), while others say Jupiter (Thursday). For some, mint is ruled by Venus (Friday) and by Mercury (Wednesday) for others. Alchemic herbalists find it efficacious to work with herbs on their ruling day, but they don't always agree on what day that is. For our work, I'm going to leave it up to you: work with an herb on the day you feel called to do so. The most important criteria is that you do it with an open heart and mind and a feeling of respect and oneness with the plant kin-doms.

Having an herb garden is great, and I look forward every year to fresh growing herbs for all sorts of purposes. However, for many reasons, fresh herbs are not always available, but there are many companies that sell organic dried ground herbs that are inexpensive. Most of the herbs listed below can be purchased in one-ounce packages for around three dollars. Listed below are some of my favorite alchemic herbs. Space does not allow me to go into detail about all the medicinal properties of these herbs, but there are unlimited resources out there for you to do your own in-depth study.

Fennel (*Foeniculum vulgare* Mill.)

Fennel was highly valued in the ancient world by Romans, Greeks, Egyptians, Chinese, and Indians for its use as a carminative and expectorant and as a talisman in rituals. Various preparations and uses of fennel were recorded in Spain as far back as 961 BCE, and the herb is employed in traditional Chinese medicine and ayurveda. The Cherokee and Pomo Indians of North America use it widely, and I have seen the Hopi smoke it as a substitute for tobacco.

Kava Kava (*Piper methysticum* G. Forst.)

There are many folktales about the origin of kava kava as it has been a traditional herb of the Pacific Islands for over three thousand years. Kava kava has traditionally been used and continues to flourish as a ceremonial beverage of Polynesian islanders and is still used quite frequently today in the Pacific Islands during social gatherings, as well as recreationally, to promote relaxation, stress reduction, and "good feelings."

Lady's Mantle (*Alchemilla mollis*)

Lady's mantle is in the rose family and has been referenced in many medicinal and magical circles since the Middle Ages. Its genus name *Alchemilla* is a derivative of the Arab word *alkemelych,* or alchemy, so called for the plant's magical healing potency. Folklore concerning lady's mantle seems to focus on the morning dew that gathers at the center of its furrowed leaves, which old-time alchemists used as a key ingredient in many alchemical formulas.

Lemon Balm (*Melissa officinalis* L.)

This herb's use goes back thousands of years to the time of the ancient Romans and Greeks; the old-time alchemists loved lemon balm, as do I. Its delicate lemony flavor uplifts the spirit and calms the heart and body. *Melissa,* the genus name, is the Greek word for honeybee, so named because of the bees' love of this beautifully scented herb.

Mugwort (*Artemisia vulgaris* L.)

I was first introduced to mugwort by one of my shamanic dreaming teachers who told me to sleep on a pillow of mugwort to help me remember my lucid dreams. There's a lot of folklore about mugwort and witchcraft, although I have found the herb to be quite friendly and useful for me. It is said Roman soldiers put mugwort in their sandals to keep their feet from getting tired, and in Holland and Germany, the plant was considered sacred to John the Baptist who presumably wore a girdle of mugwort for protection from evil.

Plantain (*Plantago major* L.)

My Lenni Lenape mentor would cringe and sometimes even cry out when she saw people spraying deadly chemicals on dandelions and plantains in their yards, which many people identify as weeds. Historically, plantain was admired by the Saxons as one of their nine sacred herbs and was an early Christian symbol. Plantain is great for bee stings and insect bites, and some cultures still consider it an aphrodisiac.

Sage (*Salvia officinalis* L.)

In medieval times there was a saying: *Cur moriatur homo cui Salvia crescit in horto?* (Why should a man die while sage grows in his garden?) Wherever sage grows around the world, it is used and revered as medicine.

Sassafras (*Lauraceae*)

One of my first plant mentors, an elder of the Lenni Lenape, adored sassafras, and she would sit and tell me folktales of how the unusual tree got its three different shapes of leaves. She would use all parts of the tree as they are all fragrant and useful, but she preferred a tea made from the roots.

Praxis 5

Dissolution and Separation

I will be using the term *laboratory work* for the alchemic processes related to the transformation of organic substances. Even though we will not employ an actual laboratory, as one is not needed, it's the best word I have. The first laboratory-type process will fulfill the first three stages of calcination, dissolution, and separation.

For the first stage of calcination, we could simply calcify any herb, but if we prepare our herbs via dissolution and separation, we have a superior and transformed herbal mass (feces or *caput mortuum*) to work with and also a tincture for later use.

Materials

    1 ounce of dried herb
    Mortar and pestle or coffee grinder
    Two 24-ounce canning jars with lids (wide mouth preferred)
    Grain alcohol 190 proof or 180 proof if illegal in your state
    Plastic wrap for barrier to metal lid
    Aluminum foil or other opaque wrap for jars when complete
    Fine mesh filter, coffee filter, or panty hose

1. In an ISC begin by grinding the herb little by little with mortar and pestle into a fine powder. If you encounter stems or roots that you can't pulverize with a pestle, you can run them through a coffee grinder. It's good to have some of every part of the plant if possible.
2. When sufficiently pulverized pour it into one of the 24-ounce jars. Add grain alcohol so the jar is one-half to two-thirds full. Be sure to not fill all the way.
3. Cover the mouth of the jar with plastic wrap so that neither the mixture nor its vapor will contact the inside of the lid. Screw the lid with the gasket on tight. To keep out light, wrap the jar in foil or other opaque material.
4. Store at room temperature. Shake the jar passionately twice a day for ten days. During the dissolving and maceration process, the fluid will turn darker day by day, which is called tincturing. I encourage you to peek at the tincture by loosening some of the opaque material once in a while and then re-covering the jar.
5. When your tincture is ready, pour your tincture into the other canning jar while filtering the macerated and dissolved plant material though a coffee filter or panty hose. At the end of the pour, press the remaining liquid out of the plant material in the filter, then put the strained plant material back into the original jar. Put the lids back on both jars.
6. In the jar with the liquid, you now have a simple tincture similar to what you might purchase at a health food store or herbal shop. In your

original jar you now have the separated plant material that we will reintroduce to the tincture after calcination.

In alchemical terms what you have just done is separated the sulfur (soul, consciousness) in the form of essential oils, fats, and waxes from the salt (the body, the solid, the vehicle) in the form of plant material by way of the mercury (vital power, spirit) in the form of the alcohol (and some water). We engage in this tangible alchemic process to see, feel, and experience the same as we will do to our own soul, body, and spirit as we move through the personal stages of transformation of chapter 6. With that said, during the whole process of making your tincture—obtaining the herbs, pulverizing, dissolving and macerating with spirit, and finally separating—be aware that you will be engaging in the same process of transformation. For this reason, it is important to treat every operation of the process with care, just as you would a small child. During the process assume an air of sacredness and awe surrounding what you are doing. The attitude of the alchemist (you) greatly impacts the process and is transferred into the results.

Praxis 6
Calcination

Now we are once again going to work with the shaman-alchemist's best friend—fire. As I stated earlier, we could have simply calcified any herb with fire to complete stage one of calcination, but now we have a personally initiated body (salt) to calcify (purify), which is enormously advantageous to our process of transformation as we are intimately connected to the herbal body we shall calcify.

The process is fairly simple and requires a few readily available tools:

Materials
Bottle of herbal mass

An outdoor barbecue grill or fire pit or an indoor fireplace

A medium-deep oblong baking dish (Pyrex works well) or other low-thermal-expansion borosilicate glass

A metal instrument to stir the burning plant material (barbecue and fireplace tools work well)

Heat-proof gloves or hot pads for moving the dish

Grain alcohol 190 proof or the highest legal proof you can obtain

Pestle

Sealable container for the incinerated ash (mason jar is preferred)

Safety glasses (recommended just in case)

A piece of metal screen (optional)

1. Enter an ISC; place the herbal mass from your making of the tincture into the dish, set the dish on the grill or fire pit, and light the mass on fire. There should be enough alcohol left in the mass to easily ignite it. Let it burn for a couple minutes then stir it some. If you need to lightly blow on it or fan it to keep it going, do so. When your fire does go out, let the salt cool and with your pestle grind the blackened feces.

2. Add a small amount of alcohol to get the fire going again and repeat the process several times. As you repeat the process you should see less plant material and more ash. (At some point, you may need to put a screen over the dish to keep the ash from blowing away.) Be sure to grind thoroughly between cooling and reigniting. After repeating the process several times, you will begin to notice the black ash turning white in places.

3. Now place the dish in a 500 degree oven (with the ash not on fire). The ash will gradually turn grayish white, which is what we want. Taking the dish out and grinding the ashes a couple of times will speed up the process and result in a higher-grade ash.

4. After a time you will see and feel that the ash isn't going to get any more white, so remove the dish and let the ash cool but not all the way. While it is still slightly warm, place it into a tightly sealed container. The warmth of the ash will prevent it from absorbing moisture while it cools in the jar.

That's it! You have now successfully completed the first three stages—calcination, dissolution, and separation. Be sure to mark your jars appropriately and keep them in a safe place. We will be using the tincture and the ash during stages to come.

Praxis 7

Conjunction—Unifying the Whole

Once the operations of calcination, dissolution, and separation are successfully completed, the most vital and authentic essences of the original matter will be contained in those two jars. For medicinal purposes the reuniting of the purified salt with extracted sulfur and the vital force of mercury matures the vibration of the resulting liquid, transforming it into a true spagyric tincture. In spiritual terms, these essences are the very soul, spirit, and body of the alchemist, and it is now time for these basic components to reunite in a new conjunction.

The conjunction is the turning point of the whole alchemical process. This fourth stage is the middle between the first three and the next three. The process of conjunction can be facilitated in a few different ways. For our purposes, the simplest way will be effective. All you will need is one more mason jar, a piece of plastic wrap, and a filter (fine mesh filter, coffee filter, or panty hose).

Remember during the conjunction to relate this physical procedure to the numinous aspects of your own psyche. Physically, we are reuniting the purified salt with mercurified sulfur. Ethereally, we are reuniting the purified ego with soul and spirit. This will become even more perceptible to you during the stages of personal shamanic-alchemic transformation in chapter 6, but for now, simply invoke the metaphor of these physical actions toward the application of personal alchemic transformation.

1. In the mind-set of earnestly caring for your inner child of soul and spirit, carefully pour half your tincture into the empty jar. In the mind-set of uniting your purified ego with your soul and spirit, carefully pour half your calcinated ash into the same jar. Seal up the other two jars containing your remaining tincture and ash.

2. Cover the top of this jar with plastic wrap and seal it tightly with the gasket and lid. Shake thoroughly while feeling the conjugation happening. Yes, in alchemy there are sexual connotations and symbols regarding the conjunction, but in this scenario, it's all about you.

3. Label and put the jar in a safe place. Now you simply let the conjugated tincture extract the soluble salts. Any remaining nonsoluble salts of the

caput mortuum will eventually sink to the bottom of the jar. Gently shake your jar once a day for a week then strain. Now you have an authentic spagyric tincture that has been used since the time of Paracelsus or even before.

4. We will be using a small amount of this tincture and the remaining ash in chapter 6, but if you are curious as to the effect, go ahead and try some now. Simply take a glass of water (distilled water is best, spring or well water will do, public tap water should be avoided unless absolutely necessary) and add a teaspoon of your spagyric tincture, stir well, and drink. The effects of the tincture will be mild, and you may or may not feel them right away. However, rest assured the spagyric tincture always affects the alchemist in some way, especially during moments of contemplation and meditation and during dreams. I regularly consume spagyric tinctures, as do my student adepts and friends.

5. Another common way to consume tinctures is to simply place a couple of drops under your tongue—a method that I usually use. This is most easily facilitated by purchasing one- or two-ounce tinted eye-dropper bottles. These are readily available and usually cost less than a dollar a piece. Simply pour your spagyric tincture into the smaller bottles with a funnel. These powerful little bottles of magic are usually well received as gifts too.

Praxis 8

Fermentation

Most of the operations involving fermentation that the old-time alchemists performed were extremely complex and required a lot more equipment than what is desirable for our work here. For example, creating alchemic essences from fermented plant material requires distillation at low temperatures under a vacuum with repeated distillations and calcinations. Complex separation of etheric oils and their fermentation also require specific equipment. If you are interested in these more complex laboratory processes, please refer to *Spagyrics: The Alchemical Preparation of Medicinal Essences, Tinctures, and Elixirs* by Manfred Junius or investigate if there are any laboratory classes or workshops in your area.

Any type of fermentation process can be described as alchemy simply because fermentation is transformation. Fermentation is the transformation of organic material by various bacteria and fungi and the enzymes and acids that they produce. One of the oldest reasons for humans to intentionally ferment something was for the preservation of foods, which has now been going on for millennia. Before there were cans, refrigerators, and freezers, fermentation was the main way people avoided spoiling food. The earliest forms of fermentation took place in pits, lined with leaves and packed full of all kinds of food: vegetables, meat, fish, grains, tubers, and fruit. The practice of fermentation is prehistory.

Most modern people usually think about beer or wine when they hear the term *fermentation*. In this case certain yeasts are used to convert the sugars in grape juice or grains into alcohol. Other forms of fermentation may use a starter culture, such as whey, a byproduct of raw milk. The practice of fermentation is widespread and exists in every culture. It is one of the most important methods to process food. According to Octopus Alchemy, an organization in the UK seeking to raise food awareness, a third of what is eaten in the world is made via fermentation. The Octopus Alchemy blog notes that few people realize the variety of popular foods and beverages that are dependent on fermentation processes, such as coffee, chocolate, vanilla, condiments (ketchup, vinegar, soy sauce, miso), and meats such as corned beef, pastrami, ham, and salami.[1]

For our work here, we are going to explore the world of lacto-fermentation. The "lacto" portion of the term refers to a specific species of bacteria, namely Lactobacillus. Various strains of these bacteria are present on the surface of all plants, especially those growing close to the ground, and are also common to the gastrointestinal tracts, mouths, and vaginas of humans and other animal species.

The bacteria that spur on the lacto-fermentation process are already present in vegetables, including *Leuconostoc mesenteroides, Lactobacillus brevis,* and *Lactobacillus plantarum.* These are halophilic (salt-loving) anaerobic organisms, so they thrive in the oxygen-free saline environment that we are going to create. (Anaerobic means that no oxygen is present in the environment.) Our bacteria friends feed on the sugars in the vegetables or fruit and multiply as they emit large amounts of lactic acid, which poisons and inhibits the growth of their competitors. Lactic acid is a natural preservative that inhibits the growth of harmful bacteria. Beyond preservation advantages, lacto-fermentation also increases or preserves the vitamin and enzyme levels, as well as digestibility, of the fermented product.

For our lacto-fermentation we will be using a salt brine that creates an anaerobic, acidic environment. For all its benefits this is a super-easy operation requiring little equipment. Here's what you need:

24-ounce mason jar. Many people I know, and that includes me, get hooked on lacto-fermentation once they try it and end up buying or making larger fermentation vessels. (My lacto-fermented biodynamic salsa made from tomatoes, peppers, and herbs from my greenhouse is now pretty much legendary.) To begin with, we can stay with the mason jars we've been using.

Disilled water. Bottled, spring, or well water also works well. Avoid tap water, as it often contains chlorine, which can inhibit the fermentation process.

Unrefined salt. Any unrefined sea salt will do, but Himalayan pink rock salt is perfect. Avoid refined salt as it contains added iodine and may be stripped of its natural mineral content.

Product to ferment. This is your choice and chance to get creative. My famous chili salsa usually has about six ingredients in the ferment, but I sometimes like to ferment single ingredients too, such as green beans and swiss chard. How it's done:

1. While in an ISC get the product ready. In some cases (like green beans and peppers), I leave the vegetables whole. Other times I'll chop or grate the vegetables or just cut them to fit the jar (like carrot spears).

2. Mix your brine. The ratio is 5 percent of salt to weight of water or roughly 3 tablespoons of salt per 2 quarts or 50 grams of salt in 1 liter of water. For a 24-ounce mason jar, I typically add 2 tablespoons of salt.

3. Put the prepared product in the mason jar and pour in the brine. Compress the product firmly until it is submerged beneath the brine and ensure that all oxygen bubbles are released. Tap the jar lightly on the table a few times to facilitate this process, or poke at the product

with a chopstick to enable bubbles to escape. Make sure all the product is under the brine. If the product wants to float, place something heavy on top of it such as a stone or something similar. Make sure there is some space between the brine and the underside of the lid—about one-quarter to one-half inch. As in our previous operations, I like to place a piece of plastic wrap over the top of my jar before tightening the lid to prevent the product or gasses coming in contact with the metal lid, but it's not absolutely necessary.

Temperature and Timing

Leave your jar in a place with an even temperature between 65 and 70 degrees Fahrenheit for up to three or four days. During the first few days, there will be a significant build up of CO_2 in the jar, and it is wise to "burp" it to release built-up gas. After a few days, move the jar to an area where the temperature ranges from 60 to 65 degrees for three or four weeks. If storing longer, move it to the refrigerator or a cool root cellar. After seven to ten days check your jar for activity (CO_2 bubbles) and taste your product to see how you like it. Fermented food can be eaten at seven to ten days, but it's usually really good around twenty days. Whether you end up eating your fermented food or not, keep at least a little of the liquid (a tincture bottle will suffice) for the final stage at the end of the book.

Remember during the whole of this operation, as in the previous ones, the fermented food represents *you*. In alchemical terms, you are the product being fermented (salt equals body), and the brine (mercury equals spirit) is the force acting on you. This operation will become even more personal during your personal fermentation in chapter 10. That's all I'll say about that for now.

Praxis 9
Distillation for Purification

Most methods of distillation (industrial and laboratory) are variations of simple distillation, which we will be employing here. This operation requires the use of a still or retort (our retort will be a teakettle) in which a liquid is heated, a condenser to cool the ethereal vapor and transform it back to liquid (we will use a bucket with coiled copper), and a receiver to collect the distillate (a mason jar or something similar is sufficient).

In both this laboratory-type process and in chapter 6, which deals with personal alchemic transformation, distillation is used as a process of purification both physically and psychically. After purification, the resulting "form" is a vessel able to receive new energy and information. For this praxis we will be distilling water to obtainer a purer form that we can then reenergize for use in shamanic alchemy operations. Learning this technique also opens the door to more sophisticated distillations and conjunctions.

Distilling Equipment

When I first became interested in distilling, I was fortunate to find an old copper still in storage in one of the barns of the farm where I live. I have used it a few times, but it is big and bulky and too large for my needs. Since then I have fabricated my own small distilling apparatuses, mostly using glass laboratory equipment that is easy to find and fairly simple to set up; however, this is rather costly if you only use it occasionally. With that in mind, I'm going to explain how to make a simple and inexpensive still that can be used for many alchemic operations.

Materials

2.5- or 5-gallon bucket (must be clean)

Teakettle

Kitchen thermometer

⅜-inch copper refrigeration tubing (sold in a 20-foot standard length of coil)

Small tubing cutter (optional)

High-temperature food-grade silicone sealant

Size 6.5 drilled rubber stopper with ⅜-inch hole

Mason jar or other receiving vessel

Drill

Two drill bits: ⁷⁄₁₆ and ⁵⁄₃₂

Fig. 5.1. Still fabrication supplies: bucket, silicone sealant, teakettle, copper coil, rubber stopper, thermometer, drill bits, tubing cutter.

These items can typically be found at a good hardware store except for the rubber stopper. I get mine from a place that sells home brewing supplies. The stopper goes inside the kettle spout. Most inexpensive kettles have a spout diameter of around 1 ¼ inches. Most stoppers sold for home brewing are tapered. The stopper shown comes predrilled with a ⅜-inch hole for your ⅜-inch tubing; it has a diameter of approximately 1 ⅜ inches at the top and 1 ⅛ inches at the bottom, which fits perfectly into a kettle spout with a 1 ¼-inch diameter.

Steps

1. Drill a hole in the bottom of your bucket with the ⁷⁄₁₆ drill bit.
2. Gently place your coil in the bucket with one end through the hole you made. The bucket I used in this photo was slightly smaller in diameter than the copper coil, so I gently fit the coil in by slightly bending the tubing. This tubing bends very easily, so be careful not to bend too hard and kink the tubing.
3. Apply a small amount of silicone sealant around the inside and outside of the hole the tubing is going through to seal the bucket.
4. Drill a hole in the front of your kettle for the thermometer. This one required a ⁵⁄₃₂-inch hole. Yours may be slightly bigger or smaller. Just compare the shaft of the thermometer with the drill bit to find the

Fig. 5.2. Copper condensing coil placed inside bucket and through hole.

right size. Put the thermometer in the hole, making sure the end of the thermometer doesn't touch the bottom of the kettle (take the lid off the kettle and look inside) and then seal it with silicone. Allow the silicone to set and dry for twenty-four hours. Push your rubber stopper into the spout of the kettle.

Fig. 5.3. Teakettle with thermometer installed and rubber stopper seated in spout.

Fig. 5.4. Homemade alchemic still completed.

5. Assemble your still by first raising your still bucket so your outlet
    (copper tube) is slightly above your receiving vessel. In this case my
    vessel was a mason jar, so the bucket only needed to be raised six
    inches or so. Now gently push the end of the tubing into the stopper,
    making sure it goes all the way through the stopper and into the kettle
    spout (with the kettle lid still off you can look inside). This will take
    a little bit of finagling and slightly bending the tubing. Again, the
    tubing bends easily; take your time and don't crimp the tubing.

    That's it! You are now ready for the magic to begin.

6. With this still configuration, I have a 1.75-quart (56-ounce) kettle, so
    for our first operation, I put 6 cups (48 ounces) of water in the kettle. I
    use a 2.5-gallon bucket because it's easy to handle and not too tall, but
    a 5-gallon bucket will work too. The colder you can keep the tubing
    coiled inside the bucket, the more efficiently your still will produce
    purified product. Cold water is fine, but cold water with ice is even
    better. Fill the bucket to the top.

7. With everything in place—water in your kettle and ice water in
    your bucket—turn on the stove and boil water as you normally

would. Pulling vapor out of the water turning it into steam and then condensing it back into distilled water takes time. Distilling 6 cups of water in the still pictured in figure 5.4 takes about an hour and a half, and you will be rewarded with about 14 ounces of purified water. For safety, be sure not to leave your still unattended, and keep pets and small children away during the operation.

8. Make sure the lid on your kettle is fully closed so you don't lose steam. Most kettles have a snap ring or something similar to hold the lid tightly in place. As steam enters your tubing, the tubing that is not bathing in the ice water will get hot. At the top of your bucket, the tubing in the cold water will get warm during the process and warm up the top layer of water. You can test the water with your finger; it will be warmish not hot. To facilitate the process, I remove a few cups of some of the top warm water and replace it with cold water or, even better, some more ice. I'll do this four to five times during the distilling process.

9. I successively set a timer during the operation for ten minutes for two reasons. First, checking the kettle every ten minutes ensures you know the level of the water in the kettle. Being careful not to have hot steam harm you, take off the kettle lid and look inside. Second, by removing the kettle lid, you change the pressure of the system, and you will normally see more product flow into your receiver for a few seconds. Make sure you put the lid back on tight after removing it.

10. As the distilled water begins to collect in your receiver, treat it as you would a little baby. It's *your* baby. Keep positive energy and vibes around your still while distilling—try not to let negative thoughts intrude from you or other people that may be close by. This is best accomplished being silent. If others are around, simply ask them to be silent or limit conversation to positive topics or the operation of the still.

With the above being said, you don't need to stand around and watch your still do its work—although I have found people do just that the first couple times as it's a unique experience. In any case, while the still is operating and I am close by, I enjoy reading a book, doing some writing, or cooking (the still only needs one burner). A perfect time for distilling is when you have already planned to take a time-out from a hectic schedule. I consider sitting by the still while it's working similar to sitting by the wood-stove on a cold day or on the beach enjoying the waves. The more passive intention you feel while distilling, the more special the process becomes.

Praxis 10
Charging Shamanic Water

Materials
   Distilled (by you) water
   Food-grade funnel (small)
   Several tinted tincture bottles (2 or 4 ounces)

1. As soon as possible after your distillation is complete, using a food-grade funnel, pour your purified water into several small tincture bottles, recognizing that you have erased all the memory from this water and it will absorb any energy it is subject to. I "charge" my pure water by placing it directly in the energy field of the entities that rule the macrocosm, thus marrying the microcosm (my pure water) with the energies of the macrocosm (sun, fire, earth, moon, and stars). This ethereal marriage lives at the roots of alchemic transformation.

   For example, I immediately take a couple bottles and bury them in the ground in my garden or other place where I strongly feel the energy of Grandmother Growth. I will leave them in the ground for a week or so. A couple of other bottles I will put in front of a Sacred Fire or even just a candle for a few hours. Grandfather Fire energizes water more quickly than Grandmother Growth. You can also place bottles outside in a quiet location to absorb the energy of the moon and stars.

2. While placing the bottles in the location of your choosing, add a blessing to kickstart the charging process. For example, while placing a bottle in the living soil of Grandmother Growth, I offer a blessing like this or something similar: "Grandmother Growth, in front of you and all my companions (everything around you), please put your ancient energy, light, and wisdom into this pure water. Help it to develop, grow, and nurture the world as you would a seed, a plant, or a tree. My offering to you Grandmother is to use this sacred water for the benefit

of others and myself for increased well-being and healing."

Blessings such as this add power to the process. With a clean heart and pure intention, prepare your blessings ahead of time or let them arise spontaneously as you place your water in your selected energetic location.

Pure water that has been charged in this manner can be safely administered in the same way as a tincture. I have seen remarkable results for example with a few drops of fire-charged water placed under the tongue of someone who is feeling down, depressed, or simply worn out. Water that has been charged by Grandmother Growth is especially good for healing both physically and psychologically. Once some students and I took Grandmother Growth water to a nursing home each day for a week, and when we told the people it was our last day, they pretty much begged us to come back. I have also witnessed remarkable results with moon-charged water, especially with young girls and women during menopause.

Energizing water in this way has been proven both through modern science (via macrophotography) and by shamans for thousands of years (via the effects of healing the troubled or ill). Unlike tinctures and other homeopathic remedies that require years of specialized training to safely and properly administer, shamanically charged water is completely safe and basically can't be administered incorrectly.

If you used a nonopaque bottle for charging (which I normally do), either transfer your water to more opaque bottles (like amber) or make sure to keep them out of sunlight after charging. Even though your water is extremely pure, you want it to stay fresh. I also like to label my bottles for myself or for when I give them to someone.

Praxis 11
Herbal Distillation for a Shamanic Elixir

This praxis is the first step for the coagulation stage, which we will complete at the end of chapter 6.

Alchemic distilling with herbs can be done in many ways; some can be very complex and require specialized equipment. Distilling of herbs by way of steam requires only two more pieces of equipment than we already have, but the apparatus for distillation by boiling is adequate for our needs.

As I am writing this I so far today have completed fabricating the new still, photographed it, distilled water with it, and now I am distilling a mixture of herbs (yes, all in a few hours). The wonderful fragrance of the herbal mixture I'm currently distilling has floated its way throughout the whole house, and I just smelled the distilled water essence in my receiving jar, and it is amazing.

The next step in distillation we would normally perform in one of my workshops would be distilling an herb of your choice. However, I'm going to skip that step here and introduce the next step, the difference being the number of herbs and the addition of the salt (body).

First, it's important to understand the difference between the terms *clyssus* and *elixir*. A clyssus is a preparation of the recombined extracts of a single plant. As we saw during the first four stages of our laboratory work, a true spagyric tincture is an herbal preparation that has been dissolved, separated, calcinated, and then recombined. In our work so far, we have used one herb at a time. If we desired to prepare a clyssus via distillation, we would also use only one herb and recombine the salt. But for a true clyssus, the whole plant is always used: roots, blossoms, stems, leaves, fruits, seeds. (See Clyssus and Elixir in the lexicon [chapter 2].)

In an elixir often several herbs are employed. The knowledge of what herbs to prepare together was of crucial significance to the old-time alchemists and continues with alchemists and herbalists today. My information for you is not so much which herbs are best to combine (that is a discipline of its own and via your DSV you can obtain such information on your own) but rather to instruct you in the proper way of preparing an elixir through distillation and conjunction.

First, let me just say that the significance of the term *elixir* has deteriorated through time. You can now read in books and online and find elixir recipes that are basically flavored blends similar to a cordial. The term *elixir* is also now used for the simple combining of essential oils and tinctures poured together. I'm sure these preparations have their own value, but here we are after the most authentic spagyric elixir preparation we can obtain with our equipment. Classic alchemic elixirs always contain the salts that are extracted through incineration and calcination of the plant residue.

This procedure begins the same way as stages one through four with a couple of minor differences. The first difference is you are going to choose more than one, but not more than three, different herbs used together to produce your elixir. The herbs I am currently boiling and distilling are organic *Melissa* or lemon balm (which I grew), organic rooibos (which I purchased), and a little bit of organic ginger root (which I purchased). For some time I was looking for an elixir mixture with the main ingredient being my favorite *Melissa* and this mixture I really like.

When you have decided which herbs to use (for instructional purposes I'll now refer to this as your elixir mixture) perform the operations of praxis 5 (dissolution and separation), praxis 6 (calcination), and praxis 7 (conjunction). However, only use half the herbs of your elixir mixture (the other half you will use after you make this tincture and be sure, as before, to retain half the ash you have calcinated).

Now you should have a new spagyric tincture of your elixir mixture for use whenever you like, half the remaining herbs of your elixir mixture, and half the ash from your elixir mixture. The remaining herbs and ashes we will use in making the elixir.

1. If your herbs are dry, soak them in water overnight. If they are fresh, you may proceed now.
2. Place your herbs in the teakettle you created in praxis 9 and cover with water, being careful not to cover the copper condensing tube in the rubber stopper. Unlike distilling only water, boiling your herbs will produce foam that can prevent steam rising into your condenser tube. Monitor your boiling, especially in the beginning, and adjust your flame if needed so the boiling liquid and froth don't cover your tube.
3. Distill as you did with plain water, and extract as much condensed herb-infused distilled water into your receiving vessel as possible without burning the plant material.
4. Now add the reserved ash from the same plants as you did in stage four conjugation, shake, and seal. Shake gently every day for a week and then strain.

You now have a spagyric elixir from the processes of calcination, dissolution, separation, distillation, and conjunction. Try your elixir now or when you feel the call. Keep this valuable product in a safe place as we use this elixir at the end of this book when we finish with the seventh stage of coagulation.

PART THREE

THE SEVEN STAGES OF SHAMANIC ALCHEMY TRANSFORMATION

The Azoth of Basil Valentine

The legendary alchemist Frater Basil Valentine is said to have been a fifteenth-century Benedictine monk; however, historians tell us that Valentine's work was more probably written by several different alchemists of the time who wished to remain anonymous. In any event, alchemic works ascribed to Valentine have been used by alchemists for centuries, and the basis for many of Valentine's work comes directly from much older sources, such as the Emerald Tablet, which could date back thousands of years.

In attempting to decipher the messages of the Emerald Tablet, ancient alchemists came up with seven operations, steps, or stages to be performed on matter. In this sense matter can be conceived as physical, psychological, or spiritual in nature. These seven steps are a mainstay to alchemy even to this day and as such may be used as a guide to shamanic alchemy practices. Frater Valentine provides us with an intricate mandala that is in reality a map that leads through the seven steps.

The symbols and symbolism of the mandala have been interpreted by many over the centuries. I'm using deciphering clues from various modern authors including Dennis William Hauck and Manfred Junius, old-time symbolic alchemists such as Maier, Custos, Faust, and the famous designer and engraver Merian, among others, and my own direct shamanic viewing of the mandala. This last source is of great importance. In an ISC, what do *you* see? How do the various symbols and symbolism make *you* feel? As important it may be to consult our elders and teachers, we have our own personal resources as well that should not be overlooked. On the contrary, we do well to embrace and enlarge our personal capacities on the path of shamanic alchemy.

The large circle and star in the center of the drawing depicts the actual steps, which we will get to shortly, but first let's look at the other important symbols. In the center of the mandala is the face of a bearded

Fig. P3.1. Azoth mandala, attributed to Basil Valentine, 1659.

alchemist with a downward-pointing triangle superimposed over his face. This is certainly the focal point of the drawing, and focusing on it is like looking into a mirror. The large triangle in back of (behind) the circle represents the three philosophical principles of alchemy (chapter 3), each depicted in a corner of the triangle. The alchemist's hands and feet are connected to the four elements: one foot is on earth, the other in water; in one hand is a torch of fire, and in the other is a symbol for air. This last symbol has caused much confusion to interpreters of the mandala because here you would expect to find a feather or something similar representing air, but he is not holding a feather. Many believe he is holding a fish bladder, which symbolizes floating (like on air) or atmospheric pressure. Where his head should be we find an image of a winged creature resembling the top of the caduceus (see definition of caduceus in the lexicon in chapter 2) that symbolizes the consciousness's ability to travel to other dimensions of reality.

The mandala includes two places where we find both sun and moon. First, we have the Sun King seated on a lion to the alchemist's right and the Moon Queen seated on a great fish to his left. In the corners of the inverted triangle behind the central mandala are the words *anima, spiritus,* and *corpus,* along with the symbols of sun, moon, and body or, in alchemist language, mercury, sulfur, and salt. Interestingly, the symbol for salt, in between the alchemist's legs, has five stars floating around it. This probably signifies the five elements, with quintessence being the fifth.

Touching the right wing of the top of the winged caduceus is a salamander engulfed in flames. Many ancient legends exist related to the salamander and fire, mostly having to do with the salamander's ability to put out fire and that its toxic skin burns one like the fire. The mystical relationship between the numinous fire and salamander and the flames touching the wing of the caduceus signifies the fire as being a means to multidimensional consciousness, as does the spirit bird touching the caduceus's left wing. Overall, the symbolism in back of the main circular of the mandala is one of the marriage of opposites, a common theme in alchemic lore, and the importance of the elements as vital role in the background.

The seven stages of alchemic transformation are diagrammed in the drawing within the large circle and star. Paracelsus often spoke of the stars in man and alluded to in the Emerald Tablet: "What is below is like that which is above, and what is above is like that which is below to accomplish the miracles of One Thing." The rays of the star are numbered, moving in a clockwise direction, and also contain both a corresponding metal and a celestial object. The circles in between the rays depict the actual alchemic processes or operations of transformation. Before each of the following stages, I will explain the symbols in the circle.

6

STAGE ONE

CALCINATION—FIRE

Fig. 6.1.
Stage one.

Star ray number one in the Azoth of Basil Valentine is the shaded ray pointing to the salt (body) cube and contains the symbols for the metal lead and the planet Saturn. Saturn is heavy like lead, slow, and stubborn. The ancients conceived salt to be representative of lower consciousness, which could be elevated through the alchemical processes. Recrystallizing this lower consciousness into a higher form is the crux of this stage.

To the left (clockwise) of the first ray is the Latin word *vista,* signifying a visit or the start of the journey, and the first circle identifying the first operational stage of calcination. The scene depicts a crow atop a skull—the Soul Bird perched on the death of the profane during the action of calcination. During laboratory alchemical calcination, a substance is reduced to ashes by heat and grinding. In shamanic terms this stage represents the burning away of negative aspects of the ego and the purifying of consciousness.

Fig. 6.2. The king suffers through calcination by the heat of the fire
and purging of his thoughts (engraving by Matthäus Merian,
from *Atalanta Fugiens* by Michael Maier, 1617).

<u>**Praxis 12**</u>

Sacred Fire Ceremony—Death of the Profane

Ceremonies with a Sacred Fire, as opposed to sitting around the camp-fire or fireplace, are widely varied in scope and purpose cross-culturally. Shamans may use a Sacred Fire in diagnosing and healing the sick, to petition for rain, see into the future, or communicate from the village to those out hunting or on a sacred pilgrimage, to name a few.

When using a Sacred Fire in my healing work, there are a few specific ceremonies and techniques I employ. In my previous book *Advanced Shamanism,* I detail a ceremony for healing energetic drains. Here I will explain a somewhat similar ceremony with the major and crucial difference being that this ceremony is more mental and the other more physical. I sincerely hope that you will engage in the ceremony for healing energetic drains. The intent of this ceremony is to clean our p-c mirrors of the mind of profane blockages that prevent us from living in our true essence.

Long before ever learning the scientific term *phase-conjugate mirrors* (p-c mirrors), I experienced this phenomena when in ceremony with Huichol shamans and can now see them at will. Many years ago I was in the Huichol Sierra of western Mexico being mentored in various aspects of shamanism. One night during a ceremony for the blessing of feathers the pilgrims would be wearing on the pilgrimage to the peyote desert, I looked across the fire to my teachers and couldn't believe what I saw. Somehow inside the heads of my teachers were beams of white-gold light reflecting and bouncing as if the light was reflecting off an intricate array of mirrors. I immediately "knew" that these light beams were in reality thoughts and memories of their minds. I looked intently at my main teacher, and in that moment he looked up at me from the fire between us and smiled at me. I knew right then that he could see that I could see these bouncing rays of light inside his energetic holographic field. Later while discussing this with him, he informed me that I had passed into another phase of my learning. Decoding the information I was seeing and then using that knowledge for healing were the next steps.

Needless to say, I was surprised to learn many years later that science had explored similar phenomena. Experiments of the pioneers of holography constructed four phase conjugate mirrors from three lasers. In this experiment two lasers meet head on; when a third is aimed into this configuration, it reflects, much like raindrops reflect sunlight to make a rainbow. Ordinary mirrors reflect light according to the angle the light strikes the mirror, but phase-conjugate (p-c) mirrors self-target—the reflection retraces the path back to its source at any angle of incidence. The reflection merges spatial and temporal information from all three input beams so data from several sources can be combined and fed back to a specific location. Mirrors form and vanish instantly as the lasers go on and off. Here we see how this light apparatus might mirror actual brain function. Imagine millions of coherent packets of light traveling through white and gray matter, meeting in strategic places, creating millions of p-c mirrors that synthesize and reflect information automatically and accurately to meaningful sites.

Remarkably similar to the holographic laser experiments, in our brain we have four ventricles linked into a winged structure. The two lateral ventricles are centered in the cerebral hemispheres, the third between the two halves of the thalamus and hypothalamus, and the fourth between the cerebellum and the brain stem. The concept of the brain communicating with itself via phase-conjugate mirrors and that coherent light energy is involved with the process of translating information from the hyperspace into sensory memory, and then into awareness and the ability of expression is based on science. However, I bring it up simply because during certain shamanic practices, we can actually view our own p-c mirrors and those of others. Some shamanic cultures like the Huichol have known and used this information long before any modern scientific explanation.

Ervin Laszlo, famous supporter of quantum theory and twice nominee for the Nobel Peace Prize has this to say with regard to phase conjugation in the brain:

> The brain does not have the capacity to store all the perceptions, sensations, volitions, and emotions experienced by an average individual in a lifetime. Computer scientist Simon Berkovitch calculated that to produce and store a lifetime's experiences the brain would have to carry out 10^{24} operations per second. Dutch neurobiologist Herms Romijn has shown that this would be impossible even if all 100 billion neurons in the brain were involved—and they are not: there are only 20 billion neurons in the cerebral cortex, and many of them have no evident cerebral function. . . . How this occurs is explained by the interactive process known as "phase conjugation."
>
> Phase conjugation means a relationship between two waves that are equal but opposite in phase to each other. Two equal waves traveling in opposite directions create a single standing wave within which they are in resonance: they are "phase conjugate." Applied to the brain, this means that when the brain receives information from its vacuum-hologram, it is in a phase-conjugate relationship with it. It emits a virtual outgoing wave that is conjugate with the incoming wave from the hologram. In this way the brain can read out the information

it has created. This information is conserved in the vacuum hologram, so that our read-out embraces the experiences we have had throughout our life."[1]

Unfortunately, throughout our lives our p-c mirrors can become tarnished, stained, and even made opaque so that they don't reflect information correctly or don't reflect at all. Removing the spots on our p-c mirrors of the mind that are not reflecting efficiently is the goal of this ceremony with a Sacred Fire.

In the Sacred Fire ceremony I mentioned earlier—dealing with energy drains—you intentionally engage in healing them by identifying, patching, and then sealing them. This Sacred Fire ceremony is much different in that we are focusing not on energetic drains but on blocks to our consciousness. These blocks stem from events in our lives that were in some way traumatic or at the least very disturbing and have left a nonreflective black "glob" on a small portion of our p-c mirrors. An experienced shaman can see these globs on our p-c mirrors and how they do not reflect information. Some of these traumatic experiences are worse the others, and the size of the glob is proportionate with the trauma of the experience. Many globs appear as tiny globules, while others are larger, typically appearing as about the size of a dime.

These nonreflective globs and globules on our p-c mirrors prevent us from being all we can be. They stunt us in certain portions of our life. Our nonreflective globs hinder relationships and advancement in education or the workplace. They stop us from trying new things and harm our physical well-being. For example, I acquired many globs on my mirrors during my midteens and early twenties. My mirrors were like the side mirrors of a car driving through mud puddles. The worst glob was created by the death of my father from brain cancer when I was fifteen. This glob affected the proper reflection of my p-c mirrors to the point that I wasn't even myself anymore. I won't get into all the crazy stuff I did because that's not really important. What is important is that aside from doing unwise things I ordinarily wouldn't have done, I also could not fully concentrate on mental activities. Physical activities were no problem, but whereas I used to be an avid reader and loved to make models and engage in various mechanic projects, I now had no interest whatsoever. All I wanted to do was travel and run from my problems.

Finally, at around age twenty-three, I met a shaman in Mexico who saw this big blob on my mirrors. That isn't how she explained to me what she saw; in Spanish she basically told me that "some of my lights were dim." With her help and the Sacred Fire, we were able clean off the blob, and my mirrors began to reflect properly again. The proof is in the pudding: I went back to school, then started my own successful business, which was very detail oriented. I dove back into books as well, and now you are holding my eleventh published book. The point isn't that I erased the painful memories of my father's death and then some miracle happened, or that the removal of that big blob solved all my problems. I still have all those memories, and I still had other blobs to clear. But after the removal of the blob created by the trauma of my father's untimely death, my mirrors were back to reflecting more efficiently, and I could deal with my life situations in a clearer way. The process of cleaning our p-c mirrors can be directly felt in our thought processes, and the results are tangible and real. In terms of shamanic alchemy, there are few better examples than this.

Steps for the Ceremony

First, you must begin by preparing for the ceremony and familiarize yourself with the technique called recapitulation. I originally learned recapitulation from Mexican shamanic researcher Victor Sanchez who developed a highly effective technique of recapitulation inspired by the books of Carlos Castaneda. Among my many years learning and teaching with Victor in Mexico on two occasions I participated in a two-week recapitulation workshop where participants spent fourteen nights sitting inside wooden boxes to recapitulate their lives. Along with that I spent many years recapitulating on my own and have utilized this technique for probably close to two thousand hours, and it has changed my life for the better. Sanchez's specific technique is covered in his book *The Toltec Path of Recapitulation: Healing Your Past to Free Your Soul*. The technique I am presenting here is a condensed and modified version, which I have adapted with the addition of the Sacred Fire as a numinous impartial teacher. In various moments during recapitulation, the Sacred Fire will act as a portal into both your consciousness and your energetic body; in other moments the Fire will be a mirror in which you can see your actions. In this ceremony, the Sacred Fire will also help you burn away the blobs on your p-c mirrors.

1. The first thing you need to do is identify the specific moments in your life that have created nonreflective globs on your p-c mirrors. Some traumatic moments you will be able to easily identify and remember; others may be more subtle and take more work to dig up. To aid you in this endeavor, I suggest you make a written list with various headings and place the specific events under that heading. Below is a small sample list from my life. Be aware this list is tiny: the list I've worked on during close to thirty years of recapitulating has over ten thousand entries. For this ceremony your list will not have ten thousand events. List the events that may have caused the biggest globs. It is important for your work with the fire that you use the names of people. In this sample list I describe my relationship to the person so that you can know what happened. For your list, you only need to write the name of the person—you already know your relationship to him or her and what happened.

Family
Death of my father (Jeno)

Tragic incident sitting in the kitchen with my mom while on acid (Irma)

Feelings of hatred toward my uncle while traveling through Europe (Frank)

Appalling feelings of disgust upon seeing human skulls on my great uncle's lawn in Hungary (Kalmanbasci)

Friends
Being punched in the face by my best friend in high school when we were drunk (Scott)

Car crash with friends that left me with a broken jaw (Scott, Tom, C.J.)

Broke my hand in a fight defending a friend (Glen)

Best friend slept with my girlfriend (Eric)

Death of my dear Huichol friend in a house fire in Texas (Rosendo)

School

Back injury during football game

Flunking out of algebra two

Rolling joints in the school parking lot to sell to other kids

Work

Falling off a ladder and injuring my neck

Losing my guiding business in Sedona

Getting fired because I came to work still drunk from the night before

Cutting my knee with a chain saw

Slicing off the tip of my finger with my machete during a fire ceremony

Falling sixty feet while guiding rock climbers

Romantic relationships

Cheated on my partner (Kelly)

Partner cheated on me (Nancy)

Partner put thousands of dollars on my credit card before leaving me (Nicki)

Partner called the police on me when she went off her medication (Sonya)

Other

Spent a night in jail for DUI

Foreclosure on my house in Arizona

Personally witnessing the aftermath of 9/11

As stated above, this is a small sample list for you to get the idea. Although we all need important and often times hard lessons in our life to grow, we also need to be aware that the trauma of certain events can block us in the way we deal with future events. This is why we want to clean our p-c mirrors and make a shamanic-alchemic transformation into a clearer mind.

2. When your list is ready and the time is right, head to the location and bring forth your Sacred Fire as described on page 94 (praxis 4 in chapter 4). Offer Fire a pinch or two of your calcinated ash as a solid representation of your seriousness and commitment to this work.

3. To begin the ceremony choose an event on your list. You can choose one at random, go through your list sequentially as written, or work chronologically—it doesn't matter. Work through your list in whatever way feels best to you.

4. While seated next to the fire, look straight into the flames and relax. When ready, state the event out loud and tell the Sacred Fire you intend to get rid of this glob on the mirrors of your mind. For example, say, "Grandfather Fire, I'm going to remove this glob placed on my mirrors from when Scott punched me in the face."

5. Now close your eyes and see the flames briefly in your mind then see the event like you were watching a movie. This should be fairly quick because you are only seeing one event. For example, when I see the event of cutting my leg with a chain saw, it only took a few moments to realize what I did. I also see a few moments of what I did right afterward (sitting down) but stop there. Anything that happens subsequently are other events. Since the movie event is quick, it may flash before your eyes a few times. Review the movie for a minute or so then open your eyes.

6. While staring into the fire stand up and relive the event. See through your eyes every detail and relive the feelings of the event. You may need to scream, cry, jump up and down, move your arms or legs, or say the words you said. The important thing is to relive the event with as much authenticity as you can; relive it multiple times if necessary to be fully present.

7. When you feel you have gone as deep as you can into the reliving the event, make a fist with your dominant hand, with your index finger and thumb extended. Bring your fist to your head and touch your forehead with your finger and thumb. Relive the event once more while throwing your fist down to the fire and opening your hand (kind of like throwing dice). While you do this, say or shout out loud "I clear you!" or "I release you!" or "Be gone!" or "I burn you away!" Do

this as many times as you like or whatever feels right (five to ten times is usually sufficient).

8. Finally, feed Grandfather an arrow to help him burn away the glob, and watch the arrow burn before going to the next event.

9. As you work through your events, your momentum and competence will increase as you become familiar with the process. You may want to go back to your first events, which you may not have thoroughly cleared.

10. When you have gone through all your globs, give your list to Grandfather Fire.

At this point you will feel different!

7

STAGE TWO
DISSOLUTION—WATER

Fig. 7.1.
Stage two.

T he second star ray of the Azoth of Basil Valentine contains the symbols for tin and Jupiter and points toward the Sun King. The jovial Sun King with his scepter and shield sitting atop a lion represents someone motivated by physical cravings or monetary gain. However, below him is a fire-breathing dragon ready to burn him if he falls too deep into this egocentric mind-set.

In the second circle we find the Black Soul Bird literally watching itself dissolve while seeing its true white essence reflected back at him. In the laboratory dissolution is the act or process of dissolving, such as separation into component parts. Dissolving something in water was probably the first form of alchemy known to humanity. In shamanic terms, dissolution works on the heart and id (instinctual drives) to open our personal floodgates, releasing inhibitions and allowing our consciousness to flow freely.

Unlike most people in Western culture, shamanic peoples consider the spirit of water to be of highest importance. My Huichol shaman mentors make annual pilgrimages to Isla del Rey near San Blas, a municipality on the Pacific Coast of Mexico, to pay their respects to Tatéi Haramara, the goddess of the Pacific Ocean (*tatéi* means "our Mother Goddess," and *haramara* means "sea"). They deliver sacred objects embedded with prayers and collect seawater to bring back to the village for blessings and healings. Some Huichol live close to the ocean, but my friends and mentors live way up in the mountains, and it is a long trip for them to make. It is both moving and hilarious to be with them during the ceremony at the sacred place on the beach. The ceremony is a solemn event, but afterward, they dive in the water and splash around, having fun. The Huichol also make pilgrimages to Lake Chapala, Mexico's largest freshwater lake, to honor Tatéi Xapawiyeme (Our Mother Fig Tree Rain Place). Numerous sacred springs dot the Huichol sacred landscape as well, including Tatéi Matinieri (Our Mother Born in the East), which is a mandatory sacred stop for blessings on the pilgrimage to the peyote desert Wirikuta—the sacred place of the east. All of these sacred water sites I have been to many times with the Huichol, and it is amazing the reverence they display.

When visiting to honor the sacred water sites, the Huichol shamans always bring some water back home with them to bless those who didn't make the pilgrimage. One of the most beautiful and profound examples of this I have ever seen happened once when I was visiting a ceremonial center deep in the Wirrarika Sierra. It was dawn on my first day there, and I had just been awakened by the sounds of someone building a fire in front of the *rirriki* (sacred hut where offerings are kept), which was next to the little hut I had spent the night in. As I sat next to the fire, I remembered the dream I had had in the night: in the dream was an old shaman whom I had met briefly a few years ago during a ceremony but who had left before I'd had the chance to find out his name. For the past few years he had frequently appeared in my dreams in different capacities, and I always hoped to meet him physically again one day.

As I sat staring into the fire and remembering my dream, a few of my friends from the village came and sat next to me, and in the course of conversation I asked them who was the current presiding shaman of the ceremonial center (this duty changes every five years). They told me his name but that he was not in the village that day. I felt a little disappointed at missing the presiding shaman, but my spirits were immediately lifted when a few small children joined us by the fire. After a few minutes they all got up and ran away to a small hill about forty yards away where a man was standing holding various things in hands, including his *muvieris* (feathered shaman's wands). I couldn't see his face as he was silhouetted by the glow of the soon-to-rise sun behind him, and I asked my friends who he was. They told me he was a *kawitero* (an elder keeper of the sacred tradition, highest ranking member of the tribe) and a powerful shaman, currently presiding over another ceremonial center close by but that he lived in this village most of the time. By the time the children reached him, he was already chant-singing to the spirits and waving his feathered muvieris in circles through the air. In the next few minutes, I would have the privilege of witnessing what truly lies at the core of shamanism.

Just as he picked the first child off the ground and held her in his arms, the first ray of light from the sun pierced the top of the hill and he put her directly into it. Then holding her in one arm he gave her a small gourd of water from a sacred spring to hold, and five times he placed his feathered muvieris into the water, infused them with sunlight, whirled them through the air while chanting, and dabbed her various body parts with the wet feathers. Then he did the same thing with the head of a beautiful flower. Five times he placed the flower in the water gourd and dabbed her body, and while chanting he gently sucked or blew his breath into various parts of her body.

The tenderness of the old shaman blessing and healing the tiny girl with sunlight, water, air, flowers, breath, and the powerful chanting in the dawn light on that special little hill touched me in such a profound way that I was moved to tears. It was like something out of a fairy tale. When he was finished with the first child, the second came and jumped into his arms like he had the most special present that child had ever seen. That little boy simply couldn't wait for the old shaman to give him his magic, and this too touched me deeply as I reflected on how children of my society must be forced to leave their video games and televisions behind to participate in spiritual blessings and communions.

As I continued to watch the scene on the hill, I gradually began to fully perceive what was going on, and by the time the shaman was with the fourth child, I could actually "see" the luminous energy that he was drawing with his muvieris from the sun, the water, the air, and the flower and infusing into the children at different parts of their body that seemed to be missing some of its radiance.

I found out later that these four children of the village were being treated by the shaman for various ailments and that he performed this type of follow-up treatment regularly at dawn for the children. When the shaman was finished with his work, I couldn't resist going to speak with him, so I walked over to the hill and as I approached him and he turned toward me, I stopped dead in my tracks. It was the old shaman from my dreams whom I had met years before! I was so happy that I almost hugged him, but he didn't seem to recognize me, so I held back my mirth and simply asked him if I could meet with him later in the day, to which he agreed.

Since that special day, he has been one of my chief mentors and teachers not only of shamanism but of life. It turns out that he did remember me and was not at all surprised that I had "inadvertently" come to his village. That day, knowing that I had "seen" his work with the muvieris and that it was of course no accident that I was there with him, he helped me to make my very first muvieri, which later in my trip was blessed and consecrated in a very powerful and ancient Wirrarika ceremony where the shamans sing and chant for hours with the feathers of the muvieri in order to call the spirits and infuse their energy into the feathers.

Water has and is considered sacred in the great religions as well. In Hinduism, ghats are traditional sites for public ritual bathing, an act by which one achieves both physical and spiritual purification. Mikvah baths for purification are a staple of the Jewish religion. In the Christian tradition, baptism is described by Saint Paul as a ritual death and rebirth that simulates the death and resurrection of Christ. In Islam, mosques provide water for the faithful to wash before each of the five daily prayers.

From a scientific perspective we know that the human body mirrors the surface of Earth, of which about 71 percent is covered with water, with the oceans holding about 96 percent of all of Earth's water. The human body is composed of about 70 percent water, and the brain is about 90 percent water. Without water we die. The body will not function optimally if it doesn't have enough water or if the water becomes too still—whether it's the great ocean that bathes every cell; the rivers of blood, lymph, and cerebrospinal fluid; the streams of the capillaries and minor nerves; the lake of the stomach; or the pools of the eyes.

Even for those, like myself, who have experienced the sacredness of water with indigenous tribes, and those that use sacred water in a religious context, the mid-1990 findings of the late Masaru Emoto are pretty mind-blowing. Emoto's pictures of frozen water show us the direct effect that emotions can have on water. Positive thoughts and feelings create beautiful crystals, while negative ones result in distorted and discolored shapes, indicating that water can receive and transmit information at an emotional level. If that wasn't enough, Emoto's experiments also confirm what shamans know—water has memory. In his book *The Healing Power of Water*, Emoto writes about how water remembers its origin.

Fig. 7.2. The king suffers through dissolution in the waters of his own unconscious (engraving by Matthäus Merian, from *Atalanta Fugiens*, by Michael Maier, 1617).

The photographs clearly showed that depending on its origins (that is, whether it came from a natural spring or from the kitchen tap), water would take on a completely different shape. This was visible proof that not all water was the same—it reacted to the "experiences" it went through during its journey and stored that information. Water from a spring formed breathtakingly beautiful regular hexagons, while water from the lower course of a river or from a dam hardly achieved a complete crystal. The most shocking results came from chloride-ridden drinking water. It can be really painful to see water that has been mistreated in such a way if you know what marvelous crystals natural water can form. . . . In light of these experiments, we can say that water has a memory. Each molecule of it carries some information, and when we drink it, that data becomes part of our body.[1]

Praxis 13

Sacred Water Ceremony— Dissolving the Chains

Here is a time-tested ceremony for deeply experiencing the amazing qualities of water. It is highly recommended that this ceremony be performed by a clean spring pool, running water, or a lake with lots of flow in and out. Dammed water or ponds with little flow are to be avoided. The very best places are rivers with rapids or waterfalls and calm pools that you can float in. My first experience with this ceremony was at the Cascadas de Agua Azul (Blue Waterfalls) in the jungle of Chiapas, Mexico. The small waterfalls with pools between them and crystal-clear water made for the perfect experience. Take your time and find your right place before doing this ceremony. As with all ceremony, set and setting are key ingredients to the experience and results. Also, I have found that when in deeper water (your feet can't hit the bottom), it's helpful to have some kind of flotation device, preferably one that will allow you to float on your back, like a life vest or something similar. Not as good but better than nothing is a floating device that you can hang on to, like a water noodle. Flotation devices will allow you to stay in the water longer without fatigue. (Don't, however, lie on a raft: you need to be in the water!) When you have found your spot:

1. In an ISC approach the water and assess its physical and subtle characteristics. Is it calm or raging, shallow or deep? Does it appear safe to enter? Are there rocks or boulders visible? How does it smell? Sit or stand quietly next to the water and soak up the unique qualities being exuded by the water, listen to its unique song. The water is a singing shaman that specializes in chanting and shapeshifting. Listen, watch, and learn.

2. Use your mind to compare your *emotional* state to the water and relate the qualities of this body of water to specific past experiences where your emotional being mirrored the feeling of this body of water.

3. Relate at a physical level by using your bodily memory of times past to remember *physical* experiences that share similar qualities to this body of water.

4. Contemplate the environmental situation of this body of water. Where did it come from and where is it headed? What are the physical threats you can see or otherwise know about that jeopardize the health of this water? Is there anything you can see, determine, or know about that actively protects this body? What do you notice about the overall health of this body?

5. Touch the water and notice how the interconnectedness of the whole body means that by touching one area of water you affect the whole body at a subtle but real level. At the same time realize and feel that the touch of the water has subtly affected your entire organism as well.

6. Retaining your ISC (check yourself—are you still perceiving three points of attention?), offer a few drops of your liquid tincture to the water as a gesture of your commitment to the work. Enter the water and open yourself to now being a part of the body of water. Feel the vibration of the water body influence your water body. Be aware of how your movements and vibrations affect the body of water. Listen, smell, and taste the unique qualities of the water. Fill your p-c mirrors of the mind with the water. Let the water infuse your organism with its unique memory and luminous energy. After a while, fifteen to thirty minutes, allow your total organism—mind, body, and spirit— to dissolve into the water. Your body water is now the same as the water you are in.

7. Feel pent-up emotions like disappointment, fear, anxiousness, and anger simply float out and away from you. Do not forcefully push them out; that will only give them energy. Simply allow them to float away. After another fifteen to thirty minutes begin to spontaneously relive moments of happiness, joy, exhilaration, and delight and let them flow out of you into the water as well.

Depending on the water temperature and other factors, I like to stay in the water for at least two hours to get the full effect of the ceremony. Your time in the water could be shorter or even longer. If you are only in the water a short time, you can still merge your p-c mirrors with the water and continue some of the suggestions for the ceremony by staying near the water, such as sitting on the shore or bank, and becoming very still.

In my shamanic workshops where we travel to ideal locations (like the Cascadas de Agua Azul) we sometimes spend ten days or more in and around certain rivers and ocean areas in order to deeply explore the unique qualities expressed by the fundamental energy of water in those locations.

8

STAGE THREE
SEPARATION

Fig. 8.1.
Stage three.

The third star ray of the Azoth of Basil Valentine points toward the torch of fire and includes the cipher for iron and Mars. The third circle shows the operation of separation in which the Black Soul Bird splits into two white birds that descend to retrieve the remains of calcination and dissolution. The action and symbolism of air is found here by the blowing of the torch and also the first time we see birds actually flying. The word *terrae* means "of the earth" and symbolically represents the tangible essences and energies that are separated out during this stage.

We experienced alchemical laboratory separation during the spagyric process of filtering the salt (body) of the plant material from the tincture during spagyrics. In shamanic terms this is a highly active (torch) stage in which we can tangibly experience other forms of being that are separate from what we are accustomed. In doing so we discover elements of

143

Fig. 8.2. During separation, the alchemist must split apart and
expose the hermetically sealed egg of self (engraving by Matthäus Merian,
from *Atalanta Fugiens* by Michael Maier, 1617).

our true essence (alchemic gold) that, when integrated in the next stage,
lead to holistic healing at an unparalleled level.

Praxis 14

Separation: Counterpractice

While dissolution is for the most part a subjective experience, the next
operation, separation, takes a more objective approach. The shamanic
alchemy approach to psychological separation involves becoming aware
of the illusions we have about ourselves and separating the personality
into its basic components. In doing so, the shaman-alchemist becomes
aware of the opposites within. With the practice of exploring opposites,
it is possible to become even more healthy, whole, and mature.

Counterpractice is term I like to use for this type of shamanic-
alchemic practice. Dealing with pure opposites is not really accurate in

defining counterpractice as it is infinitely more refined. Counterpractice involves actions that move counter, or in a contrary direction, to a habitual pattern or practice. It turns our habitual way of doing things upside down and inside out so that we can see and feel from a place other than our habitual point of view (separation). In terms of shamanism and shamanic training, counterpractice is employed specifically to enlarge and expand one's consciousness by experiencing shifts in one's perceptual point of view. Shamans accomplish this in many ways such as by exploring the consciousness of a specific animal or converting their perception to experience the energy of the wind, sun, or rain or by making solo excursions into the wilderness to obtain vision and guidance. By completely removing themselves from their normal environment, people, and food, they open the door to perceive the mystery of the world from a fresh perspective. Elders of shamanic tribes also use counterpractice when assigning tasks and roles for people in ceremonies.

For example on one of my early pilgrimages to Wirikuta (the peyote desert), two days before leaving from the village, I noticed my friend Rosendo looked all downtrodden, so I asked what was up. He told me he wasn't happy that the elders had chosen him to represent Tatéi Matinieri during the pilgrimage. I thought, wow, being Tatéi Matinieri is a real honor—it's the sacred spring in Wirikuta where the shamans sing blessings and prayers for the children back home and bless all the pilgrims with the sacred water. It is also the place where the Huichol collect the yellow uxa root, which the women crush into pigment for painting sacred designs on the faces of the pilgrims. I asked Rosendo why he was unhappy about this.

He told me that, first of all, he had never been to Wirikuta so had not been to the sacred spring either. Second, everyone knows he doesn't like water; when he went on a pilgrimage to Tatéi Haramara, he was the only one who didn't go in the water. (It's not necessary to go into the water as the ceremony is conducted on the beach.) And third, being Tatéi Matinieri was for women; he had never heard of a man doing it.

Just then Rosendo's father walked by and nonchalantly asked Rosendo, "You ready?" Rosendo watched his father walk away without responding. He became more agitated and said he was going to do something about this situation and go talk to the kawitero.

A couple of hours later I was walking by the *kalliway* (a large round main temple). In the center Grandfather Fire is almost always burning, and on this night I saw the silhouettes of Rosendo and the kawitero sitting by the fire talking. I wondered if they been talking all this time and what was going on. But it wasn't my place to ask, so I went to bed.

The next morning at sunrise I walked by the kalliway, and Rosendo and the kawitero were still talking. I knew something was up, and after a little while Rosendo came to me. He was very excited and told me how the old kawitero told him all about the pilgrimage and especially his role as the sacred spring. He also said that he and the kawitero ate some peyote, and the shaman took him on a dream ride to Tatéi Matinieri, so now he knew exactly what it looks and feels like. He was extremely elated and animated. Wow, what a change!

Out of the corner of my eye I saw the kawitero leaving the kalliway about fifty feet from us and turned to look his way. He saw me look and stopped. He glanced quickly at Rosendo, whose back was turned toward him, then back to me. He cocked his head in a comical way and then walked off. But he knew what I was thinking and knew that I knew what he had done.

By selecting Rosendo to be Tatéi Matinieri, the elders had given him two counterpractices and a homework assignment, which the kawitero had helped Rosendo to understand. Counterpractice one would be Rosendo representing water. Counterpractice two would be Rosendo carrying out the ceremonies along the way and at Tatéi Matinieri—a task normally a woman would do. Once the kawitero got him excited to be the sacred spring, Rosendo apparently couldn't get enough information—thus the all-night talking and peyote trip. The elders knew that by having Rosendo do these counterpractices for two weeks on the pilgrimage, they were helping him become more mature and balanced.

For example, I have witnessed a shaman give a person who is known to be shy or introverted the task of being one of the supportive singers during a ceremony, while a gregarious person is given a task that requires sitting still and being quiet, such as continuously stirring the sacred corn beverage, which is cooking next to the fire. In both these

cases the shaman was using counterpractice to help each person experience the ceremony from a perspective that the individual wouldn't
have if left to his or her normal habits. Although the assigning of
these counterintuitive tasks initially caused these two people anguish
and apprehension and doing the tasks was extremely challenging, there
was much laughter and feelings of accomplishment afterward as they
recounted their experiences to friends and family. This form of counterpractice is often employed by the elders is to help create well-rounded
individuals in the community.

Choosing counterpractices for yourself is much different from having a shaman that knows you well choose them for you. Luckily, when
I first starting learning counterpractice, I was part of a tight group of
people living in Mexico and learning about different forms of shamanism. As a group we would choose counterpractices for each individual
of the group. The first one chosen for me had to do with my attire,
but the real lessons were about how I felt about myself. The group
thought I spent too much energy on the way I looked, so they gave me
the counterpractice of wearing the same clothes for two weeks, which
doesn't sound so bad except for what they had me wear.

They gave me a *manta* outfit of pants and a shirt with a colorful
blue sash around my waist. Manta is mostly worn by indigenous peoples
in Mexico and is made from *cotton crudo* (wild cotton). The hardest
part of this counterpractice for me was riding the Mexico City subway
twice a day. As a gringo I already stood out, but now I was like a bea-
con. Everyone looked at me, and I overheard many conversations about
me on the subways that made me feel very uncomfortable. Some people
suggested I was looney, others that I was stoned out of my mind, or
maybe I was in some kind of a cult. The first week was really difficult, as I let go of my ego's need to present myself in public in a way I
felt comfortable. But the second week was much easier, which was the
whole point; I finally got to the point that I didn't care what people
thought, and when I went back to wearing what I was used to I had a
much more relaxed and mature attitude of myself.

Point being, if you have trusted friends or mentors, you can ask
them to help you choose counterpractices. Other people often notice

things about us that we don't. I would have never chosen wearing indigenous clothing in Mexico City for two weeks, that's for sure! It's not necessary, but if you do ask someone just be sure it's the right person. It's a delicate and very personal matter.

It is not easy to let go of our habitual ways of doing things or to convince ourselves that something like counterpractice is even necessary. This becomes especially true when introducing counterpractice to those already involved with psychology or those already on a shamanic path. It has been my experience working with folks in both of these groups that they are often the most resistant because counterpractice at some level challenges the significant amount of time and effort they have put into learning about their respective fields of inquiry. But at the same time, once members of both these groups move past a steadfast clinging to what they already know and can open to fluidly experiencing the heart of shamanic counterpractice, they are often the most deeply affected by it and the first to endorse it.

The first thing that needs to be stressed is that counterpractice cannot be overanalyzed if it is going to be useful. Counterpractice is not an exercise of thinking; it is an exercise of simply doing. There are, of course, guidelines to follow and moments when our rational mind must be engaged not only for safety's sake but also in choosing and then processing the specific experiences of counterpractice. Let's take a look at the criteria for counterpractice and how to choose a productive counterpractice.

First of all, as stated earlier, counterpractice is not at all simply doing the opposite of what we currently do. For example, the counterpractice of working at a job just to make a living is not simply refusing to work but rather working at something that fills an authentic calling from deep inside of you. Counterpractice for a nonsmoker will not include starting to smoke, just like a counterpractice for a vegetarian would not necessarily be to start eating meat. Counterpractice is a very delicate art form that requires sensible and sober judgment but in a way that allows for creative and innovative practices to be employed.

When teaching people counterpractice, I often use the phrase *luminous acts*. An authentic and powerful counterpractice is one that illuminates a side of ourselves that has been obscure or missing or seeing a side of situations that we might normally only see one side of. At the highest level, we discover qualities within ourselves we never even thought possible. Specific acts of counterpractice must be life affirming, respectful, and enlightening actions that continue the alchemic evolution of our consciousness and foster growth and heightened awareness, or else they would make no sense to practice.

There are literally hundreds or even thousands of counterpractices you could choose. To simplify choosing, I suggest you break down your life and habits into four categories: mind, body, environment, spirit. This alchemical separation is done with the knowing that they are all connected in the totality of your human organism. We are simply separating them to delve deeper into each one.

Mind

The experience of wearing ridiculous clothing, even though from the outside it seems physical, is in the realm of the mind and ego. Taken to the highest level, this would include dressing as the opposite sex (and pulling it off). Without going into a huge discussion about the Freudian term *ego,* let's determine your particular ego or personality by simply answering the question "who am I?" Typical answers to that question could be the following:

I am a nice person.
I am sincere.
I am slightly overweight.
I am a good husband and father.
I enjoy cooking.
I love the beach.
I love my dog.
I hate my job.
I'm happy with my life but know I want more.

The ego could be all these self-descriptions. Now there are two important items here. First of all, in terms of physical reality, the ego is *nothing.* When we dissect a human body, we have organs, blood, bones, glands, and, of course, a brain but no ego can be found. We were not born with an ego, and there isn't one in a corpse. When we observe that we are not born with an ego but as adults we possess one, then it seems logical that we must have picked it up somewhere along the way. Actually, life demanded that we create one, and since infancy we've been making it bigger and bigger.

Now for the good part. Since we are the ones who created it, we also have the power to alter it or even replace it. Alchemic separation in the area of mind allows us to intentionally explore new ways of being and intentionally create the ego we want. Exploring new ways of being involves forms of counterpractice, and a helpful tool for counterpractice is stalking. *Stalking* is a term borrowed from the legendary books of Carlos Castaneda, who, most people don't realize, borrowed much of his knowledge from the Huichol (my main shamanic mentors), even though he never mentions them in his books.

The word *stalking* naturally reminds us of hunting, which is perfect, except the only thing we are going to stalk is our ego. A legitimate hunter, as well as a stalker, is well versed in the difference between judgment and observation. In order to trap prey, the hunter must first observe the prey and its surroundings in order to know its habits and routines: where it lives, where it hides, what it eats, what time it wakes up and goes to sleep, its movements, and so on.

For us, in this stage of shamanic-alchemic separation, objectively stalking our habitual thoughts and actions is a valuable tool for developing counterpractices. While making your list within the four categories, you will be naturally stalking yourself. With this simple practice and the associated counterpractices you come up with, you begin a journey that can only be described as a separate reality. Traveling in a separate reality gives us the power to do much more than we ever thought possible in this reality. There are many different levels of counterpractice; at highest levels there is no way you won't be alchemically transformed. I'll cite a quick example from my life. (This is the short version; for the full story see my book *Lightning in My Blood*.)

My good friend and teacher Highwater, an old Arapaho medicine man and shaman, came to visit me. The first night he was there I had lucid dreams of thunder and lightning and a giant horse that ran right at me and struck me down. Then the horse turned and ran back and trampled me to death. Not being able to go back to sleep, I told the old shaman my dreams, and he was very excited. He explained that in his culture the components of my dreams are interpreted as a message from the "opposite ones" that demanded some of the most difficult tests for a shaman.

He said I had to become *heyoka,* a thunder being that completely reverses typical behavior, for that is how one sees the second world— the world that others are blind to. My first lesson began immediately. Highwater took me outside, made me undress, and forced me to sleep naked in the cold on my front porch. The next morning he drove me to Cathedral Rock (a famous giant red rock formation in Sedona, Arizona, where I lived) and had me walk the trail backward, naked (he allowed shoes so I wouldn't be hurt), all the way around the base (a good couple miles). Halfway through the walk I was so overwhelmed by this experience I felt like what I was doing wasn't even real. Walking naked backward in a public place known to be the site of a massive energy vortex had placed my consciousness squarely in a separate reality. This separate reality could have even been at a physical level, the proof being that although I didn't run into many people the ones that I did pass by on the trail seemed not to even see me!

After that incredible feat of counterpractice, Highwater immediately put me into another, but that's another story. The point here is that counterpractice has the power to radically change your perception of the world and what you are capable of. Like the counterpractice story I just shared with you (and I have lots more), when you actually participate in counterpractice, not just read about it and wonder or laugh, your world of possibilities grows infinite (if your head doesn't blow up).

Written Portrait

As an aid for selecting and setting up counterpractices, this exercise is very useful. It consists of writing a detailed portrait of yourself in the third person, as if you were describing someone else: "His name is

James. He prefers to be out in nature but also spends a lot of time inside on the computer. He is a professional speaker to large audiences, which he enjoys doing, but actually prefers intimate groups and being alone." Here is a sample list for a useful portrait. Remember to fill it out in the third person as factually and coldly as possible. Do this like you are neither for nor against this person; you neither like nor dislike him or her:

Name
Age
Physical characteristics
Typical manner of dress
State of health
Most common moods
Places frequented
Places avoided
Type of people attracted to
Type of people avoided
Economic situation
Types of work done in the past
Current work
Characteristics of emotional life
Kind of image projected to the world
Daily routines
Manner of speaking
Conversational themes
Ways in which free time is spent
Way in which sexuality is approached and expressed
Major virtues
Major defects
The best things accomplished
The worst things done
The best things that have happened
The worst things that have happened
Long-term cyclical patterns

Disguises

This is a wonderful counterpractice technique that anyone can perform. The counterpractice example I gave about wearing ridiculous clothes is one level beneath this counterpractice because for this one you are required to change not only your attire but your whole personality and the way you move and speak. The crux of this is to choose a mode of being that you normally wouldn't engage in or maybe even dislike.

For example, I generally dislike wearing suits (I only own one) for weddings and funerals. So for me the intentional act of wearing a suit while not at a wedding or funeral is a counterpractice. But that's only a small part of it. The real alchemy of this counterpractice is inner transformation. I must talk and act as someone who is accustomed to wearing a suit. Who wears suits every day? Executives, salesmen, bankers, and lawyers. For me, putting on a suit and then acting like a lawyer or banker in public (going to the store, the movies, a football game) soaks my conscious mind with a completely foreign experience that enlarges my view of the world.

If you dress up for work every day, take some time out and disguise yourself as someone completely different and go out in public and act it out. You could be a redneck (no offense, I'm a partial redneck who lives in the woods), a punk rocker, a goth, a farmer, a sports fan (face paint included), or, at the highest level, the opposite sex. The world is your stage!

I had to laugh when I saw an episode of *Undercover Boss,* the premise being that a high-level executive or owner of a large corporation disguises him- or herself (with the aid of professional makeup artists) and then goes undercover to really see what happens among the workers at his company. Not only do these executives find out a lot about their companies, they discover a lot about themselves in disguising themselves and playing out their new role working on a production line, installing window blinds, flipping burgers, and so on.

Telling Yourself Lies

This form of counterpractice has been proven to be very effective especially for those of us who have self-degrading thoughts.

The technique is simple. For three days keep an inventory of your thoughts that are not considered healthy. For example, you may say to yourself while in the shower, "Jeez, I'm fat," at your job, "Man, I hate this job," at school, "I'm never gonna pass this class," or at home, "Boy, I suck at cooking." Make a list of these recurring negative thoughts (what you consider to be "truths" about yourself). Next to each one, write an opposing statement (the "lies").

Truths	Lies
I am afraid to fail.	I am totally sure I will succeed.
I am so unattractive.	I'm attractive and I know it.
I have no willpower.	I finish everything I start.
I tend to repress my feelings.	I am completely free to express whatever I feel.
I am a failure to my family.	I have exceeded all expectations of my family.

When you have your list of truths and lies, every morning and before bed state your lies out loud in front of a mirror for one week. This technique, even though it may seem silly at first, has proven to improve self-confidence and reduce self-deprecation. Please be aware we are not engaging in some form of self-brainwashing or self-suggestion because we are not pretending that the lies are true. This technique of counterpractice engages us in doing something we wouldn't ordinarily do—that is what counterpractices are. Plus, when we get to the point of seeing that both sides of the list are potentially unreal, we can dispense with them altogether.

Body Sensing

Our ego attempts to control as many of our life circumstances as it can and as such becomes the controller of all of our voluntary activities. But the body, on the other hand, functions as a highly complex system of mostly involuntary actions (blood circulation, digestion, metabolism, etc.) of which we have little or no possibility of consciously controlling without specific training, such as autogenic training (which I cover in detail in my book *Advanced Autogenic Training and Primal Awareness:*

Techniques for Wellness, Deeper Connection to Nature, and Higher Consciousness). It is precisely because of our inability to completely control our body that we develop the feeling of being trapped by it, by the pain it makes us feel when we are injured or sick, and by the perceived chain of existence that promises only one final outcome of death. In response to this we become alienated from the body, and many times we long and search for means of escape, even if just temporarily.

From a shamanic alchemy point of view, modern culture has brilliantly developed to a high degree the ability to intercept and repress our body's needs and wishes. We are born from (not into) an organic reality that perfectly coincides to our physical needs, yet day after day we almost completely ignore this most primal connection. Our body needs and wants the more-than-human world. Denying and repressing this need causes a frustrated and unconsummated relationship between our bodies and our natural environment. A lifetime of these unlived and blocked experiences becomes jammed up inside our bodies to the point that it is no wonder so many of us suffer from anxiety, depression, rage, hatred, sexual dysfunction, and chronic illness.

Our bodies carry the inherited wisdom of countless generations and bear the historic past of our species right up to this very moment. The communication that our bodies employ with the world is older than words, older than intellectual thought. Through our bodies we have an inborn sense of the interrelation we have with the world, and we are made in accordance with what our bodies are expecting to receive from the environment. In this sense we are born from the world confident and adapted to the historic organismic patterns of our ancient ancestors, but if these patterns are changed or deprived, then psychic and physical distress is inevitable. This distress, the deprivation of our bodily-felt interactions and psychic connection with the natural world, is evident in countless ways by the actions and lifestyles of our modern society. We have deviated so drastically from the lifeways that have nurtured us over countless generations that we are now being born from and into a kind of ecological and cultural vacuum that prevents the complete unfolding of our life process. Without this natural unfolding and maturation, we are left with feelings of frustration, incompleteness, agitation, dissatisfaction, and a general lack of realization of both our innate bodily and psychic needs.

The end to this suffering will require us to make contact with our deeply felt bodily longings to connect with a wider view of reality than just the human hyperworld we now live in and also to work with our psychic intuition and silent knowledge to create the conditions that will allow us to unfold and fulfill our sacred niche as part of the Earth community.

An important viewpoint held by both shamans and certain forward-thinking contemporary philosophers, and one that I would like to introduce here in our search for bodily consciousness, is the psychic correspondence of flesh. In this context flesh is viewed as a primary element of the world. Just like water, air, earth, and fire, flesh is primary and elemental. Our bodies are born from the flesh of our mother, from the flesh of the world. The flesh of our body, the flesh of fruit, the flesh of the deer and whale are all one flesh, one elemental fabric of a living world.

In this sense, when flesh touches flesh, it is touching itself; when my fingers touch my body, I am touching myself. As I breathe in and out, my lungs touch the air. An exchange happens: part of the air becomes me and part of me becomes the air—and so when the air flows into my body the atmosphere is actually touching itself. When I breathe in the air I am touching myself. In this same way I touch the trees and plants and animals in my environment.

This is utterly personal and primary; it is experienced at a level deeper than thoughts or words. When I eat the flesh of an apple or the flesh of an animal, the flesh becomes me, and as I live and grow I become the flesh of Earth. The shaman-alchemist knows this. Through the reality of living experiences with the unity of body-mind, the shaman-alchemist perceives the world as a single living tissue encompassing all phenomena in a mutually informative and reciprocating body comprised of identical primary elements. There are no lines drawn, each form of life, each level of reality, is a reflection of the other. The plant, animal, human, and spirit realms flow into one another in one grand continuum of mutual multidimensional kinship.

Talking about our body would be incomplete without mentioning death. Acknowledging the psychic correspondence of flesh can also help us to deal in positive ways with our relationships to death and dying. Our repressed, blocked, and unlived experiences with our body and with the natural world results in an unhealthy body-mind-environment state in which we have not fully lived and so we are not prepared for, and even fear, death.

The human life cycle, under the best circumstances, ends with the last desire, after all others are fulfilled, to rest, to know no more, to be content. A satisfied life comes full circle as one's life projects are fulfilled; the desire to do becomes the desire to see one's offspring do, in a way that the cycle of life continues. As this happens the struggle to hang on to life loses its immediacy and is replaced by the wish to simply rest and conclude. For shamanic cultures, this manner of leaving the world is common and normal, but for us the opposite is usually the case as we try at all costs to prolong our lives with drugs and machines in the hope that one more day will allow us to feel complete. This war we fight at the end is another example of the war against our body. In the final analysis our feeble body is blamed for not giving us enough time to realize our dreams, for never being able to see our loved ones again, and we avoid the body during our lifetime because it is seen as merely the abode of death rather than the gift of life.

From the perspective of shamanic- and nature-based cultures, we avoid death so vehemently because a major part of our lives has never been fulfilled. Born from the natural world but then immediately taken from it, and then later taught precisely how to exploit it, we have missed a whole life's worth of experiences that the incomprehensible amount of living species and places of the world had for us. It is no wonder we go to our death in tragic ways or psychically kicking and screaming.

One of my indigenous shaman mentors once commented to me after being invited to travel for a few weeks to the United States and Japan that "the lives of you modern people mirror the lives of the animals in your factory farms—born inside, kept in the dark, fed artificial food, exploited for profit, and then finally when a little light seeps into the cage, it is merely the door being opened by the great huntress that ends your life."

This strong comment, said through tears of bewilderment over all the destruction he witnessed, has served as a strong reminder to me while on this path of trying to realize a more harmonious way of life and developing practices to share with others.

Counterpractices for the Body and Senses

It's quite obvious that how we treat our body is significant to leading a happy and healthy life. What we put into our body and our level of exercise affects the function of our total human organism. This is not the place to lecture on nutrition and exercise, you already know where you stand in that regard. However, in terms of counterpractice, it's not a bad idea to make an inventory and apply counterpractices to augment your health.

A simple way to do this is for one week write down everything you eat and grade that meal or snack from 1 to 10—1 being total junk and 10 being the highest quality organic food available. Only 100 percent organic food grown by you or someone you know will ever get a 10. Even if a food item is graded organic by the USFDA, you still don't usually know where it came from or how it was transported.

After your week of tallying, check out your inventory and develop counterpractices to improve your score. Do this also with your level of exercise and frequency. If you don't exercise at all, a good counterpractice would be to simply dedicate for a specific length of time to go for a walk each morning or evening. Even with regular exercise or participation in sporting activities, we can still put on extra unhealthy pounds. Counterpractices that up your exercise routine and/or scrutinize your food intake are a good idea. Here are some other suggestions:

Letting Your Body Drive Your Actions

This counterpractice technique is one that many of us wouldn't think of but is purely natural when we do think about it. It involves periodically setting aside time for intentionally listening to your body in a way that your body, not your mind, guides your actions. Many times our body gives us clear signals, but we don't listen to or attend to those signals and messages because they interfere with what our rational mind and our responsibilities are asking of us. For example, you awake in the morning still tired and your body pleads with you to stay in bed, but you have to go to work, so you get up anyway. Or, after being indoors working in an office for extended periods of time, your body is silently begging for fresh air and natural light and physical activity, but you tune it out and suppress your body's natural urges in order to keep being "productive." Our bodies have a unique way of communicating to our mind what we need to be healthy, and by renewing that flow of information and then developing and deepening the dialogue between body and mind, we place our entire human organism in a more healthy and happy position.

Setting aside specific times when you let your body "drive" your actions is the first step to developing this awareness. This can be easily done when you have time to yourself after work or on weekends or at any time when the demands of life are not totally consuming your attention. Once you have experienced the positive effects of taking a nap when you need it, prying yourself away from the computer to take a walk outside, or eat a certain food that was not on the day's menu, and you consciously feel and acknowledge the positive effects of listening to your body, you quickly learn that your human organism has its own rhythm and pattern of needs that may be much different than the schedule you are imposing on it. From these initial experiences the simple exercise of letting your body drive you can transform into an integral part of your life whereby your daily actions, as well as the habits, patterns, and cycles of yearly, monthly, and weekly activities, become more in tune to what your human organism is asking of you.

At its highest level this form of counterpractice does not conform to the rigid accounting of wristwatches or calendars and becomes much more a way of living life rather than simply another activity within our lives. Nowhere is this more apparent than in the shamanic communities in which the whole cycle of activities of the year are determined exclusively by the interaction between the environment and its human inhabitants, between the bodily felt connection and the intuition of the people themselves.

Fasting

Intentional fasting is a very healthy practice often overlooked by modern people. This is not just the skipping of a single meal but the prolonged abstinence from food that carries with it the sharp edge of awareness capable of bursting the bubble of the quick fix and instant gratification mentality of consumerism. Through conscious and intentional fasting, you create an extremely personal ritual time that at once draws your attention inward and outward.

As a form of counterpractice, abstinence is an extremely potent and obvious luminous act of cleansing and awareness. Fasting from food empties the body so that both the body and the spirit can be cleansed of toxins while at the same time an awareness separate from the time schedules of meals can be invoked. The psychological schedule of feeding is left behind and with it the rigid structure of everyday modern life. In this way the natural rhythms of your body are given the chance to meld more deeply with the natural rhythms of the world.

Although fasting is part of practically every spiritual tradition known to man, its roots go back much further and are not so much part of a spiritual tradition as simply a consequence of ancient life. The physical structure of our bodies shaped by the 99 percent of our history spent as hunter-gatherers prepares us both physiologically and psychologically for times when the belly is empty for extended periods. We humans can go only a few days without water, but we can live quite easily for a week or more without food.

While fasting you will discover how you organize your day around mealtimes and how the absence of those moments has you searching elsewhere for nourishment. You hear your empty belly talking and turning inward upon itself for food while it eats up the stores of glycogen and other bodily sources of nourishment and energy. Without the meal to occupy your time, you are given precious moments of inner reflection that can deepen your awareness to the sacredness of Earth's sustenance and the gift of life it provides.

On an outward level your awareness begins to focus on the condition of your physical body, your stomach, your genital area, your hands. You study the backs of your hands, the palms, and your fingers. They may clench with the empty shiver that clenches your jaw but that also delivers the resolute strength and clarity that comes with an empty stomach.

Start by intentionally skipping a few meals at a time. As you begin to learn how your body reacts while fasting, as well as the best things to eat for breaking your fast, gradually increase your fasting period. When you are confident in fasting for a day or two at a time, to go further it is advisable to intentionally place yourself in an environment where your physical activity level is reduced and you do not need to operate a car, machinery, or engage in any other activity where momentary lapses in concentration could be dangerous. Fasting for long periods alters your perception, as well as your physiology, significantly enough that it is best to remove yourself from normal modern activities and instead replace them with activities in the natural world like walking in nature or gardening, or inside such as reading or creating art.

Environment

Probably the most important counterpractices related to our environment have to do with our *sense of place*. The idealistic notion that one can always pick up and move for better opportunities has always been a part of the American mystique but also contributes to the existential void that many of us feel. Six out of ten Americans don't live in their hometown; however, it really depends on where that hometown is located. According to an *Inverse* article, in the Midwest more than 70 percent of residents stay in the state they were born but less than a third of those that grew up in Western states have done the same. Affluent college grads and Californians move around the most.[1] And more Americans are cramming into big cities. According to census data cited in a *Business Insider* article, half the population of the U.S. lives in just nine out of the fifty states.[2] Urban living comes with mental consequences. People living in the city have a 21 percent increased risk of anxiety disorders and a 39 percent increased risk of mood disorders. In addition, the incidence of schizophrenia is twice as high in those born and brought up in cities.

Our consumer-based lifestyles and ability to travel quickly from place to place has alleviated us of any connection to our local land for sustenance, which can lead us to believe that where we choose to live is relatively trivial. But this couldn't be further from the truth. Our immediate environment directly influences, at the most primal depths, the way we think, the way we eat, the way we dress, the way we earn a living, the things we own, the way we relate to one another, and the way we relate to the world. Our sense of place is what roots us and grounds our experience of life. Without a deeply grounded sense of place, we magnify the feelings of the existential void that accompany our modern lifestyles and can find no significant meaning to our lives. Recovering this sense of place, this rooting that is the basis for a stable psychological, physical, and spiritual well-being, is a vital task in healing many of the crises of our modern times.

Sense of Place Exercise

This counterpractice invites us to briefly separate and alchemically transform our perception of our sense of place. Dr. Mitchell Thomashow, a well-known environmental-spiritual educator, describes these types of exercises as

> a rite of passage that links ecological identity to life-cycle development . . . a process of self-reflection through which we perceive the places in which we live: the people, community, land, and species that form our networks of domesticity and exploration, the sources of sustenance and struggle. Sense of place is the domestic basis of environmentalism; it's the foundation of our deepest connection to the natural world. At the same time, we may observe how hard it is to establish a meaningful community—how places are so easily eroded, how we dwell in so many mental spaces. . . . It's about our habits of familiarity, the places we visit every day. . . . It also reflects how we earn a living, the things we do to survive, the material basis of our life. In what ways are we bonded to the landscape? What are our emotional attachments to the place we live in? How do we coexist with other people, with the flora and fauna? How do we understand the local ecosystem? How do we define our bioregion?"[3]

1. This technique begins by going outdoors and in an ISC sitting quietly. Close your eyes and take the "view from the moon" perspective of Earth, in which all the imaginary human map lines that indiscriminately carve up the world are wiped away. Then slowly zoom in on the planet to identify the connected parts of the whole, natural parts that share various organic realities such as altitude, climate, vegetation, fauna, and so on. Using the cognitive maps you already have of the planet's geography, zoom in on your continent, then your region, then your neighborhood, until you arrive at your home and the exact place you are sitting.

2. Now walk around and begin to create a new cognitive map based on the organic reality of where you are. Notice and register all of the natural features of the landscape, such as hills, valleys, individual trees, shrubs, flowers, birds, puddles, insects, rocks, and so on. Now look up and realize that you are standing in the center of your local home circle, a circle inside many other larger ecological circles. What you find inside your immediate home circle will tell you a lot about yourself.

3. The next step is to expand your awareness to include the next larger circle, which could be called your neighborhood. This might be a very small area or a mile in diameter. It might include just fifty people in a rural area or a thousand or more in a heavily urbanized area. Walk around your neighborhood and identify the geological and biological realities of the place. Notice where your smaller home circle fits within this larger neighborhood circle.

4. Now walk or even drive around inside the next larger circle, which could be called your community. Again, depending on where you live, this could include a few hundred or many thousands of people. Remember, you are working to produce a cognitive map of organic reality, so community does not simply refer to people, buildings, and streets. Inside this circle will be countless members and features of the natural community that include those in your home circle and neighborhood circle, but now at the community level you will find much more diversity of plant and animal life, bodies of water, geologic formations, and so on. Try to maintain or deepen your

ISC as your circle of awareness grows larger and larger. Don't be depressed if your community circle is detrimentally overpopulated; notice what it says about your life.

5. The next larger circle is the bioregion in which you live. At the most basic level this could be described as a large area of similar topography, or the rough boundaries of a watershed whose climate and geography supports similar types of vegetation and fauna. Even among seasoned veterans of the bioregional movement, there is still debate as to what defines a bioregion. Don't get hung up on this; we are not involved with a scientific experiment but an exercise in altering consciousness. One helpful way to determine bioregions is by investigating native tribal groups that once inhabited the area. A bioregion (absent of nonsustainable human construction) should be large enough to be relatively self-sustaining to its human occupants, and native people often formed tribal boundaries inside these realities.

6. When discerning your bioregion, keep in mind that the edges of bioregions emerge out of the land itself rather than being drawn as an arbitrary line on a map. Edges are formed by watershed divides, mountains, climate zones, fault lines, and so on. Careful and patient observation coupled with a shift in consciousness toward relating to the organic reality of place is needed when discerning the edges of your bioregion.

There are, of course, even larger natural regions that we can identify. Often called biomes and subbiomes, these large land areas include many bioregions that eventually comprise a whole continent. But for this exercise it is enough to simply acknowledge the place of your home bioregion inside the larger biome and continent without getting lost and confused. Realize and understand that continents, biomes, subbiomes, and bioregions all exist without the help of a line drawn on a political map. They are the true borders of the natural world, and we can enter into cooperation with the natural world when we learn how to live and plan our human communities while paying close attention to the organic reality of the place where we live.

Portable or Impermanent Dwelling Counterpractice

Another form of alchemical separation relating to environmental counterpractice is to get out of our modern controlled environment and spend time living for a while in a portable or impermanent dwelling, such as debris hut, tent, yurt, or teepee that contains little or no modern technology.

Why do this? Human beings have always found it necessary to shelter themselves from the infinity of space. The differences in how this is accomplished become apparent in how the shelter structures are built. For shamanic people the architecture in their lives has always been significantly associated with the sacred. For example, the tipi, hogan, longhouse, or tukupi, defines and shelters the people but also serves as a model of the world and universe. These structures establish the sacred center from where the family and community revolve both microcosmically and macrocosmically. In this sense the architecture of shamanic cultures provides a way of understanding their culture, and similarly, our relationship to architecture also serves in understanding ours. The relationship between nature and humanity can clearly be seen in the homes and buildings of each culture, and the quality of that relationship is a major indication of the character of a culture.

Our culture has the obsession of constructing "permanent" homes and buildings from raw materials mined from the earth and transformed into cement, metal, and plastic. The only living beings found at modern construction sites are humans, every other sensible creature runs away from them as fast as they can. Doesn't that tell us something about ourselves?

Working and living indoors all the time poses serious health risks especially in our modern energy efficient homes and workplaces. Indoor air pollution comes from many sources, here are a few:

Carbon monoxide (CO). This gas and other pollutants are released from fuel-burning stoves, heaters, and other appliances. Depending on how much is breathed in, CO can affect coordination, make heart conditions worse, and cause extreme tiredness, headache, confusion, nausea, and dizziness. Very high levels can cause death. Older adults, babies, and people with heart and lung diseases are even more sensitive to elevated CO levels.

Nitrogen dioxide. This gas is a product of natural gas and kerosene combustion. Like CO, it is odorless and colorless. It irritates the mucous membranes of the eyes, nose, and throat and causes shortness of breath in high concentrations. Long-term exposure to nitrogen dioxide can damage the lungs and may lead to chronic bronchitis. Exposure to low levels may worsen symptoms in people who have asthma and chronic obstructive pulmonary disease and increase other respiratory infections.

Radon. This radioactive gas can seep from the soil and rocks beneath your home. Radon can enter a home through cracks in the foundation, walls, drains, and other openings. Exposure to radon in the home is the second leading cause of lung cancer. Smoking is the first. Smokers and former smokers exposed to radon may have a much higher risk of death from lung cancer.

Secondhand smoke. Smoke from cigaretes contains trace amounts of about four thousand chemicals, including two hundred known poisons, like formaldehyde and carbon monoxide, and forty-three carcinogens.

Formaldehyde. This common preservative and adhesive can be found in furniture, carpets, drapes, particleboard, and plywood paneling. It is a respiratory irritant that causes chest pain, shortness of breath, coughing, and nose and throat irritation, according to the Agency for Toxic Substances and Disease Registry. It can also cause cancer and has been linked to an increased risk of asthma and allergies in kids. Breathing formaldehyde fumes can cause coughing, irritation of the eyes, nose, and throat, rashes, headaches, and dizziness.

Household products. A variety of common household products, such as personal care products, pesticides, household cleaners, solvents, and chemicals used for hobbies, can be harmful to the body. Exposure to these products can irritate the eyes, skin, and lungs and cause dizziness, nausea, allergic reactions, and cancer. Certain cleaning products can produce poisonous fumes.

New carpeting and paint. These can give off fumes that irritate the eyes, nose, and throat.

Asbestos. This naturally occurring silicate mineral is used in insulation, floor tiles, spackling compounds, cement, and heating equipment. These products can be a problem indoors only if the material that contains the asbestos is disturbed and becomes airborne. This also happens when the product falls apart with age. Asbestos fibers are light, flexible, and small enough to stay airborne. Because of this, fibers can be breathed in, causing scarring of lung tissue and lung cancer.

Lead. This heavy metal was a common additive in house paint made before 1978. Inhaling airborne dust from old paint that has chipped and crumbled can cause serious health problems, especially in young children and pregnant women.

Pesticides. Exposure to these can occur through normal use of sprays, strips filled with pesticides, and foggers (also called bombs). Exposure can also occur from contaminated dusts after use, especially for children who may be in close contact with contaminated surfaces. Symptoms can include headache, dizziness, muscular weakness, and nausea. Some pesticides may cause cancer.

Alchemic counterpractice must therefore include practices that put us in touch with another way to live, if even for a short time, to help counteract the effect of ecologically traumatized and unhealthy permanent structures so that we can see what we are doing from a fresh point of view and make changes accordingly. Spending time in an impermanent structure can help counteract the effect of ecologically traumatizing technology and lifeless artificial permanent structures.

Another aspect to this is how our modern structures have changed our lives so much from our ancestors. It is easy to list the ways that technology has made our lives more comfortable, but sometimes this perceived comfort masks many of the benefits that have been lost by the old ways of doing things, especially when viewed from the perspective of how we relate to the natural world at the most basic levels. Take for example the technological introduction of the central heating system.

Prior to the use of automatic heating with fossil fuels, most families relied on the heat from an old-fashioned wood fire, whether in a woodstove, hearth, or simply on the ground. The fire was not just a source of heat but was also the center of a plethora of social, physical, and psychological activities. Firewood needed to be collected, cut, and stacked, typically with each household member contributing to the work. The kindling of the morning fire marked the start of a new day, and in the evening the fire was the center for the evening meal and a place of gathering for not only warmth but of discussion, stories, music, and sharing.

This example is cited not to simply arouse the romantic feelings of the old days or suggest that we all use wood for heat. I mention it to shed light on the fact that the technology, which in this case is a heating system, has replaced not just the source of our heat but also a whole set of relationships and circumstances that for many millennia was a central focus of human life. The simple wood fire connected us to the local landscape as well as to each other. The furnace, the pipelines, the tankers, the entire enormous fuel industry has replaced whole worlds of relationships and reduced them to the flipping of a switch and the paying of a bill.

In general, this same situation applies to many of our technologies where once we related to the world in a visible give-and-take manner but now we simply push a button, turn a handle, or look at a flat screen. All this happens, many times, with the technology that we use hidden from us behind the scenes. We know how to turn the knobs and push the buttons, but most of us have really no idea how the specific technology we are using actually works. This is part of the great promise of technology—to alleviate us from the burdens of life. But so many of the so-called burdens aren't burdens at all; they are actually necessary experiences that ground and connect us to life. When we disconnect from these life-affirming experiences, we reduce some of the most important aspects of life to commodities and products that we depend on someone else to sell us.

The alchemic counterpractice implied here is that of living out of a portable or impermanent structure that will place you squarely into the natural world with a minimum layer of padding between you and the outdoors. The exercise is quite simple. First, make the arrangements necessary to spend at least a week living out of your impermanent structure. The more time you spend in and around your impermanent structure, the more you will get from the practice. In other words, try to avoid going into your house or other permanent buildings as much as possible. Figure out alternatives to meet your basic needs. The level that you do this will depend entirely on your personal situation, but the idea is to fully embody the exercise and push your limits of creativity, patience, and discipline.

This type of experience forces you into reevaluating everything in your life, starting from the simplest things, such as: Where am I going to go to the bathroom? How will I stay warm and dry? What will I eat? Facing these realities opens your eyes to all of the circumstances and experiences of the natural world that we insulate ourselves from by always being inside and also brings to light many of the activities and skills that have been lost through our dependence on technology and machines.

9

STAGE FOUR
CONJUNCTION

Fig. 9.1.
Stage four.

The fourth ray of the star is marked with the single symbol for both gold and the sun and points to the area at the top of the drawing where the right wing of the caduceus touches the salamander, which is in flames.

In the fourth circle we have the birds of soul (anima) and spirit (spiritus) lifting a five-spiked crown into the realm of the one mind. The crown symbolizing the pure essence (quintessence) reclaimed from the previous stages. This conjunction marks the turning point as we move from the anima side of the drawing to the spiritus side. The word *rectificando,* meaning "rectification," is above the circle, and the wings of the caduceus seem to be blessing the whole thing.

On a shamanic level, this conjunction is an awesomely powerful occurrence that basically changes everything. Experiences, feelings, emotions, and intuitions all become heightened states, and synchronicities and situations that you want to have happen actually do manifest. In the

Fig. 9.2. Conjunction of sun and moon
(engraving by Matthäus Merian, from *Atalanta Fugiens*
by Michael Maier, 1617).

psychological-alchemical work of Carl Jung, we can see the parallels of what he called individuation, reunifying the fragmented self (of the three previous stages), with shamanic conjunction. In the Emerald Tablet the phrase *its nurse is the Earth* describes the importance of Mother Earth's energy in this important stage of development.

Praxis 15

Pilgrimage to Sacred Sites

For indigenous shamanic cultures the land is everything, and their land-based spiritual practices are rooted in the specific places that comprise the sacred landscape. The stories of creation and the oral history of the tribe are embedded in the land. These narratives educate the people about tribal history, ethics, and spiritual values. They contain oral maps of sacred places, information about kinship with plants and animals, and most importantly they continue the cultural identity of the tribe through the retelling and passing of the stories to the next generations. Since each tribe has developed as part of its own sacred landscape, the oral stories that accompany them will, of course, be unique to each tribe. But although the stories and history may be different from one tribe to the next, one common component to shamanic cultures is the periodic visiting of places sacred to the tribe in order to honor the spirits of the places and the bones of their ancestors and to continue the sacred traditions of reciprocity with the land.

My Huichol/Wirrarika shaman mentors make pilgrimages to many sacred sites, but there are five main sites relating to the five sacred directions. The center, where the Sacred Fire was born, is located in the Huichol Sierra, so visiting this site is more like a long walk through the mountains, although the formality of the trek and the intense ceremonies at the site have the same numinous feeling as longer pilgrimages. The other four sites are much farther away and take many days or even weeks to accomplish.

The sacred site in the north is Hauxamanaka, the home of Maxakwaxi or Great-Grandfather Deer Tail, on Cerro Gordo (Fat Mountain) in Durango, Mexico. Hauxamanaka is near the top of Cerro Gordo, which, at nearly eleven thousand feet, is one of the highest points in the Sierra Madre Occidental. Along with dozens of other spiritual traditions and religions, including other native religions and in the Christian Bible, the Huichol have their own version of a great flood—the purification of Earth and its creatures so that a new and more improved world can be born. In this case, Watákame, the most ancient ancestor, is told by Nakawé to build a canoe to carry him, a dog (which later becomes human and also his wife), and seeds of the different kinds of corn and squash, along with fire. After the rains subside, Watákame's canoe lands on the high mountain of Cerro Gordo where the rirriki now stands. Together with his wife, Watákame has many children and creates a new race of people—the Huichol. The full tale of Watákame and the flood is much longer and extremely detailed. I made a pilgrimage to Hauxamanaka only once with the Huichol, but the grandeur and sacredness of the mountain is something I will never forget.

In the south is Xapawiyeme on Isla de los Alacranes (Scorpion Island) in Lake Chapala. In the west is Tatéi Haramara on Isla del Rey (King Island), near San Blas. In the east is Wirikuta near Real de Catorce in San Luis Potosí. This is where the sacred peyote cactus grows and the place where the sun was born.

My main reasons for making the pilgrimages were to enhance my knowledge of shamanic practices, to receive visions and messages for how to live my life, and to provide financial assistance for the Huichol for these trips. From my many years of living and working with the Huichol, I eventually gained their trust to the point that I became the designated photographer of the pilgrimages I went on. I always make a packet of pictures for each *jicarero* (keeper of the sacred tradition) and send them to the ceremonial center when I get home. Keeping the promise I made, I have never published in any of my books or magazine articles any of the thousands of photographs I have taken while with the Huichol.

The story I would like to share with you is a very brief recounting of my meetings with five of the sacred Blue Deer of Huiricuta while on pilgrimages with the Huichol jicareros, as these meetings demonstrate what can happen inside an ancient shamanic tradition and how these experiences have the power to enhance one's life.

It was the second night at the pilgrimage site after spending the day hunting and gathering the sacred peyote, and all the jicareros were gathered around the Sacred Fire cleaning the peyote that would be eaten that night. We had all been traveling for more than a week, purposefully eating little or no food and getting very little sleep, and had spent two full days hunting and gathering peyote in the heavy winds of the desert chaparral. But spirits were extremely high, the hunt had been good, and I prepared myself for another night of visions with the peyote, the fire, and the shaman's chanting.

Very late that night the shaman took a break from chanting, and all the jicareros, including myself, sat in silence in a circle around the fire in a deep dream state, as all of us had eaten a large amount of the sacred peyote throughout the night. Each of us was on a personal journey into the numinous realms, and a wave of gratitude passed through me that I was fortunate to be part of such a powerful and ancient tradition. I actually felt a sense of pride flowing through me, as I realized how special it was to be in that sacred place with those sacred people and included in their sacred ceremony.

As soon as that feeling of pride and the associated thought flowed through me, I heard something moving behind me. In my deep trance state, I would normally not be motivated to look and see what was making the noise, and subconsciously I knew I was being protected by the fire, the shaman, and the jicareros; nonetheless I turned around and saw a most spectacular site.

A Blue Deer stepped out of the bushes and walked right up to me. It was glowing almost as bright as the fire. For a few moments I just stared, not really able to do anything more than that. Then I turned to look at the rest of the jicareros, but they all were still sitting and all had their heads bowed, chins on chests. The shaman looked up at me for just a second and then went back to his chin on chest trance. With an almost involuntary movement, I stood up and faced the magical Blue Deer, who was standing just a few feet from me.

The Blue Deer looked down at the ground between us and seemed to be staring intently at something. When I looked down I almost gasped in surprise because the deer had somehow written in the rocky sandy soil "I am third."

I read the words and had the strong feeling that I had heard or maybe read those same exact words before, but I couldn't put my finger on where or when. At first I thought the message was about the deer and that the deer was trying to tell me something about itself. But with those thoughts, I immediately heard the Blue Deer speaking to me inside my mind. The deer began to explain to me that the message was for me. She was the Blue Deer of Humility and the message was about how to live my life. She said that we can have pride in the things that we accomplish but that too much pride is self-centeredness and that I needed to be more humble in the face of this mysterious world. If I was truly to become a medicine man and healer for my own people, I first needed to surrender to the Great Spirit and do the Great Spirit's work first. Second was my service to others—and I was third.

Our eyes met and the next thing I remember was waking up to the jicareros packing their gear. Beside me was my notebook. Sometime during the night I had sketched a crude drawing of the Blue Deer but I had no recollection of drawing. I looked over at one of the head shamans, and he smiled knowingly but said not a word. Although I can't claim to have taken the Blue Deer's advice on humility in all my actions since then, I do try to live her message that I am third and will never forget it.

The second year with the jicareros on the pilgrimage to Huirikuta was the last one for this group's cycle of five years of service to the ceremonial center, so it was especially intense. All of these men had almost completed their five years of service, for some of them this was their second or third time serving for five years, so even the youngest of the jicareros was intimately familiar with all the ceremonies and sacred sites. After the first day of hunting and gathering peyote in Huiricuta, we collected firewood as the sun set. In my mind I fully expected I would have a vision of the Blue Deer that night with the fire and the peyote I would be eating. But the Blue Deer did not appear that night. I knew from hearing many stories about the Blue Deer that it could be a trickster, so the following night before eating the peyote I reminded myself to be on the alert: the Blue Deer might simply appear in a different way this time.

Turns out I was right and wrong. The Blue Deer did appear and in a similar way as the first time. But this time it was a male deer, and right before my eyes he changed into a huge cougar. Even though I was squarely in the magical time of the peyote, I can still remember thinking to myself how unusual it was: a cougar's main diet in those desert mountains was deer! And with that thought the giant cat snarled at me, and I became paralyzed. All thoughts stopped, and my body went rigid as an oak tree.

"I am the Blue Deer of Respect and have chosen this form because I knew you would respect it, for deep respect is what you lack," I heard the cougar talking in my mind. "Oh, you no doubt think you have respect for others, and in some cases you do, but you have not yet embraced the grander scheme of respect." The deer then told me a story.

I am the king of this desert and these mountains. If the antelope or the deer catch sight of me crouching in the bush, they do not forget to run. The coyote steer clear of me; other cougars avoid me. Even the mighty humans with their guns are afraid of me. You are afraid of me. Yes, I am the most feared and respected of the animals here.

That is why I became so angry when this annoying little creature interrupted my sleep one day. I was lying in some bushes sleeping, and this tiny mouse came running and hit me right in the nose. I opened my eyes, and the mouse froze knowing I would eat him for a snack, but before I could he said, "Oh mighty king, I am terribly sorry. I did not mean to run into you. I wasn't watching where I was going. Please forgive me!"

"You have showed your king respect with your words, and I will not eat you this time," I answered.

"Thank you, thank you, thank you," said the mouse. "I hope one day to be of service to you for your kindness."

I simply laughed at the thought. How could a tiny little mouse ever help me with anything?

Then one day I wasn't paying close enough attention to where I was walking and fell into a large pit that the humans had dug and covered in order to trap large animals to eat. I tried to get out, but they also had a net in there, and the more I struggled, the more tangled I became. After a while all the other animals heard what had happened, and they came to the edge of the pit and laughed at me. The coyote came by and said that in the morning the hunters would come back and skin me.

I struggled all night to get free, but it was no use. I was exhausted and finally gave up. A few minutes later, a little pink nose appeared above me. "Now is my time to repay you mighty King," said the little mouse.

"I am grateful for your good intentions little mouse," I replied. "But there's nothing you can do. Soon the men will come and there will be a new king for I shall be dead."

With that the little mouse ran away, but within minutes dozens of the mouse's family and friends came, and in their combined effort they gnawed through the net and set me free.

"And that is how I, the king of the animals, learned to respect others. It doesn't matter if you are mighty or meek, quick or slow, beautiful or ugly. Everything deserves respect for what they are. Everything has power of its own measure. This is what you must learn, Jim."

With that the cougar turned, and as he walked away, he transformed back into the Blue Deer and disappeared into the night.

My next encounter with the Blue Deer was the following year and with a whole new group of jicareros. Some of the new jicareros were irritated at being chosen because it places so much demand on them and their families. I had seen this before with new jicareros, but always after the five years of service, they are completely changed, and I knew it would be the same with this group, and so did the elders and shaman leading the pilgrimage. But at that moment there was still tension in the group, and I found it more difficult to stay focused during the pilgrimage. However, upon arriving at Huiricuta everyone was happy. No Huichol can be in Huiricuta and not be happy no matter what is happening in the outside world. The sacred land of Huiricuta is in their blood.

On that pilgrimage I met the Blue Deer of Perseverance. He walked right out of the Sacred Fire, and like the second deer he taught me his lesson with a story.

At the top of the sacred mountain above us is the town of Real de Cortorce, and as you know that town was built because more than two hundred years ago the humans found silver there and some became very rich. Once there were two poor brothers who were mining for silver. They dug shafts deep into the roots of the mountains, breathing noxious airs and trying to survive floods and cave-ins. They hauled out the ore with their own bodies, climbing crude ladders of notched logs, carrying the heavy loads in the same blankets with which they wrapped themselves at night. For some time they were rewarded with the precious silver, but one day they found their luck had run out. They tried for a few more weeks but found nothing. Finally, in disgust and swearing at the mountain, they gave up and sold all their equipment and their claim for a few hundred dollars and went home with their tails between their legs.

The man they sold their claim to was smart, and he hired an engineer who advised him to keep digging where the brothers had left off, and just three feet deeper he found a massive amount of the precious silver. With a little more perseverance and persistence, the brothers would have been rich beyond their wildest dreams.

How much further within yourself must you dig, Jim? Do you have the perseverance to uncover your true self and the riches that lie within you?

The Blue Deer walked into the fire and left me pondering his story and questions.

My fourth deer must have known about the struggles I would be facing in my life the following year. It was a tough year, but throughout it all I remembered the Blue Deer of Perseverance, and it gave me strength. Which leads me to my fourth pilgrimage with the jicareros, the second pilgrimage to Huiricuta for this group. A pattern was emerging with my encounters with the deer, as once again the lesson was delivered with a story, and of course the story and lesson were perfect for my current life situation:

This time I was visited by a female Blue Deer. Looking me straight in the eye, she began her story.

Once there was a teenage boy who went to town with his grandfather. In the small Mexican town was a store that sold all sorts of things, and the proprietor would also make trades with the customers. The boy saw an old watch in a case and fell in love with it. Being a Huichol, he lived in the mountains and did not have any need for a watch, nonetheless he asked his grandfather if he would buy it for him. It was not expensive, but most Huichols have very little money as they live off the land and their crops. Even though his grandfather had the money from selling some of his artwork, he told the boy no, but that if he worked real hard doing chores for his neighbors, maybe he could earn enough pesos to buy it. The boy worked real hard, and in a few weeks, he had the pesos and bought the cheap watch.

Even though it didn't keep good time and he really didn't need it, he wore it everywhere and never took it off. He saw that a few of the elders of the village had watches because they had to deal with the world outside their mountains to keep their villages safe and at times traveled to the big city to talk and make agreements with the government.

The boy's grandfather was a wise old elder. He was one of the few who sometimes traveled to the big city, but he didn't have a watch. What he did have was thousands of stories, and each night he would tell one around the fire after the family had eaten and before going to bed. One night after the evening story, the grandfather came into the boy's room as the boy lay in his bed ready to sleep. "Do you love me?" the grandfather asked. "Of course, I do," replied the boy. "Then give me your watch," the grandfather said. "Oh no, not my watch, Grandfather! But you can have my machete. It's a really good one." The grandfather just smiled. "That's OK," he said. "I already have a machete. You get some sleep now."

The next week the grandfather came to the boy's room again and asked, "Do you love me, grandson?" The boy replied, "You know I do, Grandfather." And again the grandfather said, "Then give me your watch." The boy replied, "Oh no, not my watch! But you can have these beads for your artwork." The grandfather told the boy he already had enough beads and wished the boy good dreams as he left.

The following week the grandfather came once again to the boy's room. The boy was sitting on the bed and extended his hand to his grandfather. In his hand was his watch. With a grin as big as the ocean, the grandfather took the watch with one hand and with the other handed the boy a small fancy box containing a brand-new watch.

The Blue Deer of Sacrifice opened my eyes to the illusion that I think I have things I absolutely need to hold on to and showed me the new treasures of life that would be available to me if I were able to let go.

This story ends with my fifth pilgrimage to Huiricuta. One of the head shamans of the jicareros was the father of my best Huichol friend, and I knew him well. Or I should say, well enough for an American to know a Huichol shaman. Anyway, after the long days of traveling to Huiricuta and before the hunting and gathering of the peyote, he and the other shamans and elders pulled me aside and explained to me, much to my disbelief, that I was not to hunt the peyote this time nor was I to take it into my body. They explained that there comes a time when we must learn our lessons through our own inner light and connection to the Great Spirit. I was to go to a sacred hill away from the jicareros and stay there fasting for five days while the jicareros did their hunting.

The shamans took me to the hill, while the jicareros watched me leaving and shouted me blessings and good fortune, as they obviously knew what I was to do. When we got to the sacred hill, I was far from the jicareros, somewhere in Huiricuta I had never been, and I doubted whether I could find my way back on my own. A sudden fear swept over me, and the old shaman began to explain, "This is where you must use everything you have learned in Huirikuta, Jim. Only by successfully completing this task will you truly become a medicine man for your people. Throughout the years the Blue Deer of Huiricuta have given you lessons about humility, respect, perseverance, and sacrifice. The fifth deer you must encounter without eating the peyote. The peyote spirit is all around you here as you know, but you must not eat it. You must try and connect with it and everything around you on your own."

Another even older shaman then said, "This is where you shall sit, with no view of roads or fences. With no blanket to sit on you feel the earth. With no fire you shiver for your vision and look into the darkness. You slowly become the rocks, the plants, the bushes, the animals. Here you become an animal. Nothing more, nothing less. We will come back for you at sunrise after your fifth night." And with that they left, and I was all alone in the sacred desert of Huirikuta.

Space does not allow for telling all that happened during that five days, but one of the first things I learned was that I was not alone. During my days and nights, I was visited by the coyote and fox, rabbit and snake, vulture and eagle. I could feel the peyote all around me as if watching. On the third night the wind blew so strong that, as I sat there shivering, I was covered with sand and by morning was barely distinguishable from my surroundings. The boredom and loneliness of sitting in that one place, knowing the jicareros were wandering free during their hunts and bonding over stories and chants at night by the fire, was almost unbearable. My stomach felt like it was eating itself, but by far it was thirst that was driving me crazy. I had fasted before on vision quests in the wild but never without water. Those days in Huirikuta pushed and tested me way beyond anything I had ever done before.

At dawn after the fifth night, I heard something coming up the hill, but it was not the shaman as I expected. It was my fifth Blue Deer. I was so weak I could barely sit up and look at the deer. He started his story:

Once there was a Huichol man about your age who was an expert archer and won all the contests. He was boastful and arrogant about his skill and one day challenged an elder of the tribe who was well known as their greatest hunter and had no use for competitions. The archer hit the bull's-eye on the first shot and with the second shot split his own arrow. "See that old man! Try and beat me!" he boasted.

The elder simply smiled knowingly but did not shoot. He motioned for the archer to follow him and walked away. The archer was puzzled but curious, so he followed along for many miles until they came to a deep gorge with a swift running river way down below them. Spanning the chasm was a flimsy log someone had placed there to cross, and the elder very calmly and nimbly made his way to the center of the chasm, aimed his arrow at a faraway tree, and made a direct hit. "Now it's your turn," he said, as he casually walked back on the shaky log.

The archer shook with terror as he looked into the seemingly bottomless abyss. He could not force himself to step out onto the log, much less shoot at a target. "You have much skill with your bow," the elder said. "But you have little skill over the mind that lets loose the shot."

"You see, Jim," said the Blue Deer to me in the predawn light. "Both the archer and the elder had skill, but the elder also had wisdom. I am the Blue Deer of Wisdom, and my message to you is that wisdom is the antidote for arrogance, impatience, anger, and ignorance. Wisdom is the sum of our experiences: the ups and downs, highs and lows, successes and failures. Wisdom comes from the light and from the darkness, from the level of perception that only comes from experience and through our struggles. You have faced this task, this struggle, very well, and now you have its experience and the wisdom it teaches. Now, would you like a drink of water?"

As I struggled to stand up and answer the magical deer that—*yes!*—I would give anything for some water, I took my eyes off the deer and when I looked back he was gone. But coming up the hill were the shamans to collect me, and of course they gave me a little water.

Since before written records pilgrims have traveled great distances to venerate the sites most holy to them, to receive visions, instructions, and guidance. The bottom line is the interaction between the people, the land, and the spirits that reside there, that sustain a nature-based shamanic culture. And that is why shamans, whose charge it is to ensure reciprocity, regularly endure great hardships to travel the sacred road of the pilgrim. Having spent many years making pilgrimages to sacred mountains, deserts, canyons, and bodies of water, I can say that modern people can also take this road to enlarge their view of reality and seek visions for their lives.

All the world's great religions also have sacred pilgrimage sites, but for this book on shamanic alchemy, I won't delve into the that. Choosing a place to make a pilgrimage is deeply personal, but here are some suggested places for our stage four work of conjunction. I have made pilgrimage to most but not all of these.

Newgrange, Ireland

Older than both Stonehenge and the Pyramids of Egypt, the monument at Newgrange was built around 3200 BCE. Its use is a mystery, although it was most likely a religious place of worship, and there are legends that it was used as a burial chamber. The main circular mound has a passage with small chambers off it, and each year on the winter solstice, the sun travels along the passage and lights up the main chamber. Many of the curbstones at the front and stone slabs lining the passage have decorative examples of Megalithic art, with zigzags, spirals and other geometric designs. Access to Newgrange is by guided tour, and it's part of the Brú na Bóinne complex, which also has the passage graves at Knowth (on view by guided tour) and Dowth (not open to visitors). This extremely ancient and powerful site is well worth putting on your pilgrimage list. However, to see the winter solstice light show, you must enter a lottery and be chosen. I couldn't be there during the days around the solstice, so one day I will go back at that time and try my luck with the lottery.

The Salkantay Trail to Llactapata and Machu Picchu

I found out about this trail by accident while visiting friends in Peru. I was planning to make a pilgrimage to Machu Picchu via the Inca Trail but didn't know you have to reserve approximately four months in advance to be allowed on the trail. The Salkantay Trail to Machu Picchu is open to everyone (for now), and I experienced so much on my pilgrimage via the Salkantay Trail that I know I will go back again. The trail takes you past icefalls, pristine glacial lakes, and through mountain passes with condors flying overhead and has really nice lodges if you want to be spoiled. Along the way we stopped at the archaeological ruins site of Llactapata, where I had a powerful experience overlooking Machu Picchu. When we first arrived at Llactapata, some Quero men of the area gave us offerings to give to Pachamama (Mother Earth) to ensure our safe passage. That was a significant sign that we were in the right place!

Pethang Ringmo

I have not been to this place, but after hearing about it from a devout Buddhist friend that I have shared many pilgrimages with, it is definitely on my list. This is some of what he told me.

I arrived at Pathang Ringmo (4,780 meters, 15,682 feet) in a blinding snowstorm. Luckily, a friend I was with saw someone he knew—a nomadic herder who happily invited us into his tent. I will never forget the man's eyes—behind them was a calm wisdom but also a wild spirit, and he laughed often and loudly despite the severe conditions.

He gave us some tea, and we warmed up by the fire where the herdsman was melting butter, probably yak. After a short while the storm began to subside, and the herdsman jumped up with a loud ha! *and flung open the tent. We all stepped outside. I will never forget what I saw and felt. A mist began to part right in front of us as if a veil was being lifted, and the next thing I knew my breath was taken from me as the immense ice cliffs of Jomolonzo appeared shining a golden light. Towering at nearly 26,000 feet, in that moment they felt so close I could almost touch them. All thought left me, and I felt that I had become one with the mountain, one with everything. I looked toward the herdsman; he smiled and then laughed uproariously. In that moment I knew he wasn't laughing at me but with me: he knew what I was feeling, and he knew that I now knew why he lived in these magical mountains.*

Uluru-Kata Tjuta National Park, Central Australia

With an amazing number of enchanted sites to explore, planning a pilgrimage to Australia is always a good idea. I am first-generation American and only have four blood relatives in the United States. My relatives pretty much all live in Australia and Hungary. Although Australia is in many ways similar to the United States, often times visiting there seems like being in a different world.

For example, on my first visit as a young teenager, my uncle from Sydney took me in his cab to beautiful and well-known Bondi Beach. As we walked onto the sand, my uncle intentionally lagged behind because he knew what I was going to see. Almost all the girls on the beach had no tops on! I had never seen a grown female with no top on, and I just stood there flabbergasted as they walked by me like it was the most natural thing in the world (which of course it is). After a few minutes, my uncle caught up with me, and as I got accustomed to what for me was a "show," he just laughed, patted me on the back, and we went back to his cab. The ride around Sydney was almost as shocking as the beach. Several times I thought I might die of fright because the Australians drive on the opposite side of the road. On the way home, we stopped at a pub where the walls are open to the street, which is quite typical in Australia, and no one thought anything of it when my uncle ordered me a beer.

Two natural rock formations, Uluru and Kata Tjuta, are famous pilgrimage destinations. They are located in Uluru-Kata Tjuta National Park, a World Heritage Site located in Australia's Red Centre. One of the country's more recognizable landmarks, Uluru (more commonly known as Ayers Rock) is a flat-topped sandstone rock standing about 1,100 feet high and almost six miles around, with a soulful, deep-red hue that changes throughout the day. About thirty miles away, Kata Tjuta (also known as the Olgas) is made of more than thirty domes of varying rock types, including granite, sandstone, and basalt; the tallest point is almost 1,800 feet high. Both sites are sacred to the Anangu people of the Pitjantjatjara Aboriginal tribe, who believe the rocks were built during the ancient creation period and are still inhabited by ancestor spirits. (Archaeologists' work suggests there were humans in this area over twenty thousand years ago.) Owned by the Anangu and leased by the government, the park is open to the public, though tribespeople continue to perform rituals and ceremonies in various locations, such as the sacred Dreamtime track that runs near the modern hiking trail. The park also houses the Cultural Centre and Aboriginal rock art sites.

Qantas and Virgin Australia now offer direct flights from several major domestic cities. There are only a few accommodation choices in the area; however, if you are open and courteous to the indigenous Pitjantjatjara and tell them you came on pilgrimage to honor the sacred sites, you may get to stay (a few dollars always helps) in a *wiltja*, a semicircular, temporary indigenous dwelling. One word of caution, it is advised—and I advise this in any sacred site—not to take any rocks home with you. There are many stories of people who did, and their luck immediately turned so bad they shipped the rocks back to the park.

Cenote Sagrado, Chichen Itza, Mexico

Going on pilgrimage to Chichen Itza in the Yucatán Peninsula is always an intense experience, especially on the spring and autumn equinoxes when a series of triangular shadows appear and then move down the pyramid of Kukulkan, a feathered-serpent deity. Large crowds come for this show, but it's still worth it. On quieter days it is worthwhile exploring the magic and history of the ball court, skull platform, the observatory temple, and my favorite man-made structure, the temple of the warriors (which includes a *chacmool**), among many other temples and structures.

Many natural sacred sites dot the Yucatán peninsula, especially sacred *cenotes* (pronounced sen-o-tays). Cenotes are basically natural sinkholes that expose the water table to the surface. These natural alchemic sites of transformation are perfect for a conjunction pilgrimage. The most famous sacred cenote is in Chichen Itza. I suggest that you visit and feel the energy of this cenote, but don't base your whole pilgrimage on it because it has a particular vibration that is very hard, or even impossible, to figure out or grab onto. Archaeological expeditions in the murky water have found in

---

*A chacmool is a pre-Columbian Mesoamerican sculpture of a reclining male figure with his head facing 90 degrees from the front, while supporting himself on his elbows and balancing a tray or bowl on his stomach.

the cenote gold, jadeite, copal, obsidian, shell, and rubber, among many other items, including human remains left as offerings, probably to the rain god Chac. None of these natural materials are native to the Yucatán so they must have been brought from elsewhere and given as sacred offerings to the water. On my many visits to this cenote I always need a while to get my energy back and clear my thoughts; that's how powerful it is.

Not far from Chichen Itza is the Ik Kil cenote, which has quite the opposite feeling and is well worth visiting. This sacred cenote is clear and wonderful with a staircase leading down about eighty-feet feet to a swimming platform. Vines reach down from the opening at the top all the way down to the water, along with small waterfalls. Divers also frequent the clear water of this magical cenote.

Crater Lake, Oregon

This amazingly blue freshwater caldera is the deepest lake in the United States, plunging to depths of nearly two thousand feet. It formed nearly eight thousand years ago after an alleged massive eruption caused Mount Mazama to collapse. The Native American Klamath tribe has long considered the lake a sacred site; their legends retell a battle here between the chief of the above world and the chief of the below world, which led to the destruction of Mount Mazama. Many historians believe the Klamath people may have witnessed the actual implosion of the mountain. In the past, Klamath tribesmen used Crater Lake in their vision quests (tasks may have included scaling the crater walls), and it is still considered a sacred spiritual spot. The lake is now part of Crater Lake National Park.

The magnificent intense blue of Crater Lake is due to its great depth and clarity. Sunlight is able to penetrate deep into the water. The depth absorbs many of the longer rays but reflects the shorter rays of the white light spectrum, such as blue and purple. Red light is the longest wavelength and thus gets absorbed.

There are plenty of sites to visit in Crater Lake National Park. My favorites are The Pinnacles, tall spires and pinnacles of cemented ash and pumice, and the three-mile hike to Mount Scott at 8,929 feet. From the summit the views can be as great as one hundred miles, and the whole Crater Lake caldera can be seen from above. There are two campsites in the park, but be sure to plan your pilgrimage during the warm months, as the park can get ten to fifteen feet of snow.

Sedona, Arizona

Sedona is truly a magic and sacred place even with the plethora of New Age hype surrounding it. I had the pleasure of having a permitted guiding business in the Coconino National Forest (which includes Sedona) for many years. Aside from the popular "vortex" centers, there are remarkable ruins and pictograph areas off the beaten path. Upon entering Sedona my first time, I knew immediately that I wanted to stay for a long while and learn among the magnificent red rock formations. This is definitely an awesome pilgrimage site for alchemic transformation. I have hundreds of stories from clients and friends who left Sedona changed for the better—psychically, mentally, and spiritually. The many jeep tour companies can offer you a fun time riding around to see the sights, but I also suggest hooking up with a local hiking guide to take you to the more secret sacred sites.

Fig. 9.3. The author with Cathedral Rock in background, 2008.

Around the time I started my guiding business, I was driving in my own jeep with my dog, exploring the dirt roads off the beaten path in the Red Rock district of the National Forest outside Sedona. As we passed a secluded ravine on our right side, I had the sudden urge to explore it and pulled over. There was no trail in this secluded area, so we walked back along the ravine, which seemed to be an ancient arroyo leading up to a high ridge. As we walked, the sheer red rock cliffs on either side grew higher, and I had the distinct feeling that we were in a special place. After an hour or so of walking gradually up and back the spectacular ravine, we ended up in a small box canyon that was beautiful beyond words. While looking intently all around, much to my surprise I saw a magnificent cliff dwelling built way up the canyon wall. Of course, we found a way to climb up to it.

After many hours in and around the ancient cliff dwelling, we began the return trip out of the canyon and came upon an old gentleman walking up the same way we had come. He seemed surprised to see us and asked us who had told us about this secret place. I told him the truth—no one told me, the place seemed to just call to me. He laughed and said that was great but also to be very careful and respectful as this was a sacred site to his people—the Yavapai tribe. I assured him I would respect the sacred site but asked him why the word of caution. Again, he chuckled and explained that most people who are told about this place never find it. Usually nothing serious happens to them, but they tend to get temporarily lost, walking in circles for hours, and come back exhausted, disappointed, and all scratched up, with cactus quills sticking out of their clothes and boots. He said that there are powerful spirits that guard the sacred site, and only those with a clean heart and purpose may enter.

When I told him my desire to become one with the land and learn to feel the power of sacred sites like my Wirrarika mentors (conjunction), he slowly looked around the sacred arroyo, nodded to me knowingly, shook my hand, and bid us a good day. Ever after this encounter, the arroyo became one of my favorite places in all the world.

Mount Shasta, California

Mount Shasta has long been revered by the Native Americans of the area, who regard it as the center of creation, and it is a frequent pilgrimage destination for nonlocals. Native American tribes still live in the area and carry out ancient rituals in honor of the mountain. Each year, the Wintu invoke the mountain's spirit with ritual dances that ensure the continued flow of the sacred springs. Among many places to visit in the Mount Shasta area is the Shasta Abbey Buddhist Monastery, which is open to visitors and in my opinion well worth the time.

In recent decades Mount Shasta has also attracted New Age followers, who believe the mountain to be a source of mystical power. Over one hundred New Age–type sects hold various views of the sacred mountain, ranging from it being an entry point into the fifth dimension to a source of magic crystals, a UFO landing spot, the dwelling place of the Lemurians, super spiritually advanced humans who can transform from material to spiritual at will—among many others.

I have been fortunate to take a small group of my Huichol friends, including one of my shaman mentors, to Mount Shasta for a few days, and after one all-night ceremony, the shaman smiled brightly at me as he looked up at the mountain over the Sacred Fire. I can't reveal what he told me, but in a nutshell, he agreed that Shasta is a powerful holy mountain.

Uxmal, Mexico

In the jungle of the Yucatán Peninsula is the pre-Hispanic town of Uxmal, a UNESCO World Heritage Site. One of my favorite places in Uxmal is the Pyramid of the Magician. A local folktale explains the origin of the pyramid.

Long ago in Kabah, near to here, an old and powerful witch wanted a child but was not able to conceive, so by magic she brought forth a baby boy from an egg. Everyone was astounded because the boy matured into an adult and even had a beard after only a few days. But he never grew to full height; he was a dwarf. One day while his mom was out, he found a magic gong that the old witch had carefully hidden. He hit the gong many times, and it could be heard throughout the kingdom. The sound frightened the king of Uxmal as there was a prophesy that when the ancient gong was heard throughout the kingdom a new king would challenge the old one for the throne.

In fear of his position, the king found the dwarf and challenged him to a number of tests and physical feats. The dwarf equaled the king in all the tests, and the king became extremely angry and humiliated that a dwarf could match him and so he challenged him to one last test. The dwarf won that as well and became the new king of Uxmal. The first thing the dwarf did as the new king was magically erect three pyramids in one night: the Palace of the Governor to serve as his ruling palace, the House of the Old Woman for his mother the witch, and the Pyramid of the Magician for himself.

Another legend says that the magician-god Itzamna created the Pyramid of the Magician in a single night. Some believe that Itzamna, a creation deity, and the dwarf are connected or one and the same. My native friend Chon invited me to Uxmal and to speak with Itzamna. What follows is the story of my encounter with this magician-god Itzamna.

Chon told me that his grandfather has been the shaman of his village for over fifty years and has been training Chon since childhood in the ancient ways so that one day Chon will take his place. He told Chon that Itzamna is the god of the heavens and creation and that the dwarf is but a tiny offshoot of the great god Itzamna.

"He taught me when I was a small child how to talk to the magic dwarf that we call Itzamna," said Chon. "I have spoken to him hundreds of times, and he has always answered all of my questions except for one. Whenever I ask him if he really did create the three structures magically all in one night he simply smiles but does not answer . . . Do you want to try and speak with him?"

"Sure," I said, an uneasy feeling growing inside me.

For three consecutive nights we climbed the Pyramid of the Magician. When we reached the top, Chon would break an egg and speak with Itzamna, but I couldn't see or hear him. The fourth night we followed the same procedure except this time, before cracking the egg, Chon handed me a small hand-rolled cigar.

"My grandfather has prepared this special mixture for you, Jim. Inside

the cigar is the dried powder excretions from the sacred toad of the jungle," Chon said. "This will help you to meet with Itzamna."

Chon broke the egg and carefully laid the yolk beside us, being careful not to break the yolk. He instructed me to sit and smoke half the cigar and beat slowly on the gong while saying my own prayer to the dwarf king, inviting him to join us. I did as he said.

With the first puff of the cigar, my whole body began to tingle. By the time I had smoked half the cigar and put it out, I was seeing a kaleidoscope of colors and geometric figures looking out over the jungle's canopy. "Look at the egg," Chon said quietly.

I looked beside us and standing there staring at me was the dwarf king! He looked old but not ancient. He was only about four feet tall with with very dark brown skin and a long silver beard and was dressed in a simple white tunic.

"Greetings young man," the dwarf king said to me jovially in English. I couldn't speak, but even if I could I would have had no words.

He seemed to know what I was experiencing. He held out a hand to me and with a loud laugh said, "Come with me!"

I took his hand, and we walked right into the pyramid. I felt myself passing through the different layers of the pyramid and slowly sinking down into the very base of the structure. We ended up in a small room where a small fire was magically burning with no fuel for the fire to be seen anywhere. He told me to sit on a small bench next to the fire and sat next to me. The colorful geometric patterns were still floating all around but not as intensely as before. His powerful and extraordinary presence seemed to be focusing my attention entirely on him.

"Welcome to the temple of magic, Jim," the dwarf king said kindly. With that said, my voice seemed to naturally come back to me, and we had a long conversation. He was a peculiarly curious fellow and asked me many questions about what was going on in the "outside" world and with my life, even though I had the distinct impression that he already knew all that I was telling him.

Seemingly satisfied with the conversation and laughing at many things I didn't even consider to be funny, he casually poured me a mug of strong coffee from a pot I hadn't noticed before by the fire.

While I sipped my coffee, he asked, "Do you believe in magic, Jim?"

"I certainly know there are many things that I have experienced that I can't explain with my rational mind, including this," I replied.

"Very good that you realize that because the magic I am talking about is not the parlor-trick variety, Jim. It is brought about by the power and magic of intention. Your intentions create your reality. You already know this, but you have not yet fully conceived of the power in this statement," he said. "Especially from now on, since you will be taking the magic and energy of this place with you when you leave, you must be very careful with your thoughts, what you say to yourself and others, what you write, and in everything you do. You have the power to create or destroy. You must use your power wisely and with thought of how your actions and words will affect everything around you."

Just as he finished saying that, I saw for a moment the view of the jungle from the pyramid's ledge, where I had been sitting with Chon.

"Our time together is almost done, Jim. Be mindful of what I said and come back anytime! I used to have many friends come visit me. But throughout the centuries they have come less and less. Now I only have a few left. Most of the people these days don't believe in magic and therefore can't see me or don't want to."

"Can I ask you one last question?" I asked.

"Of course."

"How can you possibly know how to speak English?"

"I told you! It's magic!"

With that he threw his arms in the air, and the next thing I knew, I was sitting next to Chon on the ledge. I felt like myself again, although a little tired, and told Chon all that had happened.

"That's good advice he gave you, Jim," said Chon. I agreed, and we walked back to the village in silence. I have been back twice since then, but unlike Chon, I still need the help of the toads to meet with the dwarf king.

Since that first experience with the dwarf king, something has changed inside me, and I have found a deeper realization of how my thoughts and actions affect not only myself but everyone and everything around me both seen and unseen. And it goes without saying that I have a new

Fig. 9.4. The author overlooking the Pyramid of the Magician, Uxmal, 1999.

understanding of the word *magic* and how it manifests with every thought and action in my life.

Badlands National Park, South Dakota

The Lakota call this area Mako Sica, which means "land bad." The Badlands as we know it now was named by early 1800 fur trappers for its lack of water—which is ironic considering it used to be the bottom of an ocean.

The Badlands of South Dakota are full of power and history both in the natural and human worlds. The national park consists of 244,000 acres of sharply eroded buttes, pinnacles, and spires blended with the largest protected mixed-grass prairie in the United States. When I first visited the Badlands, I was taken aback by its true desolation; you can look for miles and see no sign of civilization. This land has been so ruthlessly ravaged by wind and water that it has become uniquely picturesque. The Badlands are a wonderland of bizarre, colorful spires and pinnacles, massive buttes, and deep gorges.

Badlands National Park also preserves the world's greatest fossil beds of animals from the Oligocene Epoch of the Age of Mammals. Prehistoric bones are still being uncovered today by park officials and sometimes visitors. The skeletons of ancient camels, three-toed horses, saber-toothed cats, and giant rhinoceros-like creatures are among the many fossilized species found here. In May 2010, a seven-year-old girl named Kylie found a fossil near the visitor center at Badlands National Park. She did the right thing. She reported her find to rangers. It turned out to be an exceptionally rare and well-preserved saber-toothed cat fossil. The area is now known as the Saber Site. Not far from the park the largest, most complete, and best-preserved *Tyrannosaurus rex* ever was discovered in 1990. It now belongs to The Field Museum in Chicago and is named Sue after Sue Hendrickson who discovered it.

Plenty of wildlife roams the park. Bison, pronghorn, mule and white-tailed deer, prairie dogs, coyotes, butterflies, turtles, snakes, bluebirds, vultures, eagles, and hawks are just some of the wildlife that can often be seen by visitors. The park has some really cool hiking trails, camping sites, and a lodge.

Another great feature of the desolate location is the lack of light pollution, a term used by astronomers to describe intrusive light in the night sky hindering the view of the heavens. Rarely do most people have the opportunity to experience the awesome dark skies afforded by this park. Two nights a week, park rangers provide telescopes for viewing the night sky. I was truly impressed by the clarity of our own Milky Way and other galaxies and also star clusters, nebulae, planets, and even the moons of Jupiter. You can also see flyovers by numerous satellites and the International Space Station.

Archaeologists speculate that humans have hunted in the Badlands for the last eleven thousand years. Paleo-Indian, Arikara, and Lakota all have a colorful history in this area. During the last two centuries the Badlands have been the site of notable clashes between homesteaders and American Indians. Among those clashes was the infamous Battle of Wounded Knee near Wounded Knee Creek, forty-five miles south of the park, which the 1890s religion of the the Ghost Dance, prevalent in the Badlands at the time, likely instigated.*

Bighorn Medicine Wheel, Wyoming

The Bighorn Medicine Wheel is a wheel-like pattern made of stones, eighty feet in diameter. It sits on top of the Bighorn Range, at an elevation of 9,642 feet—a desolate region only reachable during the summer months. At the center of the circle is a cairn—doughnut-shaped pile of stones—connected to the rim by twenty-eight spoke-like lines of stones. Six more stone cairns are arranged around the circle, most large enough to hold a sitting human. The central cairn is about twelve feet in diameter and two feet high.

Members of the Crow tribe, who have long used the medicine wheel for rituals, ascribe its creation to a boy named Burnt Face. According to the story, the boy fell into the fire as a baby and was severely scarred.

---

*The Ghost Dance was founded and led by Wovoka, a Paiute spiritual leader, and incorporated several Native American belief systems. The religion fostered cooperation among the tribes and opposed white expansion. Because it encouraged Lakota resistance against the Dawes Act, the U.S. government moved to suppress a potential uprising by killing at least 153 people at Wounded Knee. The Ghost Dance is still practiced by the Caddo today.

When Burnt Face reached his teen years, he went on a vision quest in the mountains, where he fasted and built the medicine wheel. During his quest, he helped drive away an animal who attacked baby eaglets. In reward he was carried off by a great eagle, and his face was made smooth again. For centuries, the Bighorn Medicine Wheel has been used by Crow youth for fasting and vision quests. The medicine wheel was added to the National Register of Historic Places in 1969.

Bighorn Medicine Wheel now also attracts New Age followers, who believe medicine wheels to be centers of earth energy. Archaeoastronomers have found alignments in the wheel's arrangements of rocks, cairns, and spokes, most notably arrangements pointing to the rising and setting places of the sun at summer solstice, as well as the rising places of Aldebaran in Taurus, Rigel in Orion, and Sirius in Canis Major—all bright, important stars associated with the solstice.

Please note that some Native Americans of the area resent the presence of pilgrims and visitors to the site, and some young warriors are now reluctant to go to the wheel because of the presence of white visitors. Although it is not legally necessary, before visiting a site like this, I make an effort to speak to the locals and hopefully receive a blessing from an elder or shaman. It took me many years to gain the trust and respect of the many indigenous shamans I now consider to be my mentors and friends.

Serpent Mound, Ohio

I'm including the man-made Serpent Mound in this list simply because I have never seen anything like it and I've been to hundreds of sacred sites. This spectacular earthwork effigy of a serpent uncoils along a prominent ridgetop in northern Adams County, Ohio. From the tip of its nose to the end of its tail, the serpent is 1,427 feet long—the largest such effigy in the world. When it was originally described in an 1848 account, the body of the serpent was five feet high and twenty-five feet wide. For a time, the serpent mound was dated to about 1070 CE and attributed to the Fort Ancient people, but in 2014, new research and carbon dating set construction of the mound back to about 321 BCE. It is is now considered part of Adena culture, predecessor of the Alqonquian tribes of the Ohio Valley.[1]

The serpent is slightly crescent shaped and oriented such that the head is at the east and the tail at the west, with seven winding coils in between. The shape of the head perhaps invites the most speculation. Whereas some scholars read the oval shape as an enlarged eye, others see a hollow egg or even a frog about to be swallowed by wide, open jaws. The head of Serpent Mound is aligned to the setting sun on the summer solstice and the coils may be aligned to the summer and winter solstice and equinox sunrises. These alignments support the idea that Serpent Mound had a ceremonial purpose. Serpents are a common feature in the art of the Late Prehistoric Period (900 to 1650 CE). Many native cultures in both North and Central America attributed supernatural powers to snakes or reptiles and included them in their spiritual practices. Serpent Mound may be a representation of these beliefs.

The mound conforms to the natural topography of the site, which is a high plateau overlooking Ohio Brush Creek. In fact, the head of the creature approaches a steep, natural cliff above the creek. The area's unique geologic formations suggest that a meteor struck the site approximately 250 to 300 million years ago, causing folded bedrock underneath the mound.

We can't really be sure whether this impressive earthwork was used to document celestial events, act as a compass, serve as a guide to astrological patterns, mark time, or provide a place of worship to a supernatural snake god or goddess. Numerous ancient cultures throughout the world have depicted serpents in various spiritual forms employing many different media. Earth mounds were made by the ancient Native American cultures that flourished along the fertile valleys of the Mississippi, Ohio, Illinois, and Missouri Rivers a thousand years ago, and although many were destroyed as farms spread across this region during the modern era, Serpent Mound has survived wonderfully. Without a doubt, the mound is singular and significant in its ability to provide tangible insights into the cosmology and rituals of the ancient Americans.

By walking the trail around the effigy and going up the observatory tower for a view from above, you get what many describe as "an emotional feeling of wonderment and a reverential connection with the past."[2] My first visit to Serpent Mound was on a beautiful sunny day, and the wildflowers were blooming. I received such a delightful feeling that I made many pilgrimages to this unique site during the years I lived in Pennsylvania, which was just a few hours drive from the mound. Serpent Mound is recognized as a National Historic Landmark and is protected by deed to the Ohio State Archaeological and Historical Society, now the Ohio History Connection. It has also been nominated for World Heritage status with UNESCO.[3]

Going on a Pilgrimage

A pilgrimage is fundamentally a journey, but it is a sacred journey that is infinitely more than just a there-and-back-again trip. Although each pilgrimage has its own unique dynamics, all pilgrimage experiences have eight basic steps or circumstances, which I outline below.

1. There is a reason, a calling, a longing, or some other type of hope, desire, goal, or obligation that produces the inspiration to depart on the journey to the sacred place.
2. There is preparation for the journey. This includes mental, physical, spiritual, and logistical preparations that often include ritual purification, the making or purchasing of offerings to give to the sacred place, the saving and collecting of resources, including food, clothing, and money, to make the journey, and arrangements for taking care of your affairs at home while you are gone.
3. There is the moment of departure when the sacred time officially begins. This occasion is sometimes marked with great happiness or can be very solemn depending on the circumstances. In any case, from this moment on, there is no chance that the pilgrim will return unchanged.
4. There is the journey into the mystery. No one can say what will happen to the pilgrim once he or she leaves home for the sacred place. The journey itself is full of messages and hidden meanings for the pilgrim as he or she deals with the internal and external circumstances of sacred travel. Sometimes there are other special points or places during the trip that mark significant thresholds to cross along the way.

5. There is almost always a major hardship or obstacle that creates doubt but fosters strength once it is overcome. Sometimes there are many obstacles, and if they become too great, it may be a sign that the moment is not right and the pilgrim should turn back. I have seen immense hardships, such as a baby being born prematurely to a pilgrim in the middle of the desert, that at the moment seemed like a tragedy but in the end was a blessing of the largest kind imaginable.

6. There is the arrival at the sacred place and the joy of having made it. In many cases this is just another beginning because there may be a lot of work to do once the pilgrim arrives. For example, although the trip may be exhausting and full of difficulties, when I travel on pilgrimage with my Wirrarika mentors to the sacred desert of Wirikuta, once we arrive we have two full days of hunting and gathering the peyote, at least two sleepless nights of visionary experiences with the fire, the spirits, and the shaman singing or the kawitero retelling the stories of creation, and then the demanding physical hike to the top of the sacred mountain for the making of offerings. Other times, there may be work to do to help preserve the sacred site or special duties of reverence to perform such as the building of a rirriki. In any case, during this step, the reason for the journey is addressed and the spirits of the place are petitioned and honored.

7. There is the turning around and bringing home of the gifts and/or the pain. If the pilgrim has found what he or she was seeking, this could be a joyous time, but if the pilgrim has been disappointed or injured, it could be very hard. In all cases, there are lessons to be learned and circumstances to be contemplated.

8. There is the welcome home when the pilgrim returns and integrates his or her experiences. Sometimes the pilgrim tells the story of the pilgrimage to loved ones; other times the pilgrim keeps the stories to him- or herself. But no matter what, the pilgrim has to assimilate the journey into the context of his or her current and future life.

It is good to make a serious effort to be very clear about why you are going on the pilgrimage and what you hope to find. Fasting or performing other types of purification before departure will help you gain clarity. When traveling to a sacred place in nature to ask for something important to your life, you should always make an offering in return, and it is a good idea to leave a representation of that offering in the sacred place and/or make the offering out loud in front of your companions in order to seal the deal with the sacred place in front of witnesses.

Once in the sacred place, be sure to be open and attentive to absolutely everything around you because you cannot predict in what form a message or signal might come. There is a vision of some kind waiting for you, and it is your responsibility to make yourself available and not to let it pass you by. Stay true to your reason for being there, and do not let small obstacles grow into large distractions.

There are many reasons to make a pilgrimage but none better than to seek a vision to guide your life. For this reason, I go on a special pilgrimage once a year, usually in May (the month of my birthday) to the same place if possible, and this journey marks the start of my new year, no matter what date I go on. In this type of pilgrimage, you recount your year to the sacred place. I usually do it during most of the night in the company of the Sacred Fire and some other pilgrims, if possible. Then I present a handmade physical representation of my perceived goals for the following year and petition the sacred place for any information relevant to what I aim to do. After that is done, either directly or after being witness for my companions, I go alone to the sacred place and ask the spirits of the place to communicate with me about what I have shared. Depending on what I learn from the place, I make one or more concrete offerings to carry out during the coming year.

For example, after a recent pilgrimage where I learned a great deal from the sacred place, I was guided to offer something back to the spirit of the indigenous people, specifically to the Wirrarika children. I made the offering to the sacred place but I did not know what it would be specifically. Shortly afterward, I was talking to a Wirrarika friend and he mentioned that he thought it would be great if the Wirrarika children could see the children's book I had written with two other Wirrarika friends who had the illustrated it. I immediately knew this would be my offering to the sacred place. I spent about six months arranging everything.

With the generous help of friends and fellow pilgrimagers, I acquired and donated two hundred books to the Wirrarika children.

This is just a small example of how the procedure of commitments and offerings gives strength to the whole process of learning from sacred places and especially in those moments when you have journeyed a long hard road during a pilgrimage. The pilgrimage process of conjunction can be a powerful catalyst for personal and spiritual growth, healing, honoring, and offering and a vehicle steering us into the heart of a sacred place, where our heartbeats become one with it.

10

STAGE FIVE

FERMENTATION

Fig. 10.1.
Stage five.

The fifth ray of the star points to where the left wing of the ascended essence touches the standing bird of spirit and is marked with the cipher for copper and Venus. Copper is often associated with blood.*

In the circle of operation we see the soul and spirit birds nesting in a tree awaiting the mystical event of vision. During laboratory alchemy fermentation is the introduction of new energy (usually yeast or salt) into the product of conjunction to completely "raise" and transform its qualities. On a shamanic level, after successfully uniting with sacred places during and achieving a new form of balance through conjunction, the adept now looks to the spirit world to further his development. The word *invenies* in the mandala, meaning "you will discover," and the word

---

*You will be asked to offer a tiny bit of your blood to the sacred place of your praxis in this stage.

spiritus (spirit or soul) above it asks the adept to seek discovery through the fermentation of their soul and spirit, to go beyond the possibilities of the fragile human state.

The first four alchemic-shamanic stages of operations (calcination, dissolution, separation, and conjunction) are heavy on the earth-bound processes dealing with the personality and ego with help from the Sacred Fire, water, other people, and sacred sites. Alchemists have associated three colors to the seven main stages. The first, *nigredo* (blackening), encompasses the first four stages. The associated color for this stage of fermentation and the next stage distillation is *albedo* (whitening). In additive color mixing, like light, all the colors combined create white. In alchemy a white swan or dove is commonly associated with this stage.

Fig. 10.2. Alone on an island the alchemist ferments in contemplation on a vision about life and death (engraving by Matthäus Merian, from *Atalanta Fugiens* by Michael Maier, 1617).

However, one cannot create white without first completing the work of nigredo. In this stage of the work, fermentation, we first must enter the final stage of nigredo, which is putrefaction (decomposition, decay, rot). Once putrefied we can add psychological manure to get the process of fermentation going. Putrefaction in this sense is the decomposition of the ego through realization of intrinsic deficiencies that we intentionally pile up to let rot. Alchemic putrefaction is often symbolized in drawings by skeletons, coffins, corpses, graves, massacres, rotting flesh, dung beetles, and worms, all suggesting death and decay.

This stage also includes birds descending into the light from a pitch-black sky, germination, and lush green gardens. This dichotomy reveals itself in the death-rebirth scenario where psychological death or the killing of ego allows the inner fermentation of new life spirit, a new and infinitely more mature psyche. In this way visions are obtained directly from the spirit realms and are not mistaken for the false visions of an overinflated ego.

The following three operational stages (fermentation, distillation, and coagulation) will require you to extend your consciousness beyond your individual ego to encompass aspects of the spirit world, the psyche of the numinous realms, and the transpersonal self.

In this fifth stage, through your actions, you make a plea to the mystical-spiritual powers that give life and motion to everything and that sometimes will grant visions to those who properly seek it. In this stage we will attempt to accomplish this through the process of spiritual fermentation.

Praxis 16

Shamanic Fermentation by Solitary Quest

In the days before such medicine plants as peyote, mushrooms, and datura became popular as a means of accessing visions, many shamanic tribes relied on induced suffering and hardship in the wilderness to summon up the visionary spirits that would teach them how to live. These journeys are broadly termed *vision quests.*

A person (often pubescent) would travel alone to a remote area where his or her people knew that the spirits of nature were strong and lively.

This could be a dense forest, a mountaintop, a swamp, or any other remote area where the powers dwelled. In this place the young person would stay for several days and nights, fasting from both food and water and wearing nothing but a loincloth, to endure whatever Mother Nature and the spirits had in store. In solitude and outside the sphere of village life, the initiate sat silent and alone, open to receive anything that would stimulate the mind, body, and spirit. Stripped of clothing, material possessions, and the protection of family and tribe, the initiate was forced to learn about and dive deep into his or her own physical and psychic resources to deal with the perils posed by wild animals, storms, hunger, thirst, and boredom. In this state the person was completely free of the normal social concerns of everyday life. Little by little, as the initiate became increasingly empty of human-centered wants and thoughts, the hidden abilities of the psyche would arise, and the consciousness of the initiate would expand to perceive that consciousness is all around. When this happened, visions would come.

Visions acquired in this manner must not be confused or relegated to the internal processes of the mind alone because an expansion of consciousness is happening, whereby the objects and energies of the world, normally seen as external to the human organism, are now viewed as part of a continuum that includes both what is internal and external to the initiate. In other words, there is no inside or outside of the head or mind. Both these realities meet and are bound together by what can loosely be called consciousness. In this visionary state there is little or no perceived separation among different types of living beings. Plants wave and acknowledge the vision quester, while animals and insects and birds deliver messages. In this visionary state the lines of nonverbal communication are open, and a dialogue between the human organism and the other species in the environment begins; the possibilities of this kind of communication become limitless.

This stage of shamanic-alchemic transformation will be accomplished via certain shamanic vision quest procedures along with alchemic putrefaction and fermentation by employing the use of a casket. This is a very high-level endeavor that should only be embarked on when the first four stages are successfully completed and all preparations are ready.

PREPARATIONS FOR VISION QUESTING

Frankly for many, this may well be one of the most trying things you have ever done. On the physical level, here is what is required in preparation:

Choose and prepare the place of your quest
Prepare your casket
Collect the items you will bring
Prepare for fasting
Get yourself and your casket to the questing spot
Collect firewood

On personal and transpersonal levels (among other situations) during your quest you will:

Depart from your everyday life
Feel hungry
Question why you are doing this
Feel moments of depression or self-pity
Remember repressed moments of your life
Experience insights or visions
Communicate verbally and nonverbally with everything around you
Experience a keen awareness of death
Experience a rebirth or transformation

We will now look more closely at each of these preparatory activities.

Choose and Prepare the Place of Your Quest

The place where you will carry out the quest, which you will not leave for three days, is extremely important because it is not just the physical location of the rite but also the co-creator of your experience. Optimally, it should be a location that is far enough from civilization so that no noises from human activity reach it and no other people are likely to wander into it, and you must be able to make a small fire for a short period of time. It's also a good idea to keep your casket in mind when choosing your spot and to make a place ready for it (level the ground) ahead of time. Important: never perform the quest in an area near a cemetery or an archaeological site.

Before you begin the quest, determine when you will need to enter the casket. It's best to spend approximately eight to nine hours in your casket per night, coming out at dawn. On the shorter summer nights, this period is nearly equivalent to the hours of darkness. But at other times of the year, it is dark for longer than eight hours, so you must plan to enter the casket eight to nine hours before dawn. Most weather websites provide sunrise information.

Prepare Your Casket

For those of you who are handy, this will be fairly easy; for those who are not, it will be a little more challenging but not something you can't do. The instructions are pretty simple. We don't need to create something fancy; a simple rectangular box made from wood is our aim. Remember, it doesn't have to be as strong as a real casket because you won't be carried in it.

The first casket I built was out of 15/32-inch plywood. It was light, inexpensive, and easy to build. I think most people can build a rectangle box, with a floor and lid, out of 4 × 8 sheets of plywood and furring strips, which is how I built my first casket for this praxis. If you are under six feet tall, you'll only need three sheets of plywood; if you are over six feet tall, you'll need four because you won't be able to use the scrap pieces for the end boards (you'll see what I mean as I explain the procedure). Big box hardware stores like Home Depot will usually make one cut on each of your sheets for free, which is the majority of the cutting required. You will need the following items (note that lumber measurements are given using their "common" dimensions, like 1 × 2, rather than their actual dimensions, which are slightly smaller):

Tools

    Circular saw (best), jig saw, or hand saw
    Tape measure
    Drill with a Phillips-head bit

Materials

1¼ inch drywall screws

One 1 inch × 2 inch × 8 foot furring strip

For people 6 feet tall or under: three 4 × 8 plywood sheets, ¹⁵⁄₃₂ inch thick

For people over 6 feet tall: four 4 × 8 plywood sheets, ¹⁵⁄₃₂ inch thick

Assembly

The first thing to do is have your lumber cut to the proper dimensions.

For people under 6 feet tall your required cut lumber to assemble will be:

Two 6 × 3 foot plywood (the bottom and top)

Two 6 × 2 foot plywood (the sides)

Two 3 × 2 foot plywood (the front and back)

Four 1 × 2 inch furring strips, 2 feet long (the corner posts)

1. Cut (either at the store or at home) 1 foot lengthwise off two of your sheets, leaving two sheets 3 feet wide by 8 feet long.
2. Cut 2 feet off the ends of the same two sheets, leaving two sheets 3 feet wide by 6 feet long for the top and bottom.
3. Cut 2 feet off your last sheet so you now have one sheet 6 feet long by 4 feet wide. Then cut that sheet in half lengthwise to get your two 6 × 2 foot sides.
4. You will now have three sheets 4 × 2 feet from the scraps of making the bottom, top, and sides. Cut two of these sheets to 3 × 2 feet for the front and back.
5. The last cuts are to the 1 × 2 furring strip. Cut your 8-foot-long piece into four 2-foot-long pieces.

For those of you over six feet, the length of the top, bottom, and sides will obviously need to be longer. This means you won't need to cut the length of the 8 foot sheets for the top, bottom and sides. But you also won't have any scrap pieces for the front and back so you will need to have 4 sheets of plywood instead of three.

1. Cut (either at the store or at home) 1 foot lengthwise off two of your sheets, leaving two sheets 3 feet wide by 8 feet long. These will be the bottom and top.

2. Cut your third sheet in half lengthwise, so now you have two sheets 8 × 2 for your sides.

3. To make the front and back, cut your fourth sheet in half lengthwise so you now have two sheets measuring 8 × 2. From one of these sheets, cut three feet off the length two times so now you have two sheets 3 × 2 for the front and back.

4. The last cuts are to the 1 × 2 furring strip. Cut your 8-foot-long piece into four 2-foot-long pieces.

- Begin by attaching your 2-foot-long furring strips to your bottom sheet at the corners, using the screws. But when you do this don't screw them flush with the corner—leave a space the thickness of your plywood from the corners. You can easily do this by taking another piece of plywood and marking the thickness or measure the thickness and mark it. We don't want to have the corner posts flush to the corners because when we put the sides on we want those to be flush.

- To screw the posts to the bottom—if you have a helper simply stand the sheet up on its side and while your helper holds it screw the post on from the bottom. Without a helper—prop the sheet up from the bottom high enough to get your drill under the board and screw the post to bottom from underneath. With your four posts screwed on your bottom sheet should look like figure 10.3 on page 210. Notice that the posts are not completely to the corners—I put them just slightly (the thickness of the plywood) inside the corners.

- Now screw your side sheets to the posts using 2 to 4 screws for each post, as in figure 10.4.

- And then attach the front and back as in figure 10.5.

- You needn't do anything with the top except place it on—as in figure 10.6.

- Your completed casket can easily be taken apart by taking out the screws. When you're ready to use the casket again, simply reassemble the pieces and reinsert the screws.

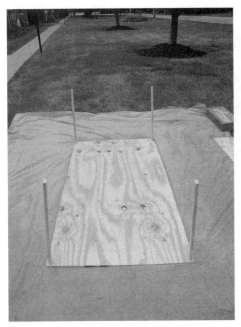

Fig. 10.3. Casket bottom with corner posts.

Fig. 10.4. Casket with two sides.

Fig. 10.5. Casket with four sides.

Fig. 10.6. Casket completed.

Collect the Items You Will Bring

Only you can decide what is completely essential to take with you on your quest. This will largely depend on your level of comfort and familiarity with being outdoors for three days and two nights. If you are new to spending time outdoors, it is a good idea to make a few trial runs at sleeping out overnight in a wooded area that is not far from civilization in order to gain confidence and increase your skills. The trick behind the whole concept of bringing gear into this type of minimalistic rite is to find the balance between what you truly need to bring and what is important to you personally (like a talisman or some other comforting or powerful object) but not necessary. For example, by my third quest I felt confident enough to lay myself as bare as I could, so I didn't bring anything except the clothes I was wearing, water, and one blanket for three nights in the mountains of Colorado in October. Needless to say, I was extremely cold at night because I didn't even allow myself the company of a fire, but my profound connection to the rising sun in the morning would never have reached the same intensity if I hadn't been so cold. More recently I haven't felt the need to be quite as extreme, and now I always have the fire for many reasons, including warmth (more on that soon). Here are some typical items to think about bringing; you really shouldn't need more. Remember, the less the better:

Materials

Notebook and pen or pencil, for taking notes
Clothes and shoes appropriate for the season and for working outdoors
Extra change of clothes and shoes just in case
Raingear (in case of wet weather)
Sunscreen if you use it
Hat for sun protection
Bottled water for three days
Work gloves
Materials for starting a fire
Sleeping mat or camping pad or extra blanket to lie on during the
    night
Sleeping bag or blanket for warmth

Pillow (optional)

Small first-aid kit

Offerings and personal items (such as photos or sacred objects); make sure to bring a needle for the blood offering on your first day

Prepare for Fasting

This stage includes two to three days of fasting (water is permissible). If you are not accustomed to fasting, you will probably find this a difficult experience not only because of the physiological responses of your body but also because of the disconnection to the regimented psychological schedule that regular feeding times provide. Hopefully you are already familiar with fasting from the counterpractice section. If not, it is wise to familiarize yourself before the quest by intentionally skipping meals for a few weeks and by eating light foods, such vegetables, fruits, rice, and fish, and skipping heavier foods, such as beef, nuts, dairy products, and oily or fried foods. It is also good to engage in rigorous physical activity outdoors and to simply pay attention to your physical and emotional needs and avoid intoxication from alcohol or drugs.

Get Yourself and Your Casket to the Questing Spot

Depending on where you will be, you will have to decide the most expedient way of getting your casket to your questing area. If possible, I suggest getting it there and setting it up before your quest so you won't have to deal with it the day of. But it's totally fine if you just bring it with you when you leave.

If you can use a vehicle to transport it to the site already assembled, go for it! If not, have a friend help carry the assembled casket, or carry the pieces with you and assemble it at the quest site. If your casket is ready to assemble, you can build it in no time. I have done this many times. If you haven't already prepared a place for your casket, this is the obvious time to do that.

Collect Firewood

You'll only need enough wood for a small Sacred Fire the night you arrive and the following night for an hour or two.

EXPERIENCES DURING VISION QUESTING

On personal and transpersonal levels (among other situations) during your quest you will likely go through the following stages.

Depart from Your Everyday Life

The first stage of the vision quest is the departure. In this stage you remove yourself from your everyday life and leave behind your family, friends, job, and responsibilities both at the physical and psychological level. When you depart on the vision quest journey, you will never come back to the same place from where you left. In this sense, with your very first step you leave your old self behind and begin walking into your new state of being. You depart from your ordinary life and cross the border into the unknown.

Sometimes it is helpful to associate this crossing with the symbolism of a doorway, threshold, gate, or passageway. There is a crack between the worlds into which you humbly pass through. There is no magical formula for making this entrance; it is purely a matter of consciousness. Just as you can't force yourself to go to sleep, but rather sleep takes you and shifts your state of consciousness, so it is when you depart on a vision quest. It is like moving through the paradox of a "gateless gate."

When you have gone into this crack between the worlds of consciousness and through the gateless gate, you arrive in a new land. This is the actual experience of the vision quest as you arrive at a chosen place in the wilderness where you will remain and fast for at least two nights and three days. In this natural setting many things will happen to you. It is vitally important to enter into a respectful relationship with the place from the very first moment you arrive. More on this soon.

During the vision quest nobody will be there to give you opinions or impose their influence on you. Your counselor is the wind, your support is the earth, your nourishment is the sun, and your only companions are the wild animals. In this sense you will transform yourself into one of your ancient ancestors who lived in a wild and untamed world free of cell phone towers, twenty-four-hour television, and high-speed Internet.

Feel Hungry

As I noted earlier during counterpractice, there is a strength and clarity that comes with an empty stomach, and feeling hungry for a short period, like a couple of days, is actually very good for us for reasons I have already discussed. New studies have also found added health benefits to fasting. Scientists are now discovering that there are physical benefits to be attained through the struggles of hunger and thirst.

> Reduced meal frequency primes the body to lose fat, while studies have shown a reduction in fluid intake for 30 days has no negative effect on people's health. Further studies have found that subjects undergoing Ramadan-specific fasting demonstrate lowered levels of LDL cholesterol and anxiety—two risk factors in the development of cardiovascular diseases.
>
> A widely-circulated research finding pointed out that fasting for as little as three days could have wondrous affects [sic] on the immune system. The researchers who undertook the study found that the fasting allowed stem cells to start pumping out brand new white blood cells, to reinforce and strengthen the immune system.[1]

Question Why You Are Doing This

It is common to initially experience periods of intense questioning as to your motives for being alone in the wilderness, fear that maybe you are simply going nuts. "What the hell am I doing here? Am I insane? What the heck was I thinking?" are all common questions that myself and probably everyone who has done this has asked themselves.

Experience Moments of Depression or Self-Pity

Denial of the reasons you are doing it, depression, or feelings of intense self-pity are completely normal and is just one of the stages that a person of the modern world must pass through to become one again with the land and the cosmos. Let those feelings out! Until you are emptied and freed from these heavy and constricting thoughts and emotions, you won't be able to soar. One of the key reasons this quest places you completely alone and fasting in the wilderness is to bring these feelings out and lay them bare before the spirits of nature and in the face of your death.

Remember Repressed Moments of Your Life

Fasting alone and spending the night in your casket is fertile ground for the flooding of memories and emotions. Don't be surprised if you experience memories you have buried. I have had many memories come to me that were blocked or repressed, especially those about my father's death. I have remembered specific events in my life that my dad and I shared before he passed, plus other severe emotional crises from my life.

Experience Insights or Visions

Be open to experiencing unexpected insights. Typically, the rational mind expects to experience some huge happening, such seeing or talking to some sort of wise old spirit. But it has been my experience that, contrary to what your ego may expect to receive, it is more common to experience many unexpected insights or visions from completely unforeseen sources.

For example, on my very first vision quest, I spent most of the first two days dealing with swarms of flies and mosquitoes. At the time it seemed like my vision quest had been reduced to me having placed myself in a position of being tortured by these aggressively savage little beasts, and I was more than a little perturbed at both the insects and myself for being there. But what eventually happened made the whole ordeal worthwhile. The flies and mosquitoes gave me exactly what I needed in that moment: they pushed my patience and my will to the absolute breaking point. Their bombardment of me was so intense that I freaked out not once but so many times that I became physically and mentally exhausted. The resulting shift in consciousness forced me to view the world in a way I had never experienced before. Seeing the world with new eyes is one of the most valuable benefits of the vision quest, and on that day, I went from seeing those irritating insects as nothing more than swarms of troublesome and annoying pests to acknowledging them as divine messengers of the nature spirits. When I finally saw what was truly going on and stopped both my internal struggle and my outward battle with the insects and just sat there with a feeling of peace and resignation, the insects ceased to be a distraction, and eventually a strong wind blew up and they were gone within an hour.

My vision was gratefully earned, and I was magically transformed from a person easily irritated by trivialities into someone who peacefully receives and acknowledges the gifts of life, which was a completely foreign state of mind to me at that time in my life. The insects delivered this vision and transformation in the most effective way possible. In this sense I was visited by the nature spirits, just not in any form that my mind would have anticipated. The outcome of my ordeal with the flies and mosquitoes was that it affected me deeply enough that I was subsequently able to physically and psychically apply the lesson I learned to my everyday life and dealings with people, both on an intentional and on a subconscious level. After my first vision quest many people who knew me well commented on how I was able to handle stressful or potentially annoying situations with much more ease and a kind of peaceful serenity. And not only did that experience affect my everyday life, it also raised my level of experience of other facets of my spiritual life.

Communicate Verbally and Nonverbally with Everything around You

On my next vision quest it became quite clear after just a few moments in my spot, which was on the other side of the country in completely different terrain than the first time, that my spirit helpers this time would be spiders. During those three days I met hundreds of spiders of many different species, and because of my previous experience with the flies and mosquitoes, this time I was able right from the start to make peace with the spiders and just let them walk right over me, under me, on top of me, and even inside my clothes and blanket. Through the powerful agents of fasting and solitude, coupled with my peaceful attitude of openness and willingness to receive without preconceived judgments, I was able to have remarkable and enlightening conversations with many different and insightful spiders. The spirits of that place had chosen to speak to me through these incredibly interesting and unique creatures. And even though I thought I was as open as possible to receiving whatever came, I have to admit that at one point, after realizing that the sheer number of spiders that were coming to me could not be mere coincidence, I felt a peculiar kind of awe that was almost frightening in knowing that I was truly at the mercy of the nature spirits of those woods and that they were really talking to me in a way I could actually understand.

With this type of experience comes a certain level of responsibility. When you are fortunate enough to receive messages, insights, or visions from the spirits of the natural world, you cannot ignore them, even if what they are telling you isn't what you want to hear or the requests they make of you seem too difficult to accomplish. In a nutshell, if you are not prepared to accept and act on the vision that the spirits of nature may have in store for you, you may want to reconsider entering into this rite of passage. Another significant consideration in undertaking this rite of passage is that the nature spirits will be asking something, or many things, of you. This is a vitally important aspect of connecting in a primal encounter with the nature spirits that rule and animate the world. You better listen to everything they are saying, not just those things you want or need to hear because they almost always ask something of you in return for their knowledge. This means that when you return from the threshold of the vision quest and step squarely back into your everyday life, you will have to accomplish the tasks given to you, no matter how difficult they may be, because if you don't, you might lose your chance for learning what they are trying to teach you.

Experience a Keen Awareness of Death

Obviously, constructing a casket and spending two nights in it will stimulate an awareness or recognition of your death. This awareness can be used in a non-morbid way to give renewed energy, urgency, and strength to your actions. Although you are not placed in any physical danger while in the casket, the implications of being in your casket will help you to not put off the things in your life that would be better done today. This is about as close as you can get to the awareness of death without placing yourself in mortal danger or having a physical near-death experience.

Experience a Rebirth or Transformation

If you follow the instructions of this quest, there is absolutely no way you will not come out of it changed. Because of the extreme circumstances you have placed yourself in, this quest can in many ways be viewed as a rebirth experience. In his book *The Unfolding Self*, Ralph Metzner, Ph.D., an expert on transformative experience, gets right to the point with respect to the implications of a death-rebirth initiation:

> Whereas in some Christian fundamentalist circles it is customary for people who have made a commitment to Christ to refer to themselves as "twice born," the original meaning of that concept goes much deeper than simply a profession of renewed faith, however sincere. It refers, actually, to the second part of a death-rebirth transformational process. The rebirth experience, to be authentic, must of necessity be preceded by an experience of metaphorically dying. This first, dying phase is inevitably anxiety provoking and problematical for most people. . . . In the mystery religions of ancient times and in many traditional cultures, "death-rebirth" was and is the name of an initiatory experience. Associated with it are the ritual practices such as entombment, profound isolation, or painful ordeal through which the initiate must pass. Afterward, the initiate customarily adopts a new name, perhaps a new garment, and sometimes a new role in society, all of which express the newly reborn being.[2]

On a personal note, when I came back from an actual near-death experience in the peyote desert, the lead shaman of the quest sat me down upon our return to the village and formally bestowed on me a new name, based on what he saw when I was dying and then resurrected: Ulu Temay, meaning "new ray or arrow of the sun."

THE QUEST

In reality, your quest began on the day you decided to do it. Your preparations before you leave home and reintegrating into your life once you return are all significant parts of the quest. In a typical vision quest experience, once you arrive at your questing site, there is really nothing that needs to get done. That's pretty much the point—physically and mentally doing absolutely nothing, including eating, for three to five days. The immediate and familiar supports of family, friends, colleagues, pets, accomplishments, and failures and all the trappings and freedoms of everyday life are severed. However, this quest is slightly different because of the added element of the casket, so I'm going to provide instructions and suggestions on what to do.

The First Day

Whether you brought your casket already built to your site or you just set it up, let's proceed with you and your casket ready to go at your site. It's best to arrive in the morning so you have a full two and a half days at your site. First, it is vitally important to enter into a respectful relationship with the place of your quest from the very first moments you arrive. The first thing you must do is explain to the land what you are doing and make a gesture of offering to the place. The most powerful way to do this is with your own blood. This can be simply done by making a small hole (where you will have your Sacred Fire) in the ground with your bare hands while talking to the land about what you are doing there. Then prick your finger with a needle and while placing a few drops in the hole, tell the sacred place that your blood is your offering and that the union of your blood with the soil symbolizes your desire and intention of becoming one with the land and the beings and spirits that inhabit it. Watch as the earth absorbs your blood, and then cover the hole. Then, if you haven't already, collect some firewood for a small fire.

With that done, this phase of your quest begins. There are simply no required activities during the day; in fact, quite the contrary, the lack of activity produces reflection and submersion in the action that is unfolding around you, and the deeper you can dive into that reality and out of your purely selfish concerns, the more profound will be your resulting experience. Beginner and novice questers are encouraged not to engage in comforting activities done simply to keep busy, such as reading, playing musical instruments, making crafts, or any other type of intentional distraction. Other than gathering firewood in an area very close to your spot during the day, the only other activities I encourage would be those that connect you directly to the land and that happen spontaneously. These could include face or body painting using materials from the land, tree climbing (just high enough to be off the ground), exposing your naked body to the wind, and talking to and listening to the nighttime fire. Simply relax and tune into your place. And do not go farther than ten yards from your casket.

The First Night

Around ten hours before dawn (you should have determined sunrise during your preparation), light your Sacred Fire (see page 94). After speaking with Grandfather Fire, it's time to get ready to go into your casket. Depending on the time of year, you may spend some time after dark in your questing area without entering your casket. As stated in the preparation, we are aiming at approximately eight to nine hours in the casket and arising at dawn.

A powerful activity before entering the casket is the writing of a short note that will act as your final words of connection to this life. The note is written just as if you knew you were going to die and never see your loved ones again. The note should include anything you want them (or the rest of the world) to read after you are gone. This note is placed under your rock in the fire circle before you put the fire out. Make sure the fire is out!

Once you enter the casket and close the lid, the material world is left behind. A threshold to the alchemic-shamanic is crossed, and a new phase of your quest begins. As you lie down in the casket, the casket becomes a sacred chamber consecrated by the concrete actions of wanting to know both self and world in new and improved ways. By lying in your casket you have formally offered your heart, mind, and spirit to the numinous aspects of the cosmos. The preparations over, now it is just you and the quest you are about to take inside and out. You are not trapped, and you will not die this night. With the closing of the casket the journey begins, a journey unique to each person, as the settling-in process continues and the fears, anxieties, hopes, and dreams begin to increase and dissipate.

Experiences in the casket are as different as the individuals, the lessons as profound as the mysteries of life. At this stage of the quest it is common to pass through a period of questioning or even rage or feelings of depression. In many cases but certainly not all, this phase is conducive to experiencing later in the night profound insights or visions. This period of doubt is another threshold to cross once one is actually inside the casket, and once it is crossed a new hallway opens up in front of you with many more rooms to explore. For some, the experience of initially lying in the casket is one of peace and comfort and feelings of depression or anxiety don't come until later in the night or not until the second night and sometimes never happen. No one can say what your experience will be like.

Once one passes through these initial phases of being in the casket, sleep sometimes comes as the person becomes more comfortable with the surroundings and with him- or herself. From this point the quester passes through different levels, from fully awake to fully asleep back to fully awake. In my experience this is usually the most productive way to spend the night during this ritual because you get to experience many different levels and states of consciousness. Although sleeping through the night in the casket (which I have done) has its own benefits, especially with regards to dreaming, shifting between being awake and asleep, and all the levels in between, has proven to be the most useful format for first-time questers.

There is an unlimited number of experiences that can occur when in the casket. It is always amazing to me how being isolated and enclosed so often leads to out-of-body or even flying experiences. During the time in your casket, it is quite common to feel like you're out of your body, looking down on your casket and questing grounds. Sometimes this leads to a feeling or perception of transition between one level of consciousness and another. Initiates also often describe moving through or down a tunnel that leads to a transition that fosters feelings of serenity, peace, unity, love, or even ecstasy.

Some people even describe seeing or visiting with dead relatives or friends. Once in a half-sleep, half-awake state in the casket, I had a significant vision and conversation with my father, who had passed when I was fifteen. During that conversation I was fourteen, and he was still alive and healthy. Other people report receiving complex yet meaningful visions about life and our connection to the living Earth—as if their casket was actually buried in the ground. (Spending the night buried in the ground is a quest I have done and also lead for clients, although it is even more work to prepare. I describe this process in my book *Advanced Shamanism*.)

Feelings or visions of disintegrating are fairly common, especially on the second night, as is the life review. This phenomenon is in many ways similar to a near-death experience, in which during the course of only a few seconds your life flashes before your eyes like a movie run at super-high speed. This type of life review spurred by a near-death experience often results in an awakening within the person that marks a major turning point in life, with subsequent changes in lifestyle and a deepening of relationships at a personal level.

Having personally passed through four separate near-death experiences (two as a result of automobile accidents, one from a rock-climbing incident, and one at the hands of the Huichol peyote) and also having had such experiences while in the casket and buried in the earth, I can say that, at least for me, there are similarities between the two experiences but also some significant differences. The near-death experience life review is superfast, even though it may seem much longer while you are living it. Although each of my four life-review experiences brought on by near-death experiences were unique in feeling, in many ways they all felt like a sort of purging of my conscious life experiences before my consciousness could move to another realm or be obliterated. In each case the awareness that the end of what I call "me" was about to happen was undeniably real, and the resulting effects (since I, of course, didn't die) were powerful to the point that in each case I came from the experience a changed person with renewed motivations and inspiration. In contrast, questers who have a life-review experience in the casket usually compare it more to what it would be like in the last few days or hours of a terminally ill person. In this case the person approaches death gradually and has the chance (if she takes it) to review her life more slowly, to make amends with people, resolve inner conflicts, and so on. In fact, sometimes afterward, questers complain that during a life-review experience they got "stuck" when reviewing a life situation they never fully dealt with, sometimes in a very uncomfortable spot. This is something I've never heard of during the life-review in a near-death experience. Also, it is often reported during the life review in this quest that life experiences that were apparently forgotten by the initiate were suddenly resurrected, and in most cases the forgotten moments were very poignant to the future growth of the person.

Emerging after the First Night

For this quest it is not imperative that you emerge from your casket at dawn on your first night; however, don't stay too much longer after the sun comes up and *definitely* come out at dawn on your second night. Hard as it is to believe, many people don't want to come out at sunrise. After spending the whole night in the casket, it has become a comfortable and safe space. When leading groups on the quest, sometimes I have to practically force some of the questers to emerge! When you do emerge, greet the world by standing up with your arms and fingers outstretched to the sky, and pronounce, "Here I am for the first time!" or something similar.

At this point you are now in the world of nature again and on a fasting quest similar to ones that indigenous people have undertaken for millennia. Spend your day in the company of nature and see what, if anything, happens.

The Second Night

When the time comes, approximately ten hours before dawn, light the Sacred Fire again, speak with Grandfather, and write another note. This time the note is not for anyone else; it is just for you. Write down (and remember what you write) things that you want to do related to what you said to people in your life in your first note. Also write down other things you want to accomplish before you die—yup, the informal term *bucket list* applies here. Like before, place your list under a rock in the fire circle before you put the fire out, and make sure the fire is out.

As before, no one can know what will happen in your casket once you are in. The only difference is this time you already know how it feels. Having anxiety about spending another night in the casket could be a blessing in disguise in terms of your quest. Feelings of comfort—the same thing. Encountering the mystery and unknown are the known knowns.

Since the second night cannot possibly be the same as the first, emerge at dawn with "Here I am for the first time!" or something similar. It's good at this point to spend a little more time in your questing area, and at some point before packing up to leave, light a small Sacred Fire and give your notes to Grandfather Fire. Watch as the numinous Fire ignites them and carries their energy into the air and up to the stars.

As much as possible, make sure to leave your questing area as you found it and thank the spirits of the place.

Return, Slowly

Returning home you will probably feel glad but also somewhat alienated. You had left home to go find something, and now that you are back, you are not the same. While you and your home were once one and the same, now you are different, and so you begin walking in two different worlds. The first world is the sacred time of the quest that you just passed through, your magic time that only you know about. But the second world of "civilized" people and schedules is calling you back, and you must go. That is the way it is—you go to the quest to submerge in the first world and be born anew into the second. Now your job begins as you walk back into the second world and try to balance it with the first. In the best-case scenario, give yourself a few days of transition between your quest and the urban jungle by staying somewhere halfway in between so that you can reflect on and digest your experience.

Upon returning to your everyday life, it is good to avoid going right back into the frantic pace of modern society and to avoid as much as possible the manipulative psychological warfare of media and especially violent movies and TV. Also, it is a good idea to intentionally avoid any situations that might make you susceptible to manipulative people because your guard will be down; your consciousness will be altered in a way that you might not recognize potentially harmful deceptions.

In the following days, months, or years, there are a couple suggestions to keep in mind so so that you don't lose what you have gained on your quest. One is to periodically spend the night in your casket. After the first few times I completed a quest, I would spend a night or two in my casket every once in a while, whenever I felt like it. I also ended up building a more "fancy" casket out of locally sourced locust boards. It is quite heavy compared to my first plywood casket, but I can easily take it apart to take on quests. Periodically reconnecting with Grandfather Fire (even with a simple candle) and remembering your quest, or even visiting your questing site (you need not go alone when not questing) are also effective ways to keep the quest alive inside of you.

11

STAGE SIX
DISTILLATION

Fig. 11.1.
Stage six.

T he sixth ray is marked with the symbol for the metal and planet Mercury
and points to the bladder of floating, symbol of air and the process of
spiritualization. In the sixth circle of operation is a unicorn lying on the
ground in front of a rose bush. The word *occultum*, meaning "secret" or
"hidden," inspires the adept to perform the necessary self-distillation process and thus reveal the secret knowledge. The pure white unicorn represents the purity obtained from the distillation process and also, according
to legend, it only lies down in the presence of a virgin. In this case, the
adept, through passing through the various previous stages, is the virgin
ready to peer into the eye of God through distillation.

In the alchemic laboratory, we created and then employed distillation
to tangibly experience on a physical level the qualities of purification and
the combining of various operations to create a potent alchemic elixir. In
terms of shamanism, distillation purifies us to the extent that doors to

Fig. 11.2. *Ut Salamandra vivit igne sic lapis* [Like the Salamander
the stone lives in the fire] (engraving by Matthäus Merian,
from *Atalanta fugiens* by Michael Maier, 1617).

realms of consciousness not ordinarily available to us open and invite us in. I know you are ready.

Intentional sweating (in alchemical terms—distillation) in a specially designed and heated hut or chamber is practiced throughout the globe, and its origins date back many thousands of years. Different forms exist including the Finnish sauna, the Russian *banya*, the Turkish *hamman*, the American Indian sweat lodge, and the Maya-Aztec *temazcal*. In shamanic cultures the sweat lodge is not only for cleansing the body by removing toxins through sweating, it is a sacred practice of inner spiritual and psychic purification.

I have experienced dozens of sweat lodges and *temazcals*. The former is a round structure formed with bent willow branches that is then covered to make an airtight chamber, and the latter is usually made of adobe bricks in a round or rectangular shape with a thatched roof. In both cases a hot fire is made outside the structure, lava rocks are placed into the fire and heated, and then the hot rocks are ceremonially brought into the dark chamber to heat the space hot enough for the people inside to sweat profusely.

Benefits of Sweating

Before getting into the shamanic-alchemic motives for distillation via sweating and the various apparatus employed, let's look at some physical realities relating to intentional sweating. You are probably well aware of the two most common methods for intentional sweating: the sauna and the steam room. Saunas provide dry heat. Although some steam can be generated in a sauna (they usually have hot rocks that water can be poured on intermittently), overall the humidity level in a sauna is considered low (ranging from 5 to 30 percent), and saunas tend to be much warmer than a steam room, ranging from 160 to 200 degrees Fahrenheit. Steam rooms create moist heat with humidity at 100 percent and temperatures typically ranging from 110 to 115 degrees Fahrenheit. For ease in explanation, I'm going to use the generic term *steam bath* in this section simply because, later in this chapter on distilling yourself, the apparatuses I suggest using all include steam, and although they can get very warm, they typically don't get as hot as a sauna. Here are some of the reasons why humans have chosen to bathe in a hot and steamy room.

Relieves Stress. Steam bathing provides stress relief in a number of ways. It's a warm, quiet space without any distractions coming from the outside. Medical studies often determine that stress in our daily lives can negatively affect our health. In fact, the vast majority of disease (e.g., heart disease) is at least partially stress related. The heat from the sauna relaxes muscles and soothes aches and pains in both muscles and joints. The heat also causes the body to release endorphins; these have a mild tranquilizing effect and can minimize the pain of arthritis and muscle soreness from a hard day's work or physical exercise. Endorphins are the body's all-natural "feel good" chemical, and their release provides a truly wonderful after-sauna glow.

Body temperature rises from the heat and causes blood vessels to dilate, thereby increasing blood circulation. This increased blood flow speeds up the body's natural healing process via soothing aches and pains and/or speeding up the healing of minor bruises or cuts.

Flushes Toxins. For those of us who don't actively sweat on a regular basis, the steam bath is a perfect way to do so. As our body temperature rises, blood begins to move toward the skin's surface; the body's nervous system then sends signals to the millions of sweat glands that cover the body to produce sweat. Sweat is produced to cool the body and is mostly water; however, sweating can detoxify the body by releasing and reducing levels of lead, copper, zinc, nickel, mercury, and other chemicals our bodies accumulate from the environment.

Cleanses Skin. Steam bathing is an age-old beauty and health method for cleansing the skin. When the body begins to produce sweat via deep sweating, the skin is then cleansed and dead skin cells are replaced, keeping your skin in good working condition. Sweating via steam bathing rinses bacteria out of the epidermal layer and sweat ducts. Cleansing of the pores has been shown to improve capillary circulation, while giving the skin a softer, healthier appearance.

Improves Cardiovascular Performance. Our heart rate increases while in a steam bath and can sink to below normal during the cool-down stage. Repeated sessions in the steam bath separated by a cool shower or a quick dip into a cool pool or lake can condition the cardiovascular system. Each time you rapidly change temperature (from hot to cool and vice versa), your heart rate increases by as much as 60 percent, which is comparable to the increase experienced during moderate exercise. People in Russia and Scandinavia have been taking "polar bear plunges" for centuries: a steam bath is placed on a frozen body of water, and the participants, after getting all heated up, jump into the freezing water through a hole in the ice. This sequence is repeated several times.

Clears Congestion. Steam baths create an environment that warms the mucous membranes and encourages deep breathing. As a result, a steam bath can help break up congestion inside your sinuses and lungs.

Temazcal or Temazcalli

The temazcal, a traditional Mexican sweat bath, which I have had the pleasure of experiencing many times, is one of my favorite types of steam baths. Some temazcals are constructed very rustically, and others are quite fancy. According to Dr. Horacio Rojas Alba, of the Instituto Mexicano de Medicinas Tradicionales,

> the traditional Mexican sweat bath differs in several ways from other types. It is not primarily used for ceremonial purposes, as is the sweat lodge of our Indians, nor for relaxation or bodily cleansing or for general well-being, as are most of the other sweat baths. It is and was, as far back as we can trace it, a therapeutic instrument, an arm of the medical practices developed in what anthropologists like to call, Mesoamerica, that vast area that now includes Mexico, Guatemala and Belize. We know it best, in its ancient forms, through the Aztecs, and Temazcal, as it is still called in contemporary Mexico, is a Nahuatl word, taken from their language.[1]

The temazcal is oriented according to the cosmic directions. The fire that heats the stones is placed toward the east where Father Sun arises. He is the light or masculine element that comes and fertilizes the womb of Mother Earth, which the chamber of the temazcal represents, and so life is conceived. The doorway through which the bathers enter and leave is oriented toward the south, or pathway of the dead, which begins with birth and ends in death.

When we enter the temazcal, according to ancient doctrine, we return once again to our mother's womb. The entrance way is low and small, and through it we enter a small, dark, warm, and humid space, in this way re-creating the uterus. We cut off the outside world and give ourselves a chance to look inside and find ourselves again. Our reemergence through this narrow opening represents our rebirth from the darkness and silence of the womb.

Fig. 11.3. Temazcal sketch (from a photo by the author,
Michoacán, Mexico, 2000).

In the previously mentioned countries, the temazcal is a powerful therapy in the treatment of many illnesses and complaints, both acute and chronic. Surprisingly, one of the most common uses of the temazcal is for women's conditions related to menstruation, pregnancy, childbirth, and the traditional forty-day quarantine following birth. It is also used to promote the flow of milk. While bathing in the temazcal is generally not recommended during menstruation itself, its regular use is helpful for treating premenstrual syndrome, irregular periods, pain and depression accompanying periods, and ovarian cysts, as well as infertility. I have shared the temazcal with women who later had what are referred to as temazcal babies. Most of these women took temazcal baths for other reasons but later confided that they had been trying to get pregnant for some time without success, and the temazcal had cured them of their difficulties.

Most temazcals are circular in shape, similar to the bread ovens still seen in rural villages, with a domed roof symbolizing the heavens. Occasionally, they are rectangular or square. They are usually small permanent structures made of adobe bricks or stone. The temazcals I have visited in ancient sacred sites such as Xochicalco, Piedras Negras, and Palenque are luxurious buildings of stone plastered with stucco and even decorated inside. A family temazcal is generally a small structure.

The traditional way to measure the dimensions for construction are to hold a string to the center of your chest (where the heart is) with one hand and hold the other hand out to your side with arm outstretched. This will give the radius of a round temazcal, or half the length of a rectangular one. I have only been in a couple of this size; usually the ones I have experienced were about the same size as a native American sweat lodge. Temporary temazcals are constructed almost exactly like a sweat lodge (which I will explain next).

Just as for a sweat lodge, it's very important to select the right stones for heating. The stones are heated until they are red hot and then are doused with water, so they must be able to withstand drastic changes in temperature without cracking or exploding. Volcanic rock is most common, but river stones should always be avoided as they will explode!

Unlike the traditional Native American sweat lodge, which uses clear water to make the steam, commonly for the temazcal a tea is prepared to make the steam. Herbs that may be used for this purpose include eucalyptus, rosemary, mugwort, or other warming or stimulating herbs such as *pericon* (Mexican tarragon). In addition, herbal branches are used inside the temazcal for directing the heat and for infusing participants; again, these branches are not commonly part of a Native American lodge. The choice of plant depends on the season and region, but eucalyptus, mullein, or the leaf of the castor bean plant are some examples of plants that are used.

My first temazcal was a very relaxing experience at a tourist resort; however, my second one was deep in the Nahuatl Sierra and was a much different experience. Leading the temazcal was a famous *curandara* and *temazcalera* (both words mean "female healer") named Xilonen (which means "goddess of the baby corn"). She was very intense and decisive in her movements and rarely spoke; but when she did, you listened. For her temazcal all the participants disrobed; they were then rubbed down with aloe and "scanned" for illnesses or injuries. After that things were pretty much the same as my previous temazcal: we crawled inside the lodge, red hot rocks were placed in the pit, and steam was made with a tea. To ensure that the temperature and humidity remained optimal, she began fanning, quite eloquently, above and all around us, while occasionally placing small amounts of tea water on the rocks.

Then one by one she came and fanned those parts of our bodies or energy field she felt or saw needed care. She seemed to be very skilled at this, and I felt enormous gratitude for being there. But then when she came over to me again, she began hitting me with the herb branches! It wasn't hard or painful, just completely surprising. Then she poured cold water over my head—another surprise as I couldn't imagine where she got the cold water. Later, after we came out, I had a chance to speak with her briefly, and she told me—very good-heartedly—that there was a woman attaching herself to me who was no good for me and she had swatted her away. I found out from my Nahuatl informants that she may or may not have been kidding about the woman; they couldn't know for sure. But they said she used the herbs all the time to hit people to infuse energy into weak or ill areas. I have been to numerous temazcals since then, and it is very common for the temazcalera (woman) or temazcalero (man) to swat participants with their herb bundles.

Russian Banya

Bathing in a banya, a Russian steam bath, is one of the oldest Russian traditions and is still extremely popular today. The word *banya* is used for both public steam baths that can hold many people or for private family steam baths, generally found at a family's summer cottage or second home. These steam baths can be a single modest-sized room or an entire building for public use in cities. All the banyas I have seen, no matter what the size, have benches built at various heights inside; the higher you sit, the hotter it gets. When you get hot enough for a break, there is always cold water from a shower, pool, or hose to cool off with, or some people go out and roll in the snow before returning to the banya. Usually, this process is repeated several times.

Probably not coincidently, the Russian banya also has a custom of smacking. This is done with small brooms called *veniks* made with the branches and leaves of local trees. The veniks are dipped in cold water and then smacked briskly all over the body. A special person called a *banschik* is responsible for the smacking. But usually people don't need a banschik's help because groups of friends typically go together and smack each other with the veniks.

Which leads me to the last point. My experiences in the banya steam baths are that they are very social in nature. In Russia the atmosphere of the banya brings people closer together and allows them to communicate and interact on a more common level. They even have a special room called a *predbannik* that is used for drinking tea and socializing during breaks from the steam bath.

Finnish Sauna

The Finnish sauna is a place to physically and mentally relax and also for hanging out with friends, much like the Russian banya, so I won't get into it here. However, it is worth noting that the Finns are crazy for their saunas and consider them not a luxury but a necessity. Here is a most revealing statistic about Finns and their saunas from a BBC news article: "Finland is a nation of 5.3 million people and 3.3 million saunas, found in homes, offices, factories, sports centres, hotels, ships and deep below the ground in mines."[2]

Native American Sweat Lodge

First, I'll just say that I don't condone people leading (copying) Native American ceremonies (including sweat lodge procedures unique to a specific tribe) that are not Native American. I actually stand with my brothers and sisters of indigenous descent that find the term *Native American* disrespectful and prefer to be called by the name of their tribe. You will notice that in all my books you rarely find the terms *Native American* or *American Indian;* I use tribal names when referring to my indigenous mentors and friends. This is a complicated subject not necessary to discuss further here—I think you get where I stand.

Second, in regard to sweat bathing, anyone is free to do it however they please. The basic structure of what is termed a Native American sweat lodge is an expedient way of fairly quickly setting up a nonpermanent sweat bath and has been used in many cultures throughout the world. I have no problem with people using designs similar to the Native American sweat lodge as long as they don't copy or steal the ceremonies of specific tribes that go with it. The portable version of the temazcal of Mexico and Belize, which I explained earlier, is pretty much exactly the same as a Lakota sweat lodge, but you don't see a temazcalero or temazcalera using Lakota ceremonies in their sweat baths! I have been fortunate throughout many years to be invited to sweat lodges of my indigenous friends and have even had them help me build my own sweat bath in a similar design simply because they knew I wasn't going to steal their ceremonies. I just wanted to sweat in a special and private place and gain the physical, mental, and spiritual benefits. It all boils down to common sense, which seems to be lacking when it comes to sweat lodges.

For example, when I lived for many years in Sedona, Arizona, my home was only a few miles from Angel Valley Retreat Center where New Age self-help "guru" James Arthur Ray (a white guy) held what he called a Native American sweat lodge that killed three people and hospitalized eighteen others in 2009. I saw all the ambulances and helicopters responding that day. My local friends of the Yavapai and Havasupai tribes were furious when they heard about it. On the rare occasions that the elders of these tribes invite nontribal members to a sweat lodge, they keep an especially keen eye on the guests and would never tell someone to stay in the lodge if they needed to get out, which is what Ray did. In 2011 Ray was finally found guilty on three counts of negligent homicide and sentenced to two years in prison, a penalty most people, especially the relatives of the deceased, found unfathomably lenient.

For these reasons and many more, when I construct a sweat bath, no matter what the design, I call it just that; *sweat bath* is a nondenominational term that carries no cultural significance. That being said, if you have access to a private sauna, steam room, temazcal, or other type of steam bath, then you can save yourself some work by using it for this stage, if that feels appropriate. For the rest of us, I provide some suggestions for creating a sweat bath.

Praxis 17

Shamanic Alchemy Distillation Bath

This alchemic sweat bath for the distillation of the human organism and psyche only needs to be large enough to accommodate one person—you.

Fig. 11.4. Willow (with side branches still on), loppers, twine, scissors, tape measure (tarp not shown).

It can be made fairly quickly and easily in a few different ways. The bath I'm going to describe is fabricated from willow saplings, twine, and a large tarp.

Here is the complete list of materials:

Materials

Willow branches for the poles, about 11 pieces, 5 to 8 feet long

Loppers or pruners, for cutting the willow

Twine, cloth, or willow bark, for fastening the poles together

Scissors or knife, for cutting the twine

Tarps, rugs, or blankets, for covering the frame

Tape measure (optional)

Rocks or wood, for holding the sides down

Several volcanic stones, larger than your fist, smaller than a shoebox

Firewood, enough for a fire lasting three to four hours

Shovel, for digging pits for the fire and hot stones

Cup or ladle, for putting water on the hot stones to make steam

Water source, hose, and 5-gallon bucket filled with water

1. Depending on where you construct your sweat bath, you may have to dig small holes for inserting the ends of the poles to brace them while you bend and them. The structure is freestanding, and if you have someone helping you, it isn't necessary to do this. But if not, it can be difficult to hold the poles up as you bend them and tie them together. Another option is to use a piece of firewood or a stone to hold one end in place as you tie. For the sweat bath in figures 11.5–11.8, you can see that I built it in the snow; by pushing the ends of the poles into the snow, I only had to use a brace for one corner.

2. Sometimes I build a sweat bath near a river. The river provides a close, convenient source of water, and the riverbed has lots of rocks for weighting the pole ends (but don't use the river stones for the fire!). Many times willow will be abundant as this tree loves water.

3. The sweat bath I made is approximately five feet high, five feet wide, and six feet deep. It is roomy enough for one person (you could have two people in it but not for this stage of your alchemy!) but small enough to heat up quickly and, without much work, keep hot. See the completed sweat bath in figures 11.7 and 11.8—and yes, I built this alone.

4. Begin by taking any side branches off a nice piece of willow five to eight feet long. Saplings are perfect for the frame as they are strong but bend easily without breaking. Do the same for another piece. Since this sweat bath is small, the second piece doesn't have to be quite as long. Secure the ends of the poles on the ground, and bend your two pieces together so the arch is about five feet high and the bottoms are five feet apart. Tie the bent portions of the poles together in as many places as needed to hold them together. This will be the entrance. Do this again three feet from the entrance (middle poles) and again for the back.

5. Next, cut and tie in some cross members for stability. For the entrance, be sure to leave enough height to get in and out. As you can see, my cross members aren't perfectly symmetrical, and they don't need to be. What I like to do (where available) is tie my cross member to places where I cut off branches on the arch poles and use the little "nub" (where the branch used to be) to help hold the cross member tight when I tie it in. Your cross members should include at least one on the top, running the length of the middle of the ceiling. When putting on

Fig. 11.5. Two arches in place.

Fig. 11.6. Completed frame.

my cross members, I find it helpful to tie on a member, even if it's too long, and then cut it. That way I know it's long enough and don't have to measure. When building something, I like to have it look as neat and pretty as possible, but here we are mainly going for strength, so if your poles aren't completely straight, don't sweat it (ha, ha).

6. Give your structure a test by gently pushing on the sides, and add cross braces where needed. The completed frame of the sweat bath pictured in figure 11.6 needed only eleven pieces to be sufficiently strong: six for the arches (two for each arch) and five for the cross braces. Be sure not to put any braces inside where you will be sitting.

7. Next, carefully cover your frame, allowing for one opening that serves as both entry and exit. I have a large 16 by 20 foot waterproof tarp bought many years ago especially for this purpose. It only cost thirty dollars, and I've used it many times. But you can piece together smaller tarps and old rugs and blankets. Put rocks or wood around the bottom of the covering to secure it.

Fig. 11.7. Side view of completed sweat bath.

Fig. 11.8. Front view of completed sweat bath, with front door open.

8. All you need now are suitable stones, fire, and water. To make steam you will need water inside the steam bath (the 5-gallon, water-filled bucket with a ladle). You will also need water for rinsing off your body in between rounds. If you have a hose nearby, perfect; if not just have another five-gallon bucket of water in addition to the bucket in the steam bath.

9. Place your fire close enough to the sweat bath to easily carry hot stones in with a shovel but not too close to injure the sweat bath, especially if it's windy (a distance of six to eight feet is good). Dig a shallow pit in the center of the steam bath (or *slightly* toward the door) for placing your heated rocks. When the rocks inside the sweat bath begin to cool, simply add a couple of hot rocks from the fire. You can easily regulate the temperature of the sweat bath by how many rocks you add to the pit inside or by closing or opening the door.

That's it! I can build this sweat bath by myself from scratch in less than two hours. When you dismantle your sweat bath, label your poles; doing this will shorten the time needed to set the bath up the next time.

The Shamanic Alchemy of the Sweat Bath

In this stage of alchemic distillation, the ferment, which is the adept (you), is purified by vaporizations (physically sweating and removing ego-related impurities) and repeated washings (physically with water, psychologically with agitating and purging psychic forces via internal heat and memory). The physical, psychological, and spiritual techniques of the distillation raise our psyche to a numinous level free from sentimentality, emotions, or even identity. What we are trying to do here is cleanse ourselves to the highest degree in preparation for the final stage of coagulation.

The formal part of this process is accomplished in six rounds of being in the sweat bath, coming out and washing (rinsing your whole body with water from a hose or bucket; for the sweat bath pictured I used snow), and reentering. The tangible power of the five previous stages of transformation you have passed through are employed here during the rounds. In each round relive the experiences of one of the previous stages, in order, while you sit with the stones and sweat, making steam with water on the hot rocks. During this process, the sweat from your body and the steam from the water are both elevated into an ethereal consistency. Relive your experiences both while in the sweat bath and during your washings.

First Round: Calcination. During the first round, relive your experiences of cleansing your p-c mirrors with the Sacred Fire.

Second Round: Dissolution. Relive your experiences of dissolving pent-up emotions and becoming fluid as the water.

Third Round: Separation. Relive your experiences of stalking your habitual thoughts and actions and then traveling in separate realities while engaging in personal forms of counterpractice.

Fourth Round: Conjunction. Relive your travels to sacred sites and energetically conjoining your human organism to the magical places and what insights or visions you obtained.

Fifth Round: Fermentation. Relive the entirety of your quest: making your casket, offering to the Sacred Fire and place, fasting alone in your questing area, writing your last words to family and friends, making your bucket list, and, of course, your experiences each night in your casket.

Sixth Round: Distillation. For the final round, relive and remember nothing. Focus on the rocks and simply allow the sweat and steam to purge all impurities of body and mind. Relax, breathe, and feel cleansed and relieved of all burdens. This is referred to shamanically as the *little death*.

But you are not dead! Quite the contrary, you are now properly distilled and ready for the final stage.

12

STAGE SEVEN
COAGULATION

Fig. 12.1.
Stage seven.

The seventh ray of the star contains the symbol for both silver and the moon and points to the watery realm of the Moon Queen. The circle of operation depicts an androgynous youth emerging from an open grave with his arms raised. The Latin word *lapidem,* meaning "the stone," joins it. This last operation in the seven-stage formula of alchemy is coagulation; the fermented Soul Child of the conjunction is fused with the sublimated spiritual presence of distillation creating the symbolic Stellar Stone manifested as the astral body. In the Emerald Tablet the power of the astral body is implied in the words: "Its force is above all force for it vanquishes every subtile thing & penetrates every solid thing."

At the shamanic level, having passed through the previous six stages, you have broken free of genetic, environmental, and even astrological restraints to your being and are free to express the bliss of your true essence—the Stellar Stone or astral body.

Praxis 18
Coagulation of the Astral Body—
The Alchemic Altar of Center

Coagulation is the final stage that culminates the six previous steps and unites them together. Successfully completing the work of calcination, dissolution, separation, conjunction, fermentation, and distillation requires supreme effort, and now that you have made it this far, it is time for you to coagulate all your new knowledge and experiences. In this sense the alchemic phrase *solve et coagula* (dissolve and coagulate) is realized as the body is made numinous and the numinous is made corporeal. On the path of practical shamanic alchemy, this is the union of realizing the esoteric truths hidden inside the stages while also honing your abilities to function at the highest levels in the objective world, finding this "center" of reality where all opposites unite. In the alchemic symbol we have been modeling, the androgyne human rises forth as all opposites become one in coagulation.

The word *lapidem* accompanying the androgyne rising from the grave represents the much-sought-after coagulated stone of the alchemist. This numinous stone is at the center of everything and something that we can metaphorically reach out for, grab, and stick in our pocket. But we must find it first, and the path leading to it is not easy, which you have bravely found out for yourself. Now that you have calcinated, dissolved, separated, conjoined, fermented, and distilled physically, mentally, psychically, and spiritually, you are at the foot of the seventh and last step of the staircase. I know that having come this far you are persistent and resilient. No one can pass through what you have been asked to do in the first six stages without possessing and/or acquiring these qualities.

So, I also know it is highly unlikely that you are reading this and thinking, "Jeez, I wonder what difficult (or absurd) project he has in mind this time?" I know this because if you truly completed all six steps leading up to this one, you are a transformed person whether *you* realize it or not, and you certainly aren't going to be intimidated or frightened by the prospect of what is going to happen next. More than likely, you are curious, as is to be expected, but in a way that at this point you really don't care because you are now prepared for pretty much anything that gets thrown your way. With the Sacred Fire you have removed nonreflective globs from your p-c mirrors; dissolved unwanted emotional attachments while floating in the magic of water; separated from the dominant side of your ego by intentionally doing things you probably would have never done; intentionally traveled to places of power with the desire to conjoin with those powers; purposefully ventured into the wild alone on a quest for vision and spent time in a casket to learn about freedom; and then distilled it all down so you could rise from the ashes (well, sweat—but ashes sounds good). Point being—you are ready, so let's begin.

Not coincidentally, I brought up the imagery of the phoenix rising from the ashes as this is a common alchemic symbol for the seventh stage. The phoenix is the resurrected adept* who has successfully passed through the multiple stages of mortification and then been put back together, resulting in a transformation that passively relishes in stable peace of mind and increased energy and confidence that adapts easily to new challenges and situations. Metaphorically, the adept has found the center.

Now, I think you know me well enough by now that even though I like metaphors, they are not the main crux of how I teach; as you have found out, neither is conventional meditation, imagination, or psychoanalysis. So you are going to find this center from where you will rise from your ashy sweat by actually going and looking for it. Then when you find it, you will coagulate everything together and fly on the wings of perception to who knows where.

Finding a Center in Nature

Before we alchemically coagulate everything into the center of our being, we are going to shamanically find a center portal in nature to perform the last stage of our work. The next few paragraphs contain key parts of an explanation I give to adepts about finding a place like this.

In the vast regions of macrocosmic space, we perceive galaxies, solar systems, planets, and stars as localized places that we can name, map, and

---

*There are many definitions for the word *adept;* for our use here, the term refers to a person who has attained a specific level of knowledge, skill, or aptitude in shamanic alchemy. For me it is also a term of respect.

therefore delineate and define. On the terrestrial landscape of our home planet, we perceive and recognize places as localized and identifiable areas, such as mountains, cities, lakes, roads, houses, valleys, and buildings. Each of these places has a boundary, whether it is clear to us or somewhat obscure, that assigns to it certain characteristics and size. Even though the border of a natural place such as a hill or forest might be debatable and not easily defined, we still nonetheless would all agree that the "place" exists, especially if we were to go to the "center" of the hill or the "center" of the forest. But since the hill, forest, mountain, or desert can't be specifically delineated because nature simply doesn't create places with a ruler or a protractor, to find the exact physical center of one of these places would be a completely abstract exercise and useless to us.

Now if we were to turn our focus away from the purely physical center and instead speak on a metaphysical or spiritual level, we could say that if we were to find the center of the hill, forest, mountain, or desert, we would encounter the core essence or spirit of the place. In this case the center is simply a metaphor, but it is an important metaphor that can assist us in encountering the spirit of a place. For example, if you were standing on a high mountain ridge overlooking a forest in the valley below, you may or may not be able to discern what you might guess to be the physical center of the forest, but if you were to journey into that forest and explore it for a long enough period of time, you would eventually be able to say where you *feel* is the center of the forest, or at least the center of a particular area of the forest. This metaphysical center is simply the core feeling or spirit of the place that is completely perceivable to us, and that will be different in every place we go.

As complex organisms of this world, we humans have the ability to feel the spirit of a place, the tangible mixture of the essences and energies unique to that place. We can say that the spirit of a place is alive and manifested by these energies and essences simply because if, for example, a particular forest is clear-cut, the spirit of that place, which we could clearly feel previously, ceases to exist in the same form as it did when the essence and energy of the forest was physically alive.

When you find the metaphysical center of a place in nature, something amazing happens—you feel the spirit of the place being aware you *and* you are aware that the spirit is aware that you are aware of it. This is what I refer to as the *first shift* in consciousness, and this shift is extraordinarily significant simply because at this level perception is no longer a one-way street but rather a two-way interaction that can lead to actual communication. The *second shift* in consciousness relating to the spirit of a natural place is feeling (perceiving) the place experiencing itself. However, this second shift that I speak of is at a level of shamanic transformation beyond anything anyone could ever write about and is certainly not the goal here. Although I have heard about adepts spontaneously reaching this second shift, for most of us it requires years or even a lifetime of connection to a specific center before we can consciously perceive a place perceiving itself. I am mentioning the second shift merely to put the first shift into a larger context for reasons of understanding.

I do believe that many people, especially those I know who have dedicated their lives to protecting certain places on Earth, can feel the second shift on the edge of their awareness, and even that small taste is powerful enough to excite the psychically and bodily felt knowing that they are part of the land feeling itself. But please note that most of these special people can sense the second shift only through having felt the first shift in consciousness in a profound way for many years, and it is the first shift, with all of its lessons both joyous and painful, that is so vitally important for people to experience because when you are aware that the spirit of a place is aware of you then everything changes. Places in the natural world cease to be simply huge numbers of diverse life-forms gathered together in an identifiable location, no matter how miraculous that may be in itself, but rather, natural areas are felt as entities imbued with their own unique form of sentience that is filled with the same form of spiritual essence that flows through our own human organism. At the shamanic level these spirit-filled places house the world's most knowledgeable metaphysical teachers that are ready, willing, and able to instruct us about the informative nature of the universe.

When you are new to finding the center of a place in nature, it is advantageous to pick a place that you like and feel comfortable with. For example, on my first pilgrimage to the peyote desert in Mexico, where I did *not* feel comfortable, if the shaman had asked me to find the metaphysical center of that vast desert with the multitude of spirits that inhabit it, I would probably have run all the way home. On the other hand, drop me off in a deciduous forest blindfolded, and I will feel totally comfortable when the blindfold is removed even if I have no idea where I am.

The first time I heard about finding the center of a place in nature was from a Yavapai friend who is an amazing tracker and, even though he is not yet an elder for his tribe, one of the wisest people I know. He was visiting me where I lived in Northern California from his home in Arizona, and I took him to Big Trees State Park where I had a job. Big Trees has two groves of giant sequoia trees and to me is one of the coolest places on Earth. I knew I would blow my friend's mind when I took him there— even the tallest pines where he lives, although very large trees, are tiny tots compared to giant sequoias, which can reach thirty feet in diameter and over three hundred feet in height. The tallest giant sequoias are as tall as the Statue of Liberty. Being among them is truly indescribable.

So we're sitting in a grove of giant sequoias (his mind totally blown now), and he starts explaining to me about the concept of the *center* of a place in nature and asked me if I knew where it was in this grove. Even though I worked there five days a week on the Big Tree Creek Watershed Forest Restoration Project, I had to admit I didn't know where the center of the grove was. He was talking about 240 acres filled with *giant* trees!

He strongly suggested I try, so I did. We walked around the forest for hours. Once in a while I would see one of the biggest trees and head to it, figuring maybe the biggest one was the center. But even though I truly *loved* every tree we stopped at, I couldn't say I felt or perceived anything different than the sheer awe of being with these wonderful old trees.

A couple of weeks later, after my friend had left and I had spent countless hours trying to find the center (even when I was working), one day I was with a local friend at the park and told her what I was trying to do. She was very interested and wanted to try too. We agreed to split up to avoid distracting each other. I had been walking around the forest for a couple hours when I came to a small tributary of a stream that runs through the park. I had been there before, and it was a gorgeous place. I climbed up on the trunk of a large dead tree that had fallen a long time ago and rested for a moment. Feeling very peaceful, I climbed down after my rest and noticed that the trunk was hollow and the little stream was flowing through the bottom of it. The hollow trunk was at least eight feet tall, so I went inside and over to where the water was flowing through it.

That's when I felt it. I can't explain how: I just knew, and the feeling was certain. Somehow or other the energy of this grove of trees was metaphysically emanating from this specific place. I sat down inside the trunk and took my boots off to place my feet in the water. A few minutes later, I heard someone coming, and it was my friend. She told me she had been following her intuition and it had led her right to where I was. I told her this was the place, and she wholeheartedly agreed. We spent a while there, and as we were about to leave, she commented on something carved into the

Fig. 12.2. The author with a giant sequoia friend, Big Trees State Park, California, 2010 (photo by Jacki Goetter).

hollow trunk near where we had been sitting, which I hadn't seen. It was a circle with an equal cross. I knew that this symbol had many meanings; it could represent the four seasons, the four winds, or the four elements. My friend added that it also commonly represented Earth in astronomy. A few days later I showed it to the park's nature interpreter, and she added that the symbol had been used since prehistoric times and many archaeologists believe it to be a solar sign for the sun. In any event it appeared quite clear to me that someone before me had also found this center of the giant sequoia grove, and I felt extremely blessed that I had too.

My friend found the center of the north grove of the Big Trees State Park the very first day she tried. It had taken me weeks, and I was much more familiar with the place than she was. Just goes to show, you never can tell what will happen. I suggest you try and find the metaphysical center of a place in nature; however, I strongly suggest that you first complete this last stage of the work as soon as possible after your distilling sweat bath, whether you feel you have found a center or not. The first time I employed the coagulation technique I'm about to describe, I didn't know about finding the metaphysical center of a place, and my coagulation went remarkably well. So, if you don't feel like you have found a center, simply choose a private spot in nature that you are comfortable with and that makes you feel good being there. This could even be the place of your fermentation.

About the Altar

This technique is called the alchemic altar of center and is fashioned of unique alchemic items of your creation that will open a personal portal for you to the center of creation. In this place you will coagulate your knowledge and experience to form an internal alchemic stone of power.

This is one of the most powerful altar configurations that I have experienced and is designed specifically to unite us with the center of creation, which has been called many names—the Great Spirit, Unkulukulu, Atman, Wakan-Tanka, Yahweh, Allah, Jah, Ngai, Brahman, Itzamna, the Universal Life Force, among countless others. It is not my intention here to discuss the similarities or differences among these names and how they are used, or to discuss monotheism, polytheism, pantheism, paganism, and the many other *isms*. But I do greatly respect the power of intentionally opening and awakening to the powerful, mystical, and numinous process of creation, especially when this leads us to be humbled and touched with awe, which can lead to states of peacefulness and harmony.

This first type of altar is designed not to support or deny any specific religion but rather to connect, bring together, or coagulate, our total human organism in a pure and direct way so our astral body can experience a portal that lies at the beginning of a new path of awareness and understanding of our role as human beings and how we might fit into the grander scheme of creation. This alchemic altar of center is specifically designed to be a portal where we can touch that which lies at the center of creation. This center might be called energy in the modern world. The ancient Maya called it *itz;* my Wirrarika mentors call it *kupuri.* What I am referring to is that which gives power to the blood or milk of humans and animals, the light and heat of the sun, an egg, the bud of a flower, and water.

For time immemorial, shamans, mystics, and holy people of all persuasions have journeyed to the place where time, matter, and consciousness meet, the place that emanates the sacred life force. This center, called Xibalba ("the place of awe") by the ancient Maya, is a real place if for no other reason than thousands of people throughout time have traveled there and have made it real.

The alchemic altar of the center is the place created by the power of our intention where we can travel to Xibalba to reunite with the sacred life force, respectfully honor the energy of creation, and realign ourselves, awakening to a life of peace and harmony.

Symbolic Components of the Altar

Those of you familiar with my book *Beyond 2012: A Shaman's Call to Personal Change and the Transformation of Global Consciousness* will see similarities between the altar I describe here and the one I explained in that book. However, when I wrote the description of that altar, I had not yet entirely put together the significant correspondences between shamanism and alchemy that, when practiced together, raise the vibrational level of transformation to an even higher level than when practiced separately. This altar, along with the practices of the previous six stages, is a powerful blend of shamanic and alchemic procedures.

The altar is constructed in the open air, for its design is all about connecting us to that which is all around us. This outdoor sacred space is much different from churches and temples, which keep nature outside the sacred structure. The foundation for the altar is four trees, usually saplings that are growing close enough together to place a small platform in between them. The four trees signify the four directions and elements, with the altar in the center representing the alchemic quintessence or fifth element.

Fig. 12.3. The alchemic altar.

A small platform is tied to the trees at the corners thus connecting it to the four cardinal directions. This platform, usually of wood, symbolizes the middle world, which is the physical reality we know of and where we live our daily lives. The ground beneath the platform altar is the underworld, where the roots of trees and plants and the billions of organisms that give life to the soil reside. This is a place of life that we normally don't see but is just as valid and important as the life above ground that we are accustomed too. And the space above the altar is the upper world, which joins our little blue-green planet, our Mother Earth, to the whirling procession of planets around our sun, and our solar system rotating within the greater galaxy.

In the center of the altar above the platform is a raised (or hanging) area for a basket, hollowed and halved gourd, or chalice that symbolizes the opening or portal from which we can travel through and where the vital life force of Xibalba pours in. This raised center area completes the ancient symbolism of the world tree or axis mundi found in so many spiritual traditions throughout the globe. For this reason, the alchemic altar of center can also be thought of as the altar of galactic center for in its symbolic construction we intentionally acknowledge the link between our planet and the center of the galaxy.

Beyond any other consideration, it is the power of intention that activates any altar. Even if you had absolutely nothing to place on the altar or physically offer, your power of intention would still be the force that opens the door to Xibalba. But there are many essences and energies that can aid us in focusing the power of our intention and assist us in our tasks. The manner in which you activate and use your altar is strictly personal, but as always I suggest that we take clues from the ancestors and then add those items and procedures that make sense to our current ways of life.

Preparation of the Altar

In an ISC stand in front of your altar and complete the alchemic coagulation of your elixir by putting a few a drops or tablespoons (depending on how much ash you have) of your liquid elixir into your elixir ash and stir it up to create a coagulated paste. Next, take a few drops of your fermentation liquid and stir it into the paste as well. In your jar of paste you now have an exceptionally tangible and manifested example of the coagulated alchemic stone.*

Congratulations, adept! Your stone is the product of the seven stages of alchemic transformation—calcination, dissolution, separation, conjunction, fermentation, distillation, and coagulation. This stone represents *you* and all the alchemic-shamanic work you have done to get to this amazing stage of your life.

With your fingers paint some of your stone onto your face, wrists, and ankles while remembering all the stages, operations, and processes you have gone through to be here.

Now that you have been metaphysically fed by the stone, begin to feed the altar with energy and actions of reciprocity. Since the altar has three main levels, all three must be fed. Among the items to feed your altar will be the essences and energies of your alchemic work of the previous six stages. For each level, you will place an alchemic offering of your work of transformation. Below are suggestions for all three levels.

The Underworld. Under the platform dig a small hole (maybe twelve inches in diameter) in the ground to acknowledge the normally unseen forces beneath us that give us life. For the underworld, place alchemic ash and waters from stage one calcination and stage two dissolution to represent the inner fire and springs of Earth. Other suggested items are:

Plant roots (from your garden or other flowers or plants). Roots signify your awareness of complex web of life and how the roots of the underground world produce the living world above.

Soil from your garden or a sacred place. Placing living soil on the altar acknowledges your understanding and gratitude that our Mother Earth is alive and that our physical body is an extension of her body.

Uncooked food items. Raw vegetables and fruits represent your thanks

---

*An alchemic stone does not have to be solid. It is *simply* a valid example of the *complex* alchemic-shamanic operations *you* have manifested.

for the bounty we receive from the energy of the underworld.

Special stones or *te'kas*. You can place these special healing stones on the ground, especially at the corners at the base of the four trees. I usually prefer to sit my te'kas on the platform because they are also my companions in the middle world.

The Middle World. On the platform we ritually acknowledge the gifts of our physical reality and the processes of illumination we are employing to be in harmonious balance with the objective world while seeking unity with all three worlds.

Place your items from the alchemic stages three and four (separation and conjunction) on the platform. Other items for the middle world platform might include:

Cooked food items. Food such as bread and stews can be placed on the altar platform to represent our human interaction with the world and can then be blessed during the activation of the altar and eaten afterwards.

Important tools, photos of special people. Thanks and acknowledgment can be given by placing on the altar tools that you use or representations of them, photos or effigies of special people, or anything that helps you or gives meaning to your life.

Objects of beauty, such as tek'as, flowers, feathers. Put on the altar objects that bring a sense of beauty to your life.

Items that represent changes you would like to make. Put on the altar objects that symbolize changes you would like to see happen in your life or in the world. We can create positive energy at this level by acknowledging things like war, oppression, extraction of fossil fuels, deforestation, and so on, and during the ceremony pray for the resolution of these situations.

The Upper World. The center basket or other types of containers (prefer using half of a hollowed-out gourd) that are placed in the upper region represent the sacred life force of creation and also connection to the numinous aspects of life.

Place your items from the fifth and sixth stages (fermentation and distillation) in the hanging container. Other items for the middle world platform might include:

Sacred fluids. Juice, milk, water, sap, blood, or infused oils can all represent the life blood of creation. Once the portal to Xibalba is opened and during the latter stages of the ceremony, these fluids can be used to bless other items in the altar with the energy of creation flowing from Xibalba and into these fluids in the center.

Sacred items or tools. Any item or tool that you use to connect with the numinous aspects of life or that you use in healing work or other spiritual ceremonies.

Activating the Altar

Now that we are ready to actively work with the altar we have created, it is important to be absolutely clear why we are doing it. I know of many people who have used the force of intention and the power of ritual to open portals to other worlds but then connected with powers that were actually harmful to them.

Throughout history, there have been shamans and priests who have intentionally called upon the forces that I refer to as anticreation to promote sickness and death in a misguided effort to elevate their own power. We must acknowledge that acts of anticreation not only exist but are also very powerful. The destructive energy that leads men to take oil and coal faster than it can be created and that imbues a false sense of power and security in those responsible for waging wars and killing millions of innocent humans and other beings is just as real as the energy that promotes peace and balance.

In activating your altar, you will feel power. It is vitally important to stay focused on channeling that power toward actions of conscious co-creation and not allow the rush of energy coming in to persuade or seduce you into harnessing it for selfish reasons. For this reason, I suggest that you now perform a formal ritual of intention. This is simply to get the energy moving and flowing in the direction that you want. I suggest that you use your voice and express through words your intentions out loud to the items on the altar, your human and nonhuman companions around you, and all the beings both seen and unseen around your altar. If necessary you can even do this while purifying the area with smoke. Historically, the use of fragrant incense—bundles of sage or sweetgrass, pieces of dried cedar, or copal resin—has been used for this and can help you switch out of your ordinary thought processes to be ready to experience the mysteries you are entering into.

Once your intentions have been clearly stated, the altar can be safely activated by a combination of movement, sonic vibration, and intention. Movement is normally initiated by walking in slow circles around the altar to join with the circular (or, more properly, elliptical) movement of our Mother Earth. As the activation proceeds, the walk can be alternately sped up or slowed down or turned into either a fast or slow dance.

Sonic vibrations are created by using instruments of sound such as the drum, rattle, guitar, violin, or any other kind of device, as well as most importantly your own voice in the form of talking, chanting, and singing.

Intention for opening the portal to the source or center is accomplished by expressing your desires, prayers, and offerings through your words, songs, and movements. Begin by making this a natural extension of your original statement of intent and then allow it to enlarge by letting your luminous self take charge and your ego sit and watch silently. What follows are suggestions for achieving this.

Foundational Phase. Express the reasons for the items you included in the altar, one by one, from bottom to top. Don't rush this process. At the deepest levels the essences and energies will eventually sing through you. You can do this as many times as necessary until you feel a shift in consciousness happening.

Experiment with the effects of raising and lowering the octave of your voice as you talk to the altar. I have found that most shamans raise the pitch of their voice in certain moments as this tends to aid power and imbue a certain quality of sacredness.

Generating Momentum Phase. Open a portal to your sacred sites, other places that have touched you, and special moments during completion of the previous six stages and relive moments of numinous connection. Feel the special qualities of the place by seeing through your eyes as you did when you were there in the past, and not just from a third person perspective. Try to experience as much of your other senses as well.

Recollect the essences and energies of the six stages and also the wind, water, soil, and fire by reliving special moments that touched you. Feel again your feet in the ocean, the wind blowing your hair, the heat and light of the fire and the sun, the sand, soil, and grass between your toes.

Acknowledgments and Prayers for the World Phase. Express your personal intentions of aligning with co-creation.

Send out your payers to our Mother Earth for the awakening of humanity so that the raping of her body will end.

Send out your prayers one by one to the individual spirits of the animals, birds, sea inhabitants, trees, and plants. Call to them by name and express your desire to be in alignment and balance with them.

Pray for the hungry and oppressed people of our world and express intentions for aid.

Acknowledge both the soldiers and the innocents that are dying right now from the misguided concepts of power and offer prayers of peace.

Pray for the awakening of our world leaders that they may shed the need for dominating others who don't share their same ideals.

Express intentions to help in the education of people in countries where human procreation is out of control to the point of major suffering.

Portal Phase. While still moving around the altar and allowing sonic vibrations and the power of intention to shift your consciousness, begin to go to the next level by uniting even further with the structure and symbolism of the altar and traveling up the central axis of the world tree.

Embody the credo of the ancient alchemists: what is below is like that which is above, and what is above is like that which is below. You are everything and everything is you. Mind and matter are ripples in the same pool. Allow your consciousness to touch the center of the pool and merge with creation . . . and do this for the rest of your life.

Fig. 12.4. The alchemist reaches the top of the seventh step and holds the world in his hands (from *The Book of Lambspring* [1599], as appeared in *The Hermetic Museum, Vol. 1*, plate 9, by Arthur Edward Waite, 1893).

EPILOGUE

WHAT'S NEXT?

The phenomena that we call shamanism and alchemy is, for indigenous cultures and modern adepts, a lifelong calling and pursuit. In this, as in most things, we can never stop learning. The azoth mandala we have been working with is circular for a reason. At the end of the seven-stage shamanic alchemy process, we arrive full circle back where we started from. However, now we are empowered with shamanic-alchemic knowledge and experiences that the uninitiated could scarcely imagine. With that said, it is my sincere hope that you pass this knowledge on to others while you continue on your path of learning.

This path begins with any of the practices in this book that you skipped or didn't give your full attention. I've found that many times the things we avoid are precisely the things we need the most. Also, because there are so many practices in this book that require long periods of time to complete or become proficient in, I always suggest to my students to keep practicing. This not a race; take your time and enjoy the new experiences, feelings, and knowledge included in the practices. Many of the more challenging or time-consuming practices I have gone through again and again, and each time I learn something new as the experiences deepen. And not to sound like a salesman, but if you found value in the shamanic alchemy practices in this book, I invite you to explore the practices in my books *Advanced Shamanism* and *Advanced Autogenic Training and Primal Awareness*. There are dozens of practices in those books that coincide with, and extend, many of the practices in this book.

Last but not least, I will leave you with this thought: you have manifested (not found) one of the shamanic alchemy stones, but there are many others to bring forth and apply in our daily lives to make the world a better place. Each time I succeed at a challenging shamanic or alchemic task, I look to the mandala and read what it says. It's not a secret but something that many overlook. The mandala has a hidden message for us that is in plain sight.

The words contained in the outer ring and that hover over the operational stages spell out what you have just experienced and what might yet come. That is for you to ponder and figure out what it means to *you*. Written in sentence form, the Latin words *visita interiora ierrae rectificando invenies occultum lapidem* translate to mean "Visit the interior of the earth, and by rectifying, you will discover the hidden stone."

NOTES

INTRODUCTION. ALCHEMY AND SHAMANISM: TOOLS OF TRANSFORMATION

1. Pagel, *Paracelsus,* 113.
2. Wolf, *Mind into Matter,* 6–7.
3. Klossowski de Rola, *Alchemy.*
4. Thompson, *The Lure and Romance of Alchemy,* 239.
5. Scot, *The Discoverie of Witchcraft,* 10208.
6. Scot, *The Discoverie of Witchcraft,* 10210–10233.

CHAPTER 1. THE DAWN OF ALCHEMY

1. Eliade, *The Forge and the Crucible,* 79.
2. Chkashige, *Oriental Alchemy,* 14–15.
3. Haeffner, *Dictionary of Alchemy,* 199–200.
4. Junius, *Spagyrics,* 12–13.
5. Eliade, *The Forge and the Crucible,* 182–83.

CHAPTER 2. A DISTILLED LEXICON OF ALCHEMY

1. Magnus, *Egyptian Secrets,* 27.
2. Magnus, *Egyptian Secrets,* 22.
3. Magnus, *Egyptian Secrets,* 20.
4. Magnus, *Egyptian Secrets,* 46.
5. Magnus, *Egyptian Secrets,* 20.

6. Jung, *Psychology and Alchemy*, 202.

7. Thompson, *The Lure and Romance of Alchemy*, 31–32.

8. Thompson, *The Lure and Romance of Alchemy*, 33–34.

9. Westfall, *Never at Rest*, 284.

10. Waite, *The Secret Tradition in Alchemy*, 33.

11. Greenlees, *The Gospel of Hermes*, xvi.

12. Mead, *Corpus Hermeticum*, 20–26.

13. Jung, *Memories*, 205.

14. Jung, *Memories*, 209.

15. Thompson, *The Lure and Romance of Alchemy*, 134.

16. Raleigh, *The Speculative Art of Alchemy*, 5.

17. Raleigh, *The Speculative Art of Alchemy*, 120.

18. Jacobi and Guterman, *Paracelsus*, 21.

19. Dobbs, *The Foundations of Newton's Alchemy*, 20.

20. Sigerist, *Four Treatises of Paracelsus*, vii.

21. Waite, *The Hermetic and Alchemical Writings of Paracelsus*, 19, 21.

22. Sigerist, *Four Treatises of Paracelsus*, 24–25.

23. Sigerist, *Four Treatises of Paracelsus*, 231–32.

24. Jung, *Psychology and Alchemy*, 304.

CHAPTER 3.
SHAMANIC AND ALCHEMICAL COSMOLOGIES

1. Endredy, *Ecoshamanism*, 7–8.

2. Wood, *Voices from the Earth*, 10.

3. Talbot, *Mysticism and the New Physics*, 122.

CHAPTER 4.
INITIATION AND THEURGY

1. Endredy, *Advanced Shamanism*, 5.

2. Endredy, *Advanced Shamanism*, 5.

3. Endredy, *Advanced Shamanism*, 6.

4. Endredy, *Advanced Shamanism*, 6.

5. Endredy, *Advanced Shamanism*, 42.

6. Endredy, *Advanced Shamanism*, 43.

7. Endredy, *Teachings of the Peyote Shamans*, 68–69.

8. Endredy, *Advanced Shamanism*, 44.

9. Endredy, *Advanced Shamanism*, 45.

10. Endredy, *Advanced Shamanism*, 47.

11. Endredy, *Advanced Shamanism*, 49.

12. Endredy, *Advanced Shamanism*, 175–76.

13. Endredy, *Advanced Shamanism*, 180–81.

14. Endredy, *Advanced Shamanism*, 182.

15. Endredy, *Advanced Shamanism*, 183.

16. Millay, *Multidimensional Mind*, 191–92.

17. Endredy, *Advanced Shamanism*, 184–85.

18. Endredy, *Advanced Shamanism*, 185–86.

19. Endredy, *Advanced Shamanism*, 186–87.

20. Endredy, *Advanced Shamanism*, 31–33.

CHAPTER 5.
SHAMANIC SPAGYRICS

1. Octopus Alchemy, "Wild Fermentation."

CHAPTER 6.
STAGE ONE: CALCINATION

1. Laszlo, *Science and the Reenchantment of the Cosmos*, 54.

CHAPTER 7.
STAGE TWO: DISSOLUTION

1. Emoto, *The Healing Power of Water*, 6–8.

CHAPTER 8.
STAGE THREE: SEPARATION

1. Sloat, "What Never Leaving Your Hometown Does to Your Brain."

2. Fu and Weller, "Half of the US Population Lives in These 9 States."

3. Thomashow, *Ecological Identity*.

CHAPTER 9.
STAGE FOUR: CONJUNCTION

1. Sea, "History Got It Wrong."

2. Robert Pond, online review of the Serpent Mound site, posted January 16, 2011 on the World Heritage Site website.

3. Glaser, "Ohio's Serpent Mound, An Archaeological Mystery, Still the Focus of Scientific Debate."

CHAPTER 10.
STAGE FIVE: FERMENTATION

1. Chowdhury, "From Ramadan to the 5:2."

2. Metzner, *The Unfolding Self,* 163.

CHAPTER 11.
STAGE SIX: DISTILLATION

1. Alba, "Temazcal."

2. Bosworth, "Why Finland Loves Saunas."

BIBLIOGRAPHY

Alba, Horacio Rojas. "Temazcal: The Traditional Mexican Sweat Bath." *Tlahui-Medic* 2, no. 2 (1996).

Besant, Annie. *Talks on the Path of Occultism.* Madras, India: Theosophical Publishing House, 1926.

Blavatsky, H. P. *Alchemy and the Secret Doctrine.* Wheaton, Ill.: Theosophical Press, 1927.

Bosworth, Mark. "Why Finland Loves Saunas." *BBC News Magazine,* October 1, 2013.

Burland, C. A. *The Arts of the Alchemists.* London: Weidenfeld and Nicholson, 1967.

Caron, M., and S. Hutin. *The Alchemists.* London: Evergreen Books, 1961.

Cavendish, Richard. *The Black Arts.* New York: G.P. Putnam's Sons, 1967.

Chkashige, Masumi. *Oriental Alchemy.* New York: Samuel Weiser, 1974. First published in 1936.

Chowdhury, Hasan. "From Ramadan to the 5:2, the Surprising Science of Fasting." *New Statesman America,* June 10, 2016.

Cockren, A. *Alchemy Rediscovered and Restored.* Mokelumne Hill, Calif.: Health Research, 1963.

Cooper, David, A. *God Is a Verb: Kabbalah and the Practice of Mystical Judaism.* New York: Riverhead Books, 1997.

Coudert, Allison. *Alchemy: The Philosopher's Stone.* Boulder, Colo.: Shambhala, 1980.

Councell, R. W. *Apologia Alchymiae.* London: John M. Watkins, 1925.

Dobbs, Betty Jo. *The Foundations of Newton's Alchemy or the Hunting of the Green Lion.* Cambridge, UK: Cambridge University Press, 1983.

Easton, Stewart C. *Roger Bacon and His Search for a Universal Science.* Westport, Conn.: Greenwood Press, 1952.

Eliade, Mircea. *The Forge and the Crucible: The Origins and Structure of Alchemy.* Chicago: University of Chicago Press, 1979.

Emoto, Masaru. *The Healing Power of Water.* New York: Hay House, 2004. Kindle Edition.

Endredy, James. *Advanced Autogenic Training and Primal Awareness: Techniques for Wellness, Deeper Connection to Nature, and Higher Consciousness.* Rochester, Vt.: Bear & Company, 2016.

———. *Advanced Shamanism: The Practice of Conscious Transformation.* Rochester, Vt.: Bear & Company, 2018.

———. *Earthwalks for Body and Spirit: Exercises to Restore Our Sacred Bond with the Earth.* Rochester, Vt.: Bear & Company, 2002.

———. *Ecoshamanism: Sacred Practices of Unity, Power and Earth Healing.* Woodbury, Minn.: Llewellyn Publications, 2005.

———. *The Flying Witches of Veracruz: A Shaman's True Story of Indigenous Witchcraft, Devil's Weed, and Trance Healing in Aztec Brujeria.* Woodbury, Minn.: Llewellyn Publications, 2011.

———. *Lightning in My Blood: A Journey into Shamanic Healing & the Supernatural.* Woodbury, Minn.: Llewellyn Publications, 2011.

———. *Shamanism for Beginners: Walking with the World's Healers of Earth and Sky.* Woodbury, Minn.: Llewellyn Publications, 2009.

———. *Teachings of the Peyote Shamans: The Five Points of Attention.* Rochester, Vt.: Park Street Press, 2015.

Fabricius, Johannes. *Alchemy: The Medieval Alchemists and Their Royal Art.* London: Diamond Books, 1994.

Feher, D. A. *The Key of Jacob Boehme.* Grand Rapids, Mich.: Phanes Press, 1991.

Flowers, Stephen Edred. *Hermetic Magic: The Postmodern Magical Papyrus of Abaris.* York Beach, Maine: Samuel Weiser, 1995.

Fortune, Dion. *Practical Occultism in Daily Life.* London: Aquarian Press, 1969.

Franz, Marie-Louise von. *Alchemical Active Imagination.* Irving, Tex.: Spring Publications, 1979.

Fu, Florence, and Chris Weller. "Half of the US Population Lives in These 9 States." *Business Insider,* June 22, 2016.

Gettings, Fred. *Dictionary of the Occult, Hermetic and Alchemical Sigils.* London: Routledge & Kegan Paul, 1981.

Givry, Grillot de. *Witchcraft Magic & Alchemy.* N.p.: Frederick Publications, 1954.

Glaser, Susan. "Ohio's Serpent Mound, An Archaeological Mystery, Still the Focus of Scientific Debate." *The Plain Dealer,* October 11, 2018. Posted on the Cleveland.com website.

Godwin, Joscelyn, and Christian Chanel. *The Hermetic Brotherhood of Luxor.* York Beach, Maine: Samuel Weiser, 1995.

Greenlees, Duncan. *The Gospel of Hermes.* Wheaton, Ill.: Theosophical Publishing House, 1949.

Guiley, Rosemary Ellen. *Harper's Encyclopedia of Mystical & Paranormal Experience.* New York: HarperCollins, 1991.

Haeffner, Mark. *Dictionary of Alchemy.* London: Aquarian, 1991.

Hall, Manly P. *Wit and Wisdom of the Immortals.* Los Angeles: The Philosophical Research Society, 1987.

Hardy, Mary, and Dotty Nonman. *The Alchemist's Handbook to Homeopathy.* Allegan, Mich.: The Sisterhood of the Emerald Fire, 2015.

Hatch, D. P. *Some Philosophy of the Hermetics.* Los Angeles: B.R. Baumgardt, 1896.

Heindel, Max. *Nature Spirits and Natural Forces.* Oceanside, Calif.: Rosicrucian Fellowship, 1937.

Hermes Trismegistus. "Emerald Tablet of Hermes." Alchemical Texts posted on Alchemy (website).

Holzer, Hans. *The Alchemist: The Secret Magical Life of Rudolf von Habsburg.* New York: Stein and Day, 1974.

Jacobi, Jolande, and Norbert Guterman. *Paracelsus: Selected Writings.* Princeton, N.J.: Princeton University Press, 1995.

Jung, Carl G. *Memories, Dreams, and Reflections.* New York: Vintage Books, 1989.

———. *Mysterium Coniunctionis: An Inquiry into the Separation and Synthesis of Psychic Opposites in Alchemy.* Princeton, N.J.: Princeton University Press, 1970.

———. *Psychology and Alchemy.* New York: Routledge and Keagan Paul, 2014.

Junius, Manfred M. *Spagyrics: The Alchemical Preparation of Medicinal Essences, Tinctures, and Elixirs.* Rochester, Vt.: Healing Arts Press, 2007. First published in 1979.

Klossowski de Rola, Stanislas. *Alchemy: The Secret Art.* London: Thames and Hudson, 1973.

Kohn, J. *The Prophesies of Paracelsus.* Edmonds, Wash.: Alchemical Press, 1993.

Laszlo, Ervin. *Science and the Reenchantment of the Cosmos: The Rise of the Integral Vision of Reality.* Rochester, Vt.: Inner Traditions, 2006.

Levi, Eliphas. *The History of Magic.* London: Rider and Company, 1951.

———. *The Science of Hermes.* Edmonds, Wash.: Alchemical Press, 1993.

Luck, George. *Arcana Mundi: Magic and the Occult in the Greek and Roman Worlds.* Baltimore, Md.: Johns Hopkins University Press, 1985.

Magnus, Albertus. *Egyptian Secrets: White and Black Art for Man and Beast.* Chicago: de Laurence, Scott & Co., 1914.

Mead, G. R. S. *Corpus Hermeticum.* Charlotte, N.C.: IAP, 2009.

Metzner, Ralph. *The Unfolding Self: Varieties of Transformative Experience.* Novato, Calif.: Origin Press, 1998.

Millay, Jean. *Multidimensional Mind: Remote Viewing in Hyperspace.* Berkeley, Calif.: North Atlantic Books, 1999.

Nollius, Henry. *Hermetic Physick.* Edmonds, Wash.: Alchemical Press, 1993.

Octopus Alchemy. "Wild Fermentation—Why It's Healthy and How to Do It." Excerpt from the Octopus Alchemy handbook, blog posted February 9, 2015.

Pagel, Walter. *Paracelsus: An Introduction to Philosophical Medicine in the Era of the Renaissance.* Basel, N.Y.: Karger, 1982.

Pauwels, Louis, and Jacques Bergier. *The Morning of the Magicians.* New York: Dorsett Press, 1988.

Prophet, Mark L., and Elizabeth Clare. *Saint Germain on Alchemy: Formulas for Self-Transformation.* Corwin Springs, Mo.: Summit University Press, 1985.

Raleigh, A. S. *The Speculative Art of Alchemy: A Textbook on the Art of Self-Regeneration.* Chicago: Hermetic Publishing Company, 1926.

Ripley, George. *Five Preparations of the Philosopher's Mercury.* Edmonds, Wash.: Alchemical Press, 1993.

Russell, Richard. *The Works of Geber.* London: J.M. Dent & Sons, 1928.

Rutland, Martin. *A Lexicon of Alchemy.* London: John M. Watkins, 1964.

Scot, Reginald. *The Discoverie of Witchcraft.* Edited by Brinsley Nicholson. London: Elliot Stock, 1866. Kindle edition published March 12, 2013 by Amazon Digital Services LLC.

Scott, Walter. *Hermetica: The Ancient Greek and Latin Writings Which Contain Religeous or Philosophical Teachings Ascibed to Hermes Trismegistus.* Boston: Shambhala, 1985.

Sea, Geoffrey. "History Got It Wrong: Scientists Now Say Serpent Mound as Old as Aristotle." *Indian Country Today,* April 27, 2017.

Serres, Michel. *Hermes: Literature, Science, Philosophy.* Baltimore, Md.: Johns Hopkins University Press, 1982.

Sigerist, Henry E. *Four Treatises of Paracelsus.* Baltimore, Md: Johns Hopkins University Press, 1941.

Sloat, Sarah. "What Never Leaving Your Hometown Does to Your Brain." *Inverse,* September 28, 2015.

South, Thomas. *The Enigma of Alchemy.* Edmonds, Wash.: Alchemical Press, 1993.

Stillman, John Maxson. *Paracelsus: His Personality and Influence as Physician, Chemist and Reformer.* London: Open Court, 1920.

Talbot, Michael. *Mysticism and the New Physics.* London: Routledge & Kegan Paul, 1987.

Telepnef, Basilio De. *Paracelsus: A Genius amidst a Troubled World.* St. Gallen, Switzerland: Zollikofer, 1945.

Thompson, C. J. S. *The Lure and Romance of Alchemy.* New York: Bell Publishing, 1990.

Thomashow, Mitchell, *Ecological Identity.* Cambridge, Mass.: MIT Press, 1995.

Tschoudy, Baron. *Paracelsus' Alchemical Catechism.* Edmonds, Wash.: Alchemical Press, 1993.

Vigenere, Blaise de. *A Discourse of Fire and Salt.* Edmonds, Wash.: Alchemical Press, 1993.

Waite, Arthur Edward. *Alchemists Through the Ages.* Blauvelt, N.Y.: Rudolf Steiner Publications, 1970.

———. *The Hermetic and Alchemical Writings of Paracelsus.* New Hyde Park, N.Y.: University Books, 1967.

———. *The Hermetic Museum.* New York: Samuel Weiser, 1973.

———. *The Secret Tradition in Alchemy.* New York: Samuel Weiser, 1969.

Westcott, William Wynn. *The Science of Alchemy: Spiritual and Material.* Edmonds, Wash.: Alchemical Press, 1993.

Westcott, Wynn. *Collectanea Hermetica.* Edmonds, Wash.: Alchemical Press, 1993.

Westfall, Richard S. *Never at Rest: A Biography of Isaac Newton.* Cambridge, UK: Cambridge University Press, 1980.

Wolf, Fred Allen. *Mind into Matter: A New Alchemy of Science and Spirit.* Needham, Mass.: Moment Point Press, 2001.

Wood, Nicholas. *Voices from the Earth: Practical Shamanism.* New York: Sterling Publishing, 2000.

INDEX

BOOKS OF RELATED INTEREST

Advanced Shamanism
The Practice of Conscious Transformation
by James Endredy

Advanced Autogenic Training and Primal Awareness
Techniques for Wellness, Deeper Connection to
Nature, and Higher Consciousness
by James Endredy

Teachings of the Peyote Shamans
The Five Points of Attention
by James Endredy
Foreword by José Stevens, Ph.D.

Earthwalks for Body and Spirit
Exercises to Restore Our Sacred Bond with the Earth
by James Endredy
Foreword by Victor Sanchez

The Lost Art of Heart Navigation
A Modern Shaman's Field Manual
by Jeff D. Nixa, J.D., M.Div.

Shamanic Healing
Traditional Medicine for the Modern World
by Itzhak Beery
Foreword by Alberto Villoldo

Speaking with Nature
Awakening to the Deep Wisdom of the Earth
by Sandra Ingerman and Llyn Roberts

The Accidental Shaman
Journeys with Plant Teachers and Other Spirit Allies
by Howard G. Charing
Foreword by Stephan V. Beyer

INNER TRADITIONS • BEAR & COMPANY
P.O. Box 388 • Rochester, VT 05767
1-800-246-8648 • www.InnerTraditions.com

Or contact your local bookseller